WIZARDS AND WIVES' TALES
ROLLING FOR LOVE BOOK 2

A LitRPG ADVENTURE

By

Kate Messick

Copyright (C) 2020 Kate Messick

Layout design and Copyright (C) 2020 by Next Chapter

Published 2020 by Shadow City – A Next Chapter Imprint

Edited by Elizabeth N. Love

Cover art by CoverMint

ACKNOWLEDGMENTS

As always, I need to take a moment to thank my cat. Her constant need for snuggles keeps me seated for long stretches of time, thus requiring a sedate hobby, leading me to typing combinations of words on a page that hopefully make sense.

Oh, right, people...none of this would be possible without my beta readers, especially Leahy Fletcher, Nick Burgoyne, Chandler Koury, Samantha Terry, and more. It's through others' eyes and feedback that I improve, not just my writing, but my talents as a cat bed.

Last, I need to thank my husband, who despite threatening it, has not thrown my cat or her human cat bed out the window...yet...

A NOTE ON TABLETOP RPGS

You do not need to have ever played a tabletop role-playing game (RPG) to enjoy this book. It's intended to be balanced between flavor text for those of us who play and explanations for anyone who does not. However, this section gives an overview of the game, if you're confused or would like the basics.

Tabletop Role-Playing Games or RPGs are wit-based games played, usually around a table, by a group of people. The players use dice and a series of rule books to guide them through a creative story-based world. There are many different RPG systems, *Dungeons & Dragons (D&D)* is probably the most well-known. *GRUPS, Pathfinder, FATE,* and *Seventh Sea* are a few more popular ones. This book uses *FATE.* Much like the many flavors of ice cream, every RPG system does something slightly different to balance the rules, and no one system is better than another. It's all just personal preference.

It's usually the GM, Game Master, (or DM, Dungeon Master in *D&D*), that picks the system a group is going 'run' in. Once that decision has been made, the GM builds a world. Everyone else creates alter egos, or characters, that will adventure in that world. Players are given free rein on what they create, but they must be made within the rules of the RPG system. Because, let's be honest, if you could create magical people who could do anything, would you give them limits? I certainly wouldn't.

Characters then go on adventures, guided by their GMs on everything from simple tasks of delivering mail to saving the world! This sounds so simple, but in reality, players often do not understand the GM's clues and just do whatever they want. The GM must then adapt, rewrite, and create new stories as players make their own terrible – er, different – decisions.

The trick to this is that all decisions, actions, and even, to a certain extent, your characters are controlled by dice. Because, if we could all make our own choices every time, we would never fail, and most of us would believe we know everything. If players want to know more about something, they can roll to see if they know. If you want to stab something with a sword, you need to roll to see if you can hit it. If you want to scare someone, you need to roll to see how scary you can be. All of this information is kept on character sheets. Each sheet is unique and gives bonuses to rolls so that everyone is better or worse at different skills, just like people.

The *FATE* system has fewer restrictions than *D&D*, and the rules for both RPG systems can be googled and found in their respective manuals.

And last but not least, for all of my RPG readers or those more curious, you can find links to the player's character sheets below.

Joe's Wizard - Ixar

Ed's Wizard - Clint
Byron's Wizard - Byke
Kevin's Wizard - Pooh

PROLOGUE

JOE SMARTIN

My eyes scan the fuzzy video chat of Dillon and Sandy on my computer screen as Dillon tells me about some project that's finally wrapping up at his work. Dillon, my best friend, looks his usual well-kept self. But Sandy, Sandy glows with pregnancy as she plays with the new engagement ring on her finger. It worries me that she hasn't put on more weight, but despite our slow internet connection, I can see a shimmer to her hair and the smallest increase in her breast size.

"We still haven't found a new GM," Dillon changes the topic of conversation, GM standing for Game Master, the leader of a role-playing group.

"I know Zack's off at college now, but we're trying to stay together – the four of us," Sandy adds. "I can't believe Lynda and I are pregnant at the same time!"

I wince at the word 'we,' but I don't think they can see it. 'We' still don't know who the child's father is, me or Dillon. I don't know if, or how, I fit into their lives anymore. My world's upside down.

I let Sandy ramble about the advice Lynda's been giving her, living in the sound of her voice. My eyes close, remembering the feeling of having her in my arms. Dillon would've undoubtedly been on her other side, letting me bounce frustrations with my new job off of his overly intuitive brain. I hadn't realized how content I'd been in Colorado until the stress of moving overseas had cleared. I'm in a parallel reality, my world just different enough that nothing feels right.

"Joe," Dillon says. I realize I have stopped listening. "I know you don't want to talk about this. But if it's yours, we would never..."

"I have work early," I cut Dillon off. "It was great to chat."

"We're looking at coming out before I get too big to fit on an airplane," Sandy says, excitedly. "I've always wanted to go to Scotland, and now you're right there!"

"Harrogate's in England still," I correct her.

Sandy bristles, still disliking being corrected, and the familiarity sweeps me with homesickness.

"I look forward to it," I tack on.

I do, I really do. Despite everything, they're still my favorite two people in the world. "You're glowing, Sandy," I add. "Pregnancy suits you."

I hang up before they can respond. My small, poorly lit apartment, 'flat' as they are called in England, gets darker as the light from my monitor dims and with it my connection to everything I love.

ONE

Campaign: Reality
Scenario One: Meet the peeps.
Scene: Various places and people.

PAULA LUBELL

I shake off the bone-chilling cold that slowly seeps its way
through my layers of brightly-colored construction wear.
The view this morning is breathtaking and so rare in the
middle of winter. Vivid pinks and oranges coat the horizon,
dotted with broken tufts of puffy clouds. Below, the
Yorkshire Dales sleeps in shades of dark green. The fields,
organized into blocks by textured stone walls, are speckled
with white sheep. The occasional bleat drifts up to reach my
ears, even so high up. A low morning fog clings to
everything, exaggerating the colors of sunrise. I feel a shiver
from winter's cold as the bone-chilling damp threatens to

sneak across my back. The chill will escort me off my high perch here soon, but not yet.

I let my gaze wander from The Dales to the radomes, buildings, and generators at my back. The radomes are a round mass of steel and white that protect the giant radar dishes, and all their parts, from the outside world. They range from the size of a small bedroom to almost one hundred feet across. Imagine two T-rex dinosaurs nose to tail, and you're about the size of my biggest baby. And my babies they are. Not that I'm happy about that.

Helmwith's the name of the secret joint military base I'm contracted with. The peaceful view from above is the opposite of the crazy mess that hides beneath its surface. Although I don't deal with it directly, the base is in the middle of restructuring and downsizing. As technology gets smaller, fewer people are needed, but too few and the base will be up shit creek without a paddle.

I wouldn't say the base's small enough that everyone knows everyone, but most people are connected by at least a friend of a friend. It makes for juicy gossip – fun, until you hear one about yourself. Yes, Radome Services is a family business. Yes, technically my dad 'got' me my job...but I didn't want it! I'd been happy in Texas building things with my own two hands instead of stuck overseas poorly managing people. But at thirty years old, I still struggle to stand up to my dad.

"Gate D to Paul," my radio makes me jump.

The wind whips through my layers as clouds start rolling back in to blanket my sunrise in gray.

"Gate D to escort manager," my radio deadpans when I don't answer right away.

"Paul to Gate D, what do you need?" I ask before Deb can get involved.

I don't work for the security escort office, but Deb is the

manager. She enables my guys to work in secured spaces. She and her team are a part of every job that happens above ground.

"We need you at gate D now," Gate D tells me.

"On my way," I say into the radio.

I rack my brain for whatever I forgot as I seal the radome's hatch behind me and drop onto the supports of the radar dish. The relentless hum of technology and the clicking of my carabiners accompanies my climb down. Part way, one of my pockets snares on a bolt and opens, spilling its contents. The harsh crack of dice hitting concrete from three stories up reaches my ears.

"Is somebody up there?" a man calls out, his voice crisp.

I'm still about two stories up as I glance down to see how much trouble I'm in. The man on the floor is lacking the usual high-visibility gear or layers of jackets. He's most likely from below ground. Maybe I won't get reported for my little unauthorized morning adventure.

"Uh, what did they land on?" I call back as I speed up my descent.

"Just the floor, they didn't hit anything," the man eventually says.

"I mean the numbers," I clarify.

"Does it matter?"

"It always matters!" I call down. "If the dice gods felt the need to leave my pockets and roll, the least I can do is heed the results."

It takes the guy a minute to find them, and I'm down by the time he does.

"Um, a twenty and a one," the man tells me.

He gives me a once over, probably similar to the one I'm giving him. Definitely from below ground, he's dressed like he works in a clean office, his black hair styled with gel that would have been utterly destroyed in my hard hat. A little taller than me, he has the build of a runner. I can see tattoos peeking out of his sleeves as he hands me the dice. "I didn't know they made twenty-sided dice."

"Well, they do," I say awkwardly.

I'm not super good at small talk, especially with good looking men not wearing a tool belt. This man is certainly both those things.

"How rude of me, I'm Luis," Luis says with a smile.

He holds out his clean hand for a handshake.

"Paula, but I won't get your nice clean hand dirty with mine," I introduce myself.

I hold up my hand and wiggle my dirty fingers between us.

Luis laughs, the sound bouncing around in the large dome. "I think the smaller dice broke," Luis points out.

I look down at my other hand. The D20 looks okay, but the standard six-sided die, D6, landed on an edge. Luis is studying me when I meet his cool blue eyes.

"Shit happens," I respond, trying not to read into the polar opposite states of my dice.

"Gate D to Paula," my radio barks.

I jump. Shit, I forgot!

"On my way," I say into the radio, quickly waving Luis a hasty goodbye as I book it for my vehicle.

The fire alarm is going off. Apparently, it's a scheduled fire drill that I somehow didn't know about. Much like the paperwork I'd filled out incorrectly this morning, meaning my contractors couldn't get into the compound to do their job. I take a few deep breaths before feelings of inadequacy can overwhelm me and I fall apart in front of my crew. I understand, logically, as one of the only women in my field, it looks bad to have all my brothers promoted before me, but I didn't want any of this.

I make sure my little office is empty before also exiting. A concrete wall sits just outside of our fire drill zone and I easily boost myself onto it, gaining some height. Sometimes it's nice to be a tall, strong woman. Maybe I can spot Luis again; it's a silly thought for such a short exchange, but on my mind nonetheless.

Like an ant colony fleeing its tunnel system, bodies pour out from the buildings, both below and above ground. People gather in their little social groups. Those that work above and below ground don't mingle together. Although contractors and government employees don't look different, they also manage to steer clear of each other. The military guys stick out in their green fatigues, but not many are left these days.

As I scan the crowd, I don't see Luis, but a set of fatigues peeks out of a long jacket. The garment is quickly removed as the guy drapes over two of his coworkers huddled next to a building attempting to keep out of the icy wind.

Even from a distance, the man cuts a fine figure, broad shoulders taper into a well-kept waistline. Muscle definition peeks out of his collar a government employees' nd disappears up his neck into a tidy brown buzz cut. Luis had been handsome, but I do love a man with broad shoulders. My mind briefly wanders back to my dice, a broken one and a twenty.

"Lisa to Deb," my radio barks.

"Go ahead Lisa," Deb's voice.

"I've got Paul on my list today, but she's not checked in," Lisa states.

"Paul to Lisa," I say quickly into the radio. "I was at the office, over."

"Did you check in with your fire drill lead?"

"Right, doing that now, over."
If one could feel eyes roll through a radio, I just felt Lisa's.
I let my eyes find Mister Fatigues one more time before jumping down. He's still chatting with the ladies, and I have the sudden urge to go introduce myself, but I need to find my fire drill lead first so they can call the all-clear. By the time I find him and get checked in, the all-clear is called, and the swarm of humanity quickly disappears. Taking Mister Fatigues with them.

Joe Smartin

I park my car outside the gym and look at the picture on my phone screen. Colorado's Rocky Mountains are behind us. My broad face is lined with ease, we all look so happy. I tower over my friends. Ex-lovers? No, I don't like that thought at all. My friends.

After all the craziness with Sandy's old boss and the drama in my *D&D* campaign, the three of us had found ourselves in a thruple, I guess that's the technical term for it. I had been happy. I'd never been happier, if I'm being honest. Until the moment that Sandy announced she was pregnant. Dillon proposed a few days later. All right, after I had gotten my orders to be shipped to England. I scrub my hands over my face and force myself to stop looking at the picture. I should change it, but I've been saying that for weeks.

I rush through the empty parking lot. Freshly leveled

buildings on either side of it attest to how small Helmwith has gotten. They've even removed all housing on base, everyone's forced to live in town.

"Joe," Jake hails me.

Taller than even my six-foot-two-inch frame, Jake's a monster of a man. Covered head to toe in tattoos, he is a retired marine turned contractor. The only acceptable type of contractor. One who put in his time first.

"Morning, Jake," I respond. "Did you have a good weekend?"

"What do you think?" Jake's gruff voice responds.

I grunt in response, and Jake snorts before returning his attention to his own sets. I hate this base. It's too small. Contractor, military, boss, underling...everyone just brushes elbows constantly. The structure I live by, largely ignored.

I slip my earbuds into my ears. As I start my warm-ups, I look around the weight room for Scrunchy. All of us regulars do. She's a regular, too – though sometimes she comes in a bit before me and sometimes after. I don't see a lot of women lifting heavy.

"She's not in yet," Jake's announcement cuts through my earbuds. I bristle at being so obviously caught looking for her. But what can I say, I've not made many friends.

Scrunchy's probably about five inches or so shorter than me. She has long silver-blonde hair that she wears in a high ponytail with bright scrunchies, hence the nickname. Her round face is always red from exertion and often clashes terribly with her seemingly random sports tops of every color. Like me, she takes her lifting seriously enough to change into weight lifting shoes as she comes in from her cardio.

I look at my phone once more before attempting to push Colorado out of my mind. I should be in a better mood than this. Tonight, after a month-and-a-half, I finally found a role-playing game.

I usually love to run games, but I don't want to be a GM right now. Too much work's what I'm claiming. It is a lot of work, but it's also that I don't want to think about Sandy. I was her GM and so much more. Being a player should be perfect.

TWO

Campaign: Reality
Scenario One: Meet the peeps
Scene: Together we build a world.

PAULA LUBELL

I'm late for my own game. Well done me. I would worry, but hopefully, no one by now expects me to be on time. Except maybe the new guy, but he'll learn soon enough. I think they actually changed the start time to later and didn't tell me.

Byron's wife, Carmen, greets me at the door. She's stunning, as always. Long wavy black hair, petite features on her tall frame, coordinated outfit and everything. Every time I see Carmen, I struggle to connect her to her husband. Byron's her opposite. Always dressed in tacky Hawaiian shirts that pull in the middle. His beard could rival Santa Claus and his handlebar mustache is always on point.

"Would you like some chili?" Carmen asks, her Spanish accent is thick, she talks fast.

"Of course," I answer. I'm sure she's offering me chili.

Carmen's a godsend on gaming nights; it's not just me that has to rush from base to Byron's house to get here early enough to make it worth running on a weeknight.

I stick my gaming bag onto one arm. Trainers off, chili in hand, I easily find my way to THE CAVE.

"Hey, Paul," Kevin says the moment I enter the room.

His usual mop of brown hair is neater than usual, accenting his round ears and oval face. Like me, he comes straight from base, though his job below ground keeps him a hell of a lot cleaner. He looks tired behind his large round glasses.

"Hey," I echo keeping my face neutral.

I scuttle to my place at the head of the table. We've gone on three dates, and I've not been overly impressed. We don't have another date set up, and I'm leaning toward keeping it that way. I shouldn't have let him talk me into the first one. I'm so bad at saying no.

"Paul, this is Joe," Byron introduces me to the new guy.

Joe finishes whatever he was doing on his phone before he acknowledges me.

I can't help but bit my lip. I'm pretty sure Mister Fatigues gives me a tired smile. Broad shoulders are covered by an Air Force hoodie and corded neck muscles hint at his weight lifting hobby. A few love lines crinkle the sides of his eyes, which are set in square chiseled face. He's probably in his early thirties, like me. A five o'clock shadow covers his straight jaw and thick brown hair that, despite being so short, is somehow still disheveled on his head, adding to his tired brown eyes.

"Restructuring get'n too you?" I ask Joe as a wave of nervous energy hits me. Stupid good-looking men.

"What a mess," Joe starts to say, but stops himself looking around the room.

I chuckle, definitely military if he's watching what he says.

"It's getting to me too, Paul," Kevin sticks in trying to get my attention. "And Byron, we all have insane workloads."

"My teenagers will kill me first," Byron laughs, before more seriously adding. "But something important is going to fall through the cracks soon. There is no doubt."

"I don't deal with the computer stuff below ground directly," I give Joe what is hopefully a reassuring smile. "But we're all in this together, well maybe not Ed, our token Brit."

"Yet, you discuss it so often, I feel I am somehow involved," Ed respond lightly.

Ed's the tallest Brit I've ever met. Maybe in his mid-fifties, his salt and pepper hair is cropped very short and matches his simple black rimmed square glasses.

Chuckles go around the room, and Joe relaxes slightly.

"It's nice to meet you," I add with a smile. "I hear you just came over the pond a month ago?"

"You heard right," Joe states.

Joe has an amazing voice, low and rumbly. I want to hear him talk again.

"What a terrible month to arrive," Byron adds.

"He'll survive," Kevin says, stressing the rhyme.

I spare him a glance; he's grinning at me like he's given me a gift. I like accidental rhymes. He's really trying too hard.

Instead of interacting, I sit. One by one I pull out the tools of my trade. The *FATE Core* guides, notes, my laptop, and miniatures soon fill the space in front of me. I take a sip of whatever liquor Byron poured for me. Tastes like whisky tonight, and load up my dice into my personal dice tray. Like magic, a confidence I don't feel outside of role-playing nights descends upon me.

"This room's incredible," Joe tells Byron.

"It really is," I agree.

I pick up the tablet that controls the room and share a conspiratorial look with Byron. We're seated around a large glass table covered in a white sheet. At my command a map of Harrogate appears on its surface from the projector sunk into the hard wood flooring below it.

I dramatically lower the lights, drawing Joe's attention to the flickering LED sconces in the corners and the back lit wood bar at the far end. A huge flat screen 64-inch TV flairs to life with a picture Harrogate bathed in sun. I let Stray FM filter lowly through the room's speakers.

"It took me seventeen years to finish putting it together," Byron announces proudly.

"You've been here for seventeen years?" Joe repeats.

"No plans to leave either. I want all my kids to finish their A levels here," Byron continues. A light tension fills the air as we wait for Joe's response. Byron not only just announced his contractor status, but that he is a lifer, a contractor who flits from contract to contract so he can stay on foreign soil. Most military have a problem with that.

"I see," Joe says neutrally.

Although, I'm the GM, Byron's who actually brought us together and set up everything up. He would be who Joe got his invite from. Awkward…

I raise the lighting back up in the room so we can actually see our character sheets and Byron laughs, chasing away the tension. "Everything's different over the pond," he chuckles before launching into his story about building THE CAVE. It's very long and even Joe's giving me subtle 'help me' signs by the time I interrupt it to begin my game.

"All right," I say. "Here's the plan. We're using the *FATE* system this time around. I have a bag full of *FATE* dice here, two sides blank, two sides a plus sign, and two sides a minus. Plus and minus signs cancel each other out, obviously."

I wait until I get nods of understanding from the rest of

the table. Good, it looks like everyone read through the rules already. I reiterate the most important bits.

"If you want to do something above and beyond your abilities, you must spend a *FATE* chip. You only start with three, but you can earn more by failing things on purpose, making the game harder for yourself. It creates a system of checks and balances that allows us to pit our creative wills against each other. All of us, me included, need to be constantly spending and earning new *FATE* chips to have a healthy game economy."

"The setting will be present-day Harrogate, but in the summer because I'm sick of British winter already," I continue. "Life's exactly as you know it, except supernaturals live hidden amongst us. They have no government, no policing body. Some humans are in the know, others are not. It's pretty much the world for every urban fantasy novel or movie out there. We'll build our characters in three stages. Stage one is your high concept and a SHORT back story. Any questions?"

"I'm making a kung-fu wizard," Kevin immediately announces, pulling out a character sheet and holding it out to me.

"That doesn't give us much to go on," Joe adds dubiously, looking up from his phone.

"Well, you've walked around town, right?" I ask Joe. He nods. "Great, so it's an old spa town. Victorian manor houses, plumbing on the outside, no straight roads, lots of cute shops and too much money...oh! I know you've not seen it in the summer yet, but North Yorkshire is *stunning*. So green it will hurt your eyes."

"That's not really what I meant," Joe says slowly eyeing me.

I grin and nod extra big. Oh, I know it's not. He wants more details about my supernatural world. But I'm not ready to give those out yet.

Joe and my stare down's interrupted by Kevin shaking his character sheet to get my attention. I take it from Kevin and look it over as Byron and Ed get into the discussion. I'm not great and multitasking and I lose track of the conversation as I check that all of Kevin's concepts are legal.

"Your backstory's where your character derives its meaning," Joe's rumbly voice is explaining. I give Kevin an approving smile, handing him his character sheet back, and turn my attention to Joe as he continues. "It's what you base your character's skills and personality on. I think it's worth spending more time and space on it than this tiny square." He gestures to the very limited space on his character sheet, a character sheet I didn't make; it's from the rule book.

"Sure," I answer easily. I don't disagree, but that's not how I set up this game. "I did send out an email explaining that this game is intended to be fast, fun, and over in a few months."

Joe gets out his phone, again, maybe he didn't get the email. I know people's backstories are important to them, but I'm not reading any novels this time around. I shouldn't be judged for how I want to run my game.

I take a minute to remove one of my sweaters, finally starting to warm up. "Take the week, but write more than two paragraphs and I won't read it. Not to get all philosophical or anything, but all we can ever do is play aspects of our own personalities, that we will literally modify with dice rolls."

"The point of role-playing is to embody someone else," Joe insists. "To be creative in a world nothing like reality. Not in the city I'm currently living in."

"And you get to do that still," I respond evenly, our eyes meeting for a stare off once more.

His brown eyes are skeptical as I try to will him to just go with it. Sure, Harrogate isn't a faraway land, but I'm still going to fill it with bad guys and magic. We're still on step one of three in character creation! He needs to have some faith in his GM, me. Even God didn't create the universe in thirty minutes. Though I see his point with the back story. Should I be a merciful god of *FATE*?

"All right," I say, looking away first.

I give him what I hope is a winning smile. "I'll meet you halfway. Your back story can be as long as you want. But for every paragraph after two, I take away one of your starting *FATE* chips – happy to go negative."

JOE SMARTIN

I had looked twice when it was Scrunchy, the woman from the gym, who walked in and sat down at the head of the table. It caught me off guard. Our obvious difference in play styles bothers me, though she seems organized enough. I have to remind myself that it's her game, I'm not the GM here.

After about an hour, Scrunchy has removed two of her sweaters and calls for a 'powder break.'

I feel my eyes linger on her backside as she leaves the room. Scrunchy's – I'm not calling her Paul, that's for damn sure – ass looks a lot better in her spandex at the gym. Her hair is a mess, falling out of its French braid, and plastered to her head like she spent the day in a hat.

"She's not single," Kevin announces as soon as she's out of earshot.

"Really?" Byron laughs. "That's new, who's the unfortunate victim?"

"She's just not on the market," Kevin reiterates, his smile falling.

Byron and Ed exchange a knowing look that I can't decipher.

"This feels really sandboxy," I say instead of interacting with Kevin.

"Paul likes to give us worlds to hang ourselves in," Byron chuckles.

"What does sandboxy mean?" Ed asks politely.

I half-listen to Kevin explain that in role-playing, some GM's give their players a set path to go down and others just make a world and the players have to figure it out. Scrunchy's obviously just giving us a world...I prefer to make a set path for my players. I want to see them learn and work together. It's what I had win my game with Sandy...

I look down at my group chat the hundredth time tonight, my complaints about Scrunchy's gaming style already met with love and support from my two best friends. I wish they were in this game. Do I wish that? I promised them that we were friends first, no matter Sandy's decision at the end. And, at the end, she chose Dillon. If I say I'm cool with it often enough, it will be true. It has to be.

"We should make four wizards," Kevin announces, pulling my attention away from my phone and thoughts of Colorado.

"Why?" Ed asks.

"It actually could be really fun," Byron adds, twirling his mustache in thought.

"I was thinking I would play whatever would round out the party, balance-wise," I add.

"I wouldn't worry so much about balance. Just play whatever makes you happy," Byron tells me.

I cringe a little inside, making a balanced party is what would make me happy. I like rules and teamwork. Scrunchy's game logic is the exact opposite of what I love about tabletop gaming. She seems to be running on pure story and chaos, and her usual players are eating it up.

"My kung-fu wizard's element's going to be ice," Kevin interjects. "His name is Pooh-Bah."

"Ah, the Lord High of Everything Else!" Edward exclaims.

The room is silent.

"I think you're alone in your humor," Byron chuckles.

"Bloody uncultured Americans," Ed grumbles.

I turn my phone over on the table and attempt to focus on the new people, maybe friends. Being a part of a role-playing game is what I'm used to. It's normal for me. I need something to feel normal.

PAULA LUBELL

I blink at the woman in the mirror. She's me, a version of me. I need to look at myself before game night starts. There is a line of dirt across one cheek that I'm just now noticing. Face washed, hair quickly brushed and twisted up in a clip. Paul 2.0 looks satisfactory enough in the mirror.

Joe's not on his phone, for once, when I come back. I pull a flannel button-down out of my gaming bag. It's too cold down in Byron's cellar for just my black tank top, but I hate putting my work sweaters back on once they are off.

"We are making four wizards!" Kevin exclaims as I rejoin the table.

His grin literally makes the lights of the room seem brighter. He's one of those all or nothing type people, and tonight he's all happy, thankfully.

Joe doesn't seem super excited, though his nose is buried in the *FATE* book, so it's hard to tell. It takes about another hour for all four of them to sort themselves. Joe's wizard concept is fun, but walking the borderline of what is overpowered for my game. I give him a warning and he acknowledges it, his brain seeming to work overtime as he sticks his nose back in the rule book.

"Do you have another question?" I ask him.

"Nope," Joe deadpans without looking up.

"Interesting," Ed's voice grabs my attention. "I can combine weapons and magic?"

Twenty minutes later, most questions have been answered and character sheets are filled out. Joe's made his wizard even more overpowered, and I shake my head. "All right. We have us a party of four wizards, very different wizards, but wizards."

"We do, indeed," Byron speaks for the group.

"Nine days shy of two years ago," I begin setting my scene theatrically, "the world as you know it was destroyed."

"I knew it," Kevin interrupts.

I continue like he didn't speak.

"Two of the gods of old rose from their slumber to battle it out. This created a ripple effect, and suddenly, the supernatural world sprung into the spotlight. It became harder to hide. Fear of the unknown led to violence. And magical abilities that can heal and do things humans only ever dreamed of became sought after." I dramatically lowered the lights of the room. "Every country dealt with this differently. Generally, borders closed up. Travel is limited. No gods have awoken in England, but the government swiftly took control."

"This is how we know it's a fantasy game," Ed says knowingly, referring to the words 'swiftly' and 'government'.

"Right?" I say the word slowly both in question and agreement before continuing. "Supernaturals can now function in society in three ways. First, as a branch of the government force known as the MPD – Magical Police Department. Second, as registered supernaturals just living their lives. Third, as unregistered supernaturals trying not to be discovered as supernaturals. The government's attempt to control the use and trade of magical items has, of course, created a violent black market. This includes a subset of supernatural people who are deemed 'too powerful' and are hunted down and either forced to join the MPD or killed.

"Supernaturals are also organizing for the first time, but not as one force. Similar types are bonding together, the equivalent of gangs, to stay safe. The registration system doesn't protect supernaturals, and it certainly attempts to weaken them by removing the most powerful and unique. The registration system is managed and enforced by the MPD. Despite magical ability, humans still outnumber supernaturals 1000 to 1."

I start drawing on the tablet, and it shows up on the map. I love THE CAVE.

"Three factions exist in Harrogate," I point as I explain. "The druids, their magic's strong with the earth and elements, reside and control the South East and most of the Stray. The faeries, who hide their dark magical nature behind glamor and magical disguises, control the West, including all of Valley Gardens and old town, up to Betty's Tea House. And the smallest piece of the pie goes to the trolls. Or that's what they are called. The most diverse group, with unknown leadership. They hold the North."

I draw the borders on the map; it leaves a few blank sections and I point them out. "Those belong to the MPD and are effectively neutral territory. Or, if you're unregistered, really, really dangerous areas.

"Final piece for tonight," I continue. I look at each of them in turn. "All of you are in some business relationship together. It can be anything you want: black market smugglers, PI's, the same office at the MPD. Whatever, but you need to agree on it."

I take a deep breath. "Oh, and I need to know how you found yourself to be in Harrogate. It can be as simple as 'I was on vacation when the borders closed,' for everyone except Joe."

I turn to our newbie and give him an apologetic smile. I'm not trying to pick on Joe; all these rules were already in place before I had any idea what my players were going to make. "Ixar," I say, using Joe's wizard's name. "You've picked one of the subsets of powers deemed 'too powerful'. You're an unregistered wizard hiding from the MPD, unless you guys choose to join the MPD. I'm not pinning in your character. You can be good or evil or anything you want, but Ixar's a little overpowered."

"So, no real back story, and I start the game with a high concept that's not my choice," Joe deadpans.

I think I see a corner of his mouth twitch into a smile, but I don't know him well enough. He did ignore my warnings...is he messing with me?

"Yes," I say slowly. A bit of self-doubt fills my voice as I study his handsome face.

"I want to write a real back story," Joe demands, his voice almost a growl. "Consequence free. Otherwise, I roll a new character."

My cheeks hurt with the size of my grin. He's bartering with me! A core part of *FATE*. I can't tell if he's getting into the system early or just really, really into his backstories. Either way, I love it.

"Fine," I say, quite pleased. "But if it's stereotypical and emo, you owe me at least two beers."

"Sounds like a win-win to me," Joe agrees too quickly. Little butterflies flutter in my stomach, are we flirting? Did he build an overpowered character just to barter a backstory out of me?

Joe breaks our starring contest first, his eyes returning to his phone. I'm starting to hate that phone. I can't get a read on Joe at all, and I want to.

"Last phase of character building," I announce before I can dwell on Joe. "One more interaction that ties you all together in a nice little bow. Joe, er, Ixar included, with his unregistered limitations." There are some grumbles, but discussion begins again. I keep an eye on the time. As we get toward 11 PM the group seems to be settling on their own PI agency. And I'm happy enough with that. I start gathering my stuff.

"All right," I announce. "I need to go."

"Already?" Kevin whines.

"Yup. I've got a team in, pulling cables, they have to be done by Monday or else one of your precious server rooms won't work right," I tease Kevin. "So, it's bright and early for me. You're almost done. Just email pics of your sheets, and we will go over the hows and technical details next week."

"We will send the emails, boss," Byron says, giving me a mock salute.

I glance at Joe, looking at his phone again. Figures. Kevin gets my attention and makes a motion with his fingers like he's texting. I don't acknowledge him as I head back through Byron's house, stuffing myself into my coat to brave the walk home.

The damp cold is like a wall. My confidence drains. My joy from being around people is washed away by the abysmal weather. I'm not really doing so well alone, but maybe Joe's looking for a friend too. His soft brown eyes fill my memory, making the rain feel just a little bit warmer.

THREE

Campaign: Reality
Scenario Two: The world around us.
Scene: Life on Helmwith Base.

JOE SMARTIN

I peek into the cardio room on my way into the weight room Monday morning. Scrunchy, oblivious to the world, is watching something on her phone as she runs up steps on the stair stepper. I adjust my plan so that I can keep the only door that connects the two rooms in sight.

Despite our differences, I didn't hate her game on Friday. Yes, it had started rough, but Scrunchy had impressed me. My plan to make a character just to show her that her system was flawed had backfired. Not only that, she'd run with it. I'd spent some time making little adjustments to Ixar over the weekend. He was actually kind of cool, though only time would tell, I guess. There's not another open game so it's either this or nothing.

As predicted, she comes in about fifteen minutes later,

dripping with sweat. She finds her usual spot in the corner to change her shoes and wrap her wrists. I casually make my way over as she stands.

"Ah, hi," I say.

She blinks and then takes out one of her little earbuds.

"Hey," she says back.

Her eyes narrow and then she snaps her fingers. "Joe, from my game."

"That's me," I respond, searching for whatever I wanted to say next. "The *FATE* system's interesting."

"Different then what you're used to?" Scrunchy asks, one eyebrow raised.

"Yup."

"I hope I didn't make you uncomfortable."

"It's all a learning process," I answer unsure why I even brought up the *FATE* system. "We've been working out at the same time for about a month now."

"Creepy that you know that," she laughs. "Sorry I didn't recognize you. One of those different people, different places things."

"You don't need to apologize. What are you lifting this morning?"

"Back and shoulders, my favorites," she answers. "You?"

"The vanity pack." That's chest, arms, and core, but I assume she already knows that so I don't say it. Sandy was always quick to point out my mansplaining. I feel my face drop thinking of Sandy and try to push her out of my thoughts.

"Cool," she responds with an over-exaggerated nod. There's an awkward pause, and I realize she's waiting for me to say something else.

"Well, if you need a spot, let me know," she says before I can think of anything to add.

"Will do," I say lightly.

I'm not sure what I expected from this conversation, but this wasn't it. Her earbuds are already back in as she brushes past me to get started. Like all weight rooms, this one is covered in mirrors. Although it's meant as a tool for form and to help keep the gyms well lit, this morning I use it to watch Scrunchy. Despite my unease with our conversation, I'm happy to find her eyes doing the same.

PAULA LUBELL

Managing has one perk; I make my own schedule, well sort of. As I had needed to work over the weekend, I give myself Friday off.

My cat, Lord, greets me with meows when I come in from my hike in the Dales. About a year old, he's a gray British shorthair with vivid orange eyes and thick, soft fur. He might be a little overweight. And by that, I mean he's fat as shit. I just leave food out for him all the time and he vacuums it up.

A quick shower warms me up, and I sink into my overstuffed couch. My flat is small but adorable. With no room for a kitchen table, I pretty much live on my couch. The mismatched coffee table shows it, covered in papers and technology.

I post a few pictures from my hike into my family's group chat. The chilly morning left a layer of frost and ice on everything, and there's a great one of frozen moss, overlooking one of the reservoirs. I flip my chat over to my individual messages with my second oldest brother, Mason, and send him probably the most artful cow shit I've ever taken a picture of. The crystallized grass behind it, a hint of wafting steam coming off it. I can't remember when we started sending pictures of feces back and forth, but it's been escalating for years. This one tops them all.

A sting of loneliness tries to wriggle its way into me, and I push it away. My family's really close, and it's hard to have them literally a world away. I fill my life with people and activities. I do love them and I'm not unhappy, but...there's always a "but." I also wish I was sharing these pictures with someone in person. I don't like being alone, being one of five siblings, the house was always busy and full of activity. Not the peaceful, stale silence of my flat.

I narrow my eyes as I push aside my unhappy thoughts and realize that my *FATE* books are not on the table. I must have left them at the office. That's 20 minutes' drive and three security checkpoints. Ugh. Maybe I can use Byron's or, actually, maybe Joe's?

Joe and I exchanged numbers on Thursday after spending most of the week eyeing each other in the mirrors. I'm pretty sure Joe's just looking for a friend, maybe a workout buddy. Despite having my digits, he hasn't contacted me.

Luis, on the other hand, the saint who didn't report me for my rule breaking morning excursion...We have a coffee date set up for Saturday. I'm not sure how he got my number. He was so polite on the phone, even telling me he could lose my number just as easily if he'd made me uncomfortable. His voice was not quite as low as Joe's, but it rumbled with his excitement to see me again.

My phone gives me a messenger notification, and Kevin's message asking about another date comes through.

"What's going on?" I exclaim to Lord.

The gray ball yawns and stretches. I've been overseas for a year now, an entire year! Murphy's law, everything's happening all at once. Lord wanders into my lap, and I push my bizarrely active "love" life to the side to prepare for my game.

Four wizards. Ed's the funniest – Clint Northwood. His overall arching character ideal, called a high concept, is Gunslinger Bounty Hunter Wizard. Tall, thin, and dressed in the tackiest cowboy clothing known to man. He casts most of his magic by enchanting his weapons and wild west tech.

Kevin's gotten confused about what a wizard is. His high concept is Discipline of the Ice Snake, Professional Ass Kicker. Pooh-Bah is a kung fu master who blends elemental ice magic into his martial arts. He described his character as looking like Jet Li but with cool swirly blue tattoos. He also only wears a shirt when absolutely necessary.

Slyltyrd Byke, who I will be calling Byke, as I have no idea how to pronounce that, matches Byron's personality to a "T." His high concept is Goblin Artificer, tinkerer in things large and small. He describes himself as a short goblin with green skin, a round potbelly, and long, pointed ears. He wears a charm on his neck that projects an illusion of a dark-skinned human, similar in shape, though still with his unnaturally orange hair.

And last, I look at Joe's sheet again. It's the shortest, though I've been promised a longer back story. Joe's made a Summoning Wizard named Ixar Oleus. The high concept I forced upon him is "Unregistered and needs to keep a low profile." Although he's min-maxed his numbers to make his wizard as powerful and well connected as possible, Ixar's void of a personality. I wonder if it's Joe's way of not committing to my game. Though, I'm not sure why he's role-playing if he isn't. It's a time-consuming hobby, well at least for the GM.

I flip through my notes and glance at my phone. In a few hours, I need to be ready to lose myself in a world of my creation, to inflict my will upon those daring enough to attempt to navigate it. I can't wait!

FOUR

Campaign: Where is your god?
Scenario One: The world is our oyster.
Scene: To be or not to be.

PAULA LUBELL

"**3**14 PI Services, really?" I groan.

"It's funny because 3.14 is the start of a mathematical constant for PI and Private Investigator," Ed explains. I blink at him.

"I never would have gotten the terrible pun if you hadn't been there for me," I respond sarcastically.

"I would've thought you knew that," Ed states, completely serious. Kevin suddenly can't breathe, he's laughing so hard. Byron has to wipe his eyes. Even Joe chuckles, though he looks just as tired and skeptical as last week. I splutter for a moment and feel a flush come to my cheeks.

I finally gather myself. "All right, moving on." I have the

outline of an office up on Byron's projector. Everyone has chosen a random miniature to represent themselves.

"Your detective office is located above one of the many pubs in the middle of old town. The front is accessed through a slip of a door between the pub and the dry cleaners next door. Although each of you has keys, guests must ring and be buzzed in. Upon entering, the front room is lovely, clean, and well kept. You have enough regular business for a local cleaning company to take care of it. Fish tank and all. But the back room, the back room is a different story..."

THE OFFICE CAT

Character description: huge, fluffy Maine coon, white face but tortoiseshell in coloring.

Despite its current occupants, this is my office, I was here before they moved in, and I will be here after they leave. Although, they are quite entertaining and I get fed at least four times a day, usually. I don't mind that at all. I guess I can call them my tenants, for now.

It's late morning, the summer sun has moved, and I stretch, my spot no longer purrrrfect. This room is lofty. The majority of the light comes from the dusty chandeliers and the skylights, at least sixteen feet above us. I have tried in vain to reach them. They illuminate the dented, cracked, and magic-scarred walls and floor. Honestly, it looks like a war zone, but I don't mind. There's usually lots of debris for me to play with. Not today, though.

I consider moving to the front room, I do love the fish,

but I just don't feel like getting my paws wet at the moment. I wander over to Byke's desk.

It's the biggest, painted black, in a modern style "L" shape and tucked into the corner. Shelves going all the way up the high ceilings are filled with things for me to knock over. Which I do, often. Especially if he's watching and has his hands full. Today, he's boring, just sitting in front of his computer, reading or whatever goblins do to rot their brains.

Clint is next on my list. Clint loves me. He always knows the best places to stroke me, and I can often smell other animals on him. If it's the ones I like, I rub against him. If it's the ones I don't, I hiss and pee on his shoes. He should know better by now. I jump up on Clint's desk, the thick antique wood faded under my paws. He's not big on modern technology, so there's no warm surfaces to lie on, but he usually has lots of loose bullets for me to play with.

I bat one to the floor, and there's a loud banging noise that frightens me. I jump down, scampering for safety. That happens often when I play with Clint's stuff, and it scares me every time, but I still do it.

"Tarnation," Clint's voice comes from near my hiding spot in between two of Pooh's bean bag chairs.

Pooh desk is my favorite. Low to the ground, it's surrounded by soft things. The opposite of in Byke's in every way, it lacks anything I can knock off it. Pooh spends a lot of time sitting still with his legs in the perfect cat bed shape, he's often my heated pillow. I guess he calls it a wizard trance to help him practice and focus his magic. But he will learn its true purpose someday.

"Would you stop leaving bullets on your desk for the cat?" Byke demands.

"We could just get rid of the cat." Pooh's large warm hand stroke my head as he says it.

He would never really want to get rid of me. He even

made a little ladder with a bed on it so I can watch out the window on the side of the back door. Before my tenants can argue, said door opens.

Ixar walks in, coffee cups in hand. Ixar always looks like someone just made him kill his puppy. Some cross between sad and angry that's hard to balance. Maybe it's because he doesn't have his own desk in the back? I've also never seen him play with the fish, so there's that.

"How long has the front door been buzzing?" Ixar asks.

"The door's buzzing?" Clint asks, surprised.

Ixar growls something about incompetence and stalks toward the front room. His clean, boring white desk is out there; he's the front man of their little business. Probably for the better: Byke, Clint, and Pooh are not so good with people. I make my way up to my highest perch and sit regally, observing the world that I rule over with my divine benevolence.

IXAR - JOE'S WIZARD

"Sir," the woman of the trio now standing before me says. "I must insist, I was standing and buzzing for a solid fifteen minutes. My issue is time-sensitive."

Three clients have jockeyed their way up our narrow staircase at the same time and now fill our small waiting room. The woman, who introduced herself as Isabella Blackwell, is dressed the nicest. Her pixie-cut brown hair and large blue eyes pull your attention away from her comically large feet covered in chunky loafers and poking out of a green pants suit. The two men are unremarkable. One is dressed in a business suit, the other looks to be wearing a uniform from the local kitchen supply shop.

"I'm sorry," I try to smooth things over. "We don't have a camera on our door, so I've no way to verify your stories. Ah, is there some way you can work this out yourselves?"

"I was here, 8:00 AM sharp," the uniformed man explains. "I didn't see any sign of this woman at all. My job is pressing, and I can pay."

"Pressing? I need to get to the office," the man in the suit bellows.

"Please calm down…" I start but am cut off.

"I know you're unhappy," Isabella cuts me off, her voice sweet. "I can see it all over your face. Maybe we can get a coffee and you can talk to me about it."

"Ixar isn't unhappy," I break character to add.

"Well, Joe," Scrunchy says. "If you don't want me to describe your character as unhappy maybe you could at least try a smile? GM's need love too."

"The point of role-playing is to embody someone else," I insist.

"We had this exact conversation last week," Scrunchy reminds me. "And I didn't disagree with you. Embody a happy Ixar, and my NPC's won't describe you as being unhappy," Scrunchy explains, using the acronym NPC (non-player character) when referring to Isabella. I flash a petulant fake smile with too many teeth in her direction. I'm not used to being told how to act, I don't like it. Scrunchy rolls her eyes.

"I demand service first!" *Scrunchy says shrilly, in her voice for Isabella.*

It pulls the room's attention from me and back into her game.

"How 'bout we done split uhp and each tawk t' one awf ya?" Clint's voice comes out of the back room, followed by his person.

Unlike my tailored dark suits, Clint's American cowboy get-up is as outrageous as his accent.

"I think my job requires more attention than that," the uniformed man insists.

"Mine probably doesn't," the man in the suit quickly adds.

"Does anyone need some asses whooped?" Pooh asks as he also joins us, cracking his knuckles.

I look up at the ceiling as my two coworkers are undoubtedly about to make this more complicated than it needs to be.

"We should work on these one at a time, as a team," I press. My comment is ignored, and I soon find myself on my own, seated across from Isabella in the empty pub below us.

PAULA LUBELL

Well, the first thing my players do is split into three groups. I'm not surprised. I half-expected it. This is their chance to learn about the world, they don't need to do it together. Joe's openly unhappy about the arrangement, going so far as to verbally challenge my choice to let the party split.

"What do you expect me to do about it, Joe?" I ask.

Joe picks up his phone in response with a disapproving shake of his head. I bristle, more upset than I expected to be. This is my game, not his. I set this up to give them a foundation of world-building. You don't have to do every fucking thing together. Joe's getting under my skin, and I realize that I'm letting him because I want his approval. I quickly squash it down.

I decide to resolve Pooh's "job" first as I focus on Kevin. The man in uniform takes Pooh over to the local kitchen supply shop where he's introduced to Audry Lakeland, the owner. Mrs. Lakeland is having trouble as all of the trash on the block keeps "magically" ending up outside her shop. Pooh easily follows the magical trail of the culprit. I'm sure to point out that the Mrs. Lakeland's shop is in troll territory, and the trail he finds is clearly faerie magic.

Pooh decides to take on the faerie, giving me the perfect opportunity to demonstrate how combat works and how players keep track of injuries. It's called the consequence tier, and it's in three levels: mild, moderate, and severe. They are exactly what they sound like. On his own, the faerie easily escapes, leaving Pooh with a moderate injury. Her lovely laugh is filled with the promise of return.

Next, I get Ed and Byron's attention. Clint and Byke's target is every PI's cliché, a man who wants to know if his wife is cheating on him.

"You follow the wife as she goes about her day to day business," I describe, "You notice that Harrogate is busting at the seams with people, odd but not uncommon for this time of year. Several known druid shops are being heavily trafficked. Despite it being day out, you can see some odd lights coming from Betty's Tea House. You pass two different gyms, the people coming out of them stumble a little, like they just had an amazing leg day."

"Leg day?" Ed asks me.

"It's when you lift a bunch of weights with your legs at the gym," Scrunchy explains. "An amazing leg day is when your legs feel like wet noodles when your done and walking up stairs becomes a daunting challenge."

"How is that Amazing?" Kevin asks in disbelief.

I look over at Joe for back-up, but he's looking at his phone. Sigh. "You'll have to take my word for it."

Clint nor Byke focus on the oddities, instead keeping their eyes peeled on the wife. I move onto Joe.

Joe rolls to see if Ixar can calm my crying, two-faced half-troll he thinks is just a normal human girl. He manages, just. I offer to let him spend a *FATE* chip to make her feel more comfortable, but he doesn't bite. I blink a few times when he doesn't question her, just asks for her story. Joe doesn't even roll to see if she's telling the truth or check to see if she's magical. Is he that uninterested in my game?

She might be dressed all classy, but I described her entire bottom half as looking like a troll, she has fucking clown feet, tucked into loafers yes, but they're still comically huge! What is Joe doing?

"Um, Joe, roll Empathy," I ask Joe, throwing him a line.

If he makes this roll, I can tell him something seems off and maybe it will encourage him to investigate Isabella's story a bit more. Dice fly, and every single one lands on a minus sign. I blink. Or maybe Isabella is an even better actress than even I realized. I guess if Joe and the dice want to just believe everything she says...

"Isabella summarizes that her best friend's missing," I explain, keeping my voice even. "Well, her best frenemy. They were super competitive. She's terrified to alert the MPD because she thinks they will blame her for it, and Teresa, her friend, is a faerie. Ixar knows that faeries take care of their own, but things can get complicated. Teresa's last known location was at Hotel du Vin, right at the edge of druid territory. She's offering 5000-pound reward for you to find her."

"I tell her it's not enough information for me to guarantee anything," Joe explains. "But I will take a 500-dollar, er pound, deposit from her and learn what I can. If action needs to be taken, I will need the rest of my team with me."

I nod and make a few notes for myself. Well, that went very well for me, also known as, my character is getting what she wants. Which is not necessarily the best for the health of my players or my story line, honestly.

JOE SMARTIN

"Your team?" Kevin scoffs at me.

"Yeah, my team," I reiterate. I've relaxed a little as the night's gone on.

"You can't just say something's yours," Kevin declares.

I chuckle. I don't know why I'm finding this so funny, but I am. Kevin's a spit-fire, he is at work too. Although we haven't acknowledged it, Kevin's a contractor on one of the teams I manage. I seem to have rubbed him the wrong way immediately in both locations. He has had quite a few biting remarks for me tonight. Though he phrases a lot of them with humor, I know they are meant to hurt my ego.

"Only time will tell," I say, leaving the argument open.

"Should I pull out my dick and get in on this pissing contest?" Scrunchy asks sarcastically, motioning to her pants.

I smile and laugh for real this time. I might not agree with her GMing style, but Scrunchy's refreshing. I realize no one else laughed and calm myself. Scrunchy gives me a calculating look, as if she's putting together a puzzle.

"All right," Scrunchy intones. Kevin's phone makes an obnoxious noise, and he immediately picks it up. "We will call it here for tonight."

"Paul!" Kevin exclaims quickly. "My sky scanner binged. Up for a trip to Dublin tomorrow? Eighteen pounds round trip flight."

"Kevin, that's such a bad idea," Scrunchy answers.

"Eighteen pounds?" I can't stop from commenting. "That's like 25 dollars, to fly somewhere?"

It's Byron who quickly fills me in on the small airport, about twenty minutes away, and the amazing thing that is budget European airlines. The biggest perk of living overseas is being able to travel, though I haven't taken advantage of it yet. I just haven't had a moment to spare. No, I'm lying to myself. My new boss has overloaded myself and my teams, but I also don't want to travel alone.

"If I go with you, I'm…" I hear Scrunchy start to list off conditions. "Taking a nap. That flight's in seven hours. You're buying the first round. I'm not sharing a hotel room with you. And I'm hiking Sunday."

"I can agree to all those terms," Kevin chirps happily.

"Joe, you want to join us?" Scrunchy asks me.

I look up, surprised she would ask but also grateful. I see the corners of Kevin's mouth tighten, and I realize he's into Scrunchy. I think for a moment.

"Isn't Dublin a different country?" I ask hesitantly, still struggling with the concept.

"It's too spur of the moment for military brains," Kevin comments. His voice is playful, but I can see in his eyes and body language, it's just another barb at my background. "Does not compute," he adds in a robot voice. Fuck it.

"What do I pack?" I ask.

Scrunchy cheers and attempts to get Byron and Ed on board as well, but they have commitments already. Kevin's shooting lasers out of his eyes at me, and I feel something lighten. The old Joe, the Joe before Sandy and Dillon, would have done spontaneous stuff like this, and enjoyed messing with Kevin. I even would have thrown some insults back at him.

I shoot my group text with Sandy and Dillon an excited message about my sudden trip. A few minutes later, I'm handing Kevin a twenty-pound note and filling in my passport info on his phone. To Dublin I go.

FIVE

Campaign: Reality
Scenario Three: Expanding friendships.
Scene: What happens in Dublin, stays in Dublin.

PAULA LUBELL

We all split a cab to the airport. Joe and I, both being used to our morning workouts, are pretty chipper, but Kevin's not a morning person and declares his intention to sleep on the flight right before he nods off in the taxi. We prod him awake to get him through security, and I soon find myself squished in between Joe and Kevin in a row towards the back. Our little overnight packs shoved into the compartment above.

"Thanks again for the invite," Joe says as he puts his phone in flight mode.

"Are you going to survive the forty-five minute flight with that turned off?" Kevin asks with a yawn. Joe doesn't respond to Kevin's grumpiness.

"I brought music," Joe tells me. "But I was wondering if we could chat about the *FATE* system?"

"No games on your phone? No book?" I tease.

"I have been trying to read the same book for about a year," Joe admits a little sheepishly.

"I'm in a similar boat," I add. Joe gives me a half-smile that I return. "What did you want to talk about in *FATE*?"

"I don't quite understand what all the skills do, is Empathy being able to feel someone's emotions?" Joe asks, making a logical assumption.

"No, it's knowing if someone is being truthful, recognizing signs if they are lying or not," I correct.

We pause our conversation as the plane accelerates and takes off into the air. Kevin manages to nod off again as the plane evens out, not remotely interested in the details of a system he's already familiar with.

Joe's a different person with his phone off. His questions slowly morph from innocent details about *FATE* to more specific questions about my GMing style. He seems truly interested when I mention my family plays together, but the concept of a family all working together seems to make him even more sure that I should be creating a fixed path for my players to go down.

"Look, I just don't run games that way," I find myself reiterating as the flight is landing. I feel like we just took off. My grin is so wide it almost hurts my face.

I enjoy conversations about things that make you think. I enjoy having my view challenged. It doesn't mean I will change my mind, but having honest, open conversations is how people improve. Despite not knowing each other well, Joe has dived right into it with me!

"But you can't deny when everyone works together, it's the best part of role-playing," Joe reiterates his point.

"I don't deny it! I even agree with you," I counter. "But,

the harder people have to work for things, the sweeter the victory. Role-playing isn't about getting from point A to point B, it's all the shit that happens in between. It's trying to figure out what point B even is, and if you can't figure it out, it's creating point T. Your decisions should affect the storyline, even if that mucks up my plans!"

"But it needs to be a story, still," Joe says, sticking to his guns. "Characters need to grow and players be entertained. Not just mucking about goallessly."

"You will just have to trust me," I finish. "And stop trying to bully me during my game, it's not going to work." Joe gives me a confused look as I turn and poke Kevin awake, I can't believe he slept through landing.

"What time did you go to bed?" I ask him as he rubs the sleep out of his eyes.

"I don't know," Kevin mumbles.

We get a few coffees into Kevin and soon find ourselves on a bus into Dublin city center. By the time we exit the bus, Kevin has returned to his excited chipper self and shows off his late night of research in the form of a walking tour. He takes his role as tour guide quite seriously. Joe isn't a man of many words now that we're not discussing *FATE*, but he has some clever puns. Kevin's quick to point out how bad they are, but I bark out a laugh at each one. Like me, Joe's laid back as we follow Kevin around the cobbled streets of Dublin.

We walk by castles and cathedrals, their flying buttresses grand against the grey sky. It's not raining, yet, but it's in the forecast. We do a quick wander through a Viking museum, Joe and Kevin both humor me as we try on helmets and snap a few selfies. Their issues with each other put aside so we can enjoy the day. I have to fight the urge to grab Joe's hand and pull him towards anything and everything that excites me. I like seeing the smile on his face in place of his usual frown, it makes him look younger. Even more good looking, if that's possible.

I officially have a crush, like a teenage girl crush. Joe's handsome, thoughtful, even holding the door like an old-fashioned gentleman for both me and Kevin. Though I get the feeling he's doing it to Kevin to mess with him.

We find our way to the River Liffey and catch a bus toward the Guinness Storehouse. While on the bus, Joe's phone begins to ding.

"Your friends in Colorado?" I ask him.

I don't know much about them, but he mentioned them a few times on the flight.

"Yeah, Dillon just woke up," Joe answers absently.

That fast, Joe's smile from the morning's activities dims and the Joe that came out of his shell to play with me vanishes into his screen. I have to physically pull Joe off the bus, he almost didn't notice we got off it, as it comes to our stop. By the time we make it up to the top story of the massive seven-story interactive beer museum that is the Guinness Storehouse, I find Kevin at my side, not Joe. Kevin's happily leading us through the throngs of people, enjoying the glass-encircled panoramic viewing room while Joe trails after us, mostly attempting to message on his phone and carry a pint at the same time.

Joe Smartin

I'm relieved when Dillon messages me back. Although I'm having fun, something about the day just doesn't feel right, and I realized it's because I'm with the wrong two people.

Scrunchy's growing on me, a little, and Kevin's tolerable, but it isn't the connection and playfulness that I'm used to.

That I miss. I let myself hang back, sending pics from the morning and catching them up on my 'adventure,' as Scrunchy keeps calling it.

I get a great picture of my pint with Dublin sprawling below it before finding Scrunchy and Kevin again.

"Ready to go?" Scrunchy asks me sharply.

I look at my half-full pint and then at both their empty ones, clearly not ready to go.

"We'll be in the gift shop," Kevin gloats, stressing the word we.

"I'll find you there," I respond.

Kevin almost possessively tries to put an arm around Scrunchy's waist, but she doesn't notice. Her long strides already taking her out of his reach and toward the stairs. I really should clear the air with Kevin, as much as I enjoy winding him up. I'm not interested in Scrunchy. She's almost as tall as me, her shoulders, though feminine, are almost as wide as my own. Physically she's not my type, and even if she was, a piece of me is still holding out for something. I angrily scrub my hand through my hair. I don't even know what I'm holding out for – Sandy made her choice. She and Dillon are official and I'm chopped liver. But if the baby's mine...

I knock back what's left of my pint and force my thoughts back on the here and now. I'm in Dublin, seeing the world. My phone plinks again, Sandy's up now and gushing over my pictures, with me in spirit, if not physically here.

I can't believe how much these two can drink. I'm not sure what pub we're in now. The world's a little blurry around me, and the noise is deafening. I'm not a big drinker, I love sampling micro brews and enjoying the taste of things, but I'm not a big fan of being drunk. I thought I could at least keep up with Kevin, he's half my size! It seems I was wrong. I take out my phone and try to send a message to Sandy, but the keypad's really small.

"Why did you invite him?" I hear Kevin ask.

His and Scrunchy's voices come in and out with the rolls of sound in the pub.

"He looks like he could use friends," Scrunchy responds. "You remember what it was like when you first moved. At least we had the fucking sun."

"He's been a gloomy shadow following us all day," Kevin whines. "And he treats you like shit during your game. It's your game. He shouldn't be telling you how to run it."

"He was pretty cool this morning, but I won't argue with you about recently," Scrunchy answers, her voice bitter. "I don't know about my game, I'm handling him so far. Byron invited him, if he gets too bad, Byron can un-invite him."

I reach forward and find my half-finished beer, taking a big gulp. I must look really out of it. Maybe I am. Only half of what they are saying makes sense. The band starts their next song, is this "Sweet Caroline" again? I thought we were in Ireland? The overly happy covers of pop music with Irish flute and fiddle were entertaining for a while. But now everything's just a blur.

"Another?" Kevin asks Scrunchy, I'm assuming. Why would he be asking me?

"No, I'm going to get Joe to his room," Scrunchy sighs.

I reach for my beer again, but before I can drink it, it disappears.

"Just leave him, he's an adult," Kevin says offhandedly. "I know you tried to make this a group thing, but I was hoping we could spend time together."

"Kevin, I like you, you make me laugh," Scrunchy says warmly. "But even you aren't cold enough to abandon Joe in a foreign country."

"It's Ireland. It's our backyard."

"Really, Kevin?"

"It feels like it," Kevin relents. "Look, you're right, I don't really think we should abandon Joe. I'm just having fun, you know me, I get very caught up in the moment."

"You do, and when it's a good moment, you're so much fun," Scrunchy says with a laugh.

"And I'm fun right now!" Kevin exclaims. "Joe can be just as drunk in a pub as in his hotel room."

"Oh my god," Scrunchy laughs. "Go get yourself another beer and go mingle. I'm getting Joe out of here."

"I don't want to mingle," Kevin whines. "I'm bad at mingle. It's why I spend all my time gaming and hanging out with other gamers. Just leave Joe. He's a mingler."

"You don't know that," Scrunchy says quickly. "Just because he doesn't look super nerdy doesn't mean he's not."

"He's not one of us, Paul!" Kevin insists. "He's even military. They're brainwashed."

"He's in my game. He's one of us."

"No, he's not. And you know it, just look at him."

There is a pause and I realize my head is resting on the table. When did I put it down?

"Then I'm not either," Scrunchy's voice is like steel. I feel an arm start to pull me up from my seat and I let it.

"You know I didn't mean it that way," Kevin backpedals.

"Have a good rest of your night," Scrunchy clips.

"Paula…"

I lose track of him as the arm guides me through the colorful moving crowd. I feel hands help me put on my rain jacket. The freezing cold drizzle helps me sober up a little, but I'm still struggling to walk straight. I feel Scrunchy's strong arm slip around my waist to steady me.

I think I ask Scrunchy to send a message to Sandy and Dillon on my phone. Are we walking? I'm not really sure what starts it, but at some point, I realize that it's not just the cold drizzle on my face but tears and my mouth is running. I'm talking. I think about stopping, but I can't focus enough to even know what I'm saying.

PAULA LUBELL

The night attendant gives me a pitying look as I collect both my and Joe's keys from him. Joe to stops talking and focus enough to navigate the stairs in the ancient building. I love being strong, and right now, I'm thankful for every workout. Joe's fucking heavy, even when he's supporting some of his own weight. Every flight up leaves behind more of the noise and chaos that fills Temple Bar.

I almost just dump Joe on the floor in his room and leave. This morning had been wonderful and fun, but once his friends in Colorado started messaging him, that was it. Even when he wasn't on his phone, his thoughts were far away.

I rescheduled coffee with Luis for this. Luis is actually interested in me. Honestly, so is Kevin, though I haven't felt a real connection there. Why is my stupid brain stuck on Joe?

I let this almost stranger ruin my day, hoping for some vague sign that he would be interested in me too. Like some lovesick puppy. I need to take better care of myself. Joe stumbles into the room, and his hand grabs my arm. He awkwardly clings to me for balance, his babbling slowing as his stream of consciousness stops. Joe's brown eyes find mine and hold them.

"I'm angry," I hear Joe's words clearly this time. "I'm lonely. I always was and just didn't know it."

Those words break my heart, and I realize I can't just shove him in his room and leave. He's soaking wet from our walk home and fucked up from drinking too much. No matter how mad I am, I can't do that to anyone. With four brothers, I've dealt with my fair share of drunken emotional turmoil, and this is exactly what's going on.

With a sigh, I pull off my shoes and coats before helping Joe with his. I find two bottles of water before making myself comfortable on his bed, a pillow supporting my back as I lean against the headboard. Joe sloppily joins me, and I let him settle with his head resting in my lap. His cropped hair is as thick as it looks, and wet from our walk in the rain as I run my fingers through it. Joe wraps an arm around my legs, his lost soul searching for comfort.

"It will be ok," I tell him soothingly.

"I just don't know," Joe says.

Calmer, but still slurred, Joe starts to talk again, and like a puzzle, the pieces of his life slowly slide into place.

"Did you sleep with Joe?" Kevin asks me. "Is that why this is happening?"

"Oh, sweetie, no," I respond to Kevin's jealousy. "Joe was so drunk he couldn't have gotten it up even if he had wanted to."

"Then why don't you want to go on another date with me?" Kevin presses.

We're seated across from each other at the Little Ale House. My favorite pub. The Victorian building is decorated with old wood panels, the tables and chairs made of the same. The bar has twelve, always local, taps on. The best part is the cellar. Decorated with reeds, sconces, and old barrels, it honest to god could be a medieval pub.

I spent many an afternoon here hoping a group of adventurers would show up and invite me on their quest... no such luck. Turns out, even in England, the only real quests you get are the ones you find for yourself.

"Kevin," I explain. "Honestly, romantic feelings are just not there for me. I like you, I want to stay your friend, but I don't feel a spark. And, no offense, but I don't think you really feel it either."

"Maybe it just needs to grow," Kevin sighs. "We have so much in common. Give it time. We have been on what, three dates?"

"Yeah, three dates," I say the word three much differently than Kevin does. "And we haven't even kissed. Look, I want love. Romance, the shit you read about books. You deserve someone to be just as starstruck about you. That's not me."

I want someone to love me as much as Joe loves Sandy, I think but don't say out loud.

The man's a mess, his world in pieces. Because he put his heart out there. He found someone he truly loves. Even if it ends with me crying in some stranger's lap in a hotel room, I want that too.

"Paul, Paula, I really like you," Kevin tries again.

"Kevin," I cut in. "You really like the idea of me, and I like the idea of you, but, at least on my side, I'm just not feeling it."

"Paula…"

"Alright, let's try it this way," I cut him off. "It's not me, it's you. Wait. Right, it's not you, it's me. The tragedy of it all." I put the back of my hand against my forehead dramatically. I get my desired response and Kevin chuckles. I give him a minute to think and sip my beer.

"Friends," Kevin confirms.

"We better be. We play in two campaigns together," I remind him.

Kevin sticks out his hand, and I give it a shake.

"Did you hear about Harrison's shakedown with Smartin?" Kevin asks, changing the subject.

I happily slide into base talk. Apparently, Joe's not making friends as he attempts to reorganize the massive workload now on his teams, all four of them. Wow, I hadn't realized he was managing a double load.

"He's trying to change everything," Kevin complains. "We already know two of those systems can't handle less admins, we learned that under George last year. And I can't get pulled off Gettlin, because no one else knows the code it's so old. He's doesn't listen to us though! Mister 'I serve my country' by having muscles and making everyone else's jobs harder."

"Oh, shit, you're on one of this teams?" I confirm. "That must put some weird dynamics on game night."

"It does," Kevin confirms. "He's just doesn't really fit in with us."

"Kevin," I warn. "You've no idea what's going on in Joe's life. I know he's your boss and he looks like someone that stole your lunch money in middle school, but seriously, I'm giving him a chance."

"I don't know why," Kevin responds glumly.

"Because everyone deserves at least one," I say, unwilling to breach Joe's drunken trust.

"I wish you'd given me a chance," Kevin brings us full circle.

"I gave you three!" I exclaim.

Kevin grins at my outburst and stands picking up our empty beer glasses. "Same thing?"

"What makes you think I'm staying?" I ask.

"Because you're spending the rest of the evening helping me set up my online dating profile," Kevin responds.

I laugh, "Bouncing back there quick."

"You're a foot taller than me anyway," Kevin says off handedly. "If I'm rolling a new character, I want to put in a request for one that I don't need to stand on my toes to try and kiss."

SIX

Campaign: Where is your god?
Scenario Two: Druids & Disorder
Scene: Farmer Brooks and his sheep.

JOE SMARTIN

The door to Byron's house swings open when I ring the doorbell. A girl, maybe fourteen, opens the door and immediately yells for Paul before scampering off.

I quickly step in and shut the cold out behind me, stripping off my wet layers and shoes. I understand why every house in England seems to have a wet room now. I don't think it has stopped raining since I got here.

I've been in a good mood, despite the weather. Scrunchy and I chatted a little at the gym this week, and something just feels lighter. Ever since coming back from Dublin – I can't really explain it.

"Hey, Joe, can we chat for a minute?" Scrunchy asks, appearing in the hall.

She's dressed like she just came from work, smudges of dirt, hat hair, and all.

"Of course. Is everything ok?"

"It's fine," Scrunchy answers, and we move into the little dining room off the side of the kitchen.

"I've no idea how to bring this up," Scrunchy starts. She takes a deep breath and crosses her arms defensively over her chest. "Last Saturday you asked me to take your phone from you during my game. Now, I'm not rehashing anything out. And I'm not going to take it from you if you don't want to give it to me. But you told me a lot. That you feel stuck. That your life should be back with Sandy in Colorado and that your phone is your link to that. Everything you do with us you're sending back to them, but it doesn't make you happy."

She gives me a minute to speak, but I can't. I don't remember any of this. I'm not sure what to say. A few memories of soothing hands running through my hair drift to the front of my mind. They surprise me and set off a little cascade of more images. My mouth running as the blur of Temple Bar goes by us. Scrunchy's arms wrapped around me as I cried. How did I not remember any of this? When I don't move, she continues.

"Now, this is just my thinking," she explains. "And opinions are like assholes, everyone's got one. But, when you're in my game, you're with us. Not Sandy, not Dillon, not whatever complicated shit you're buried in. I'm a half-decent GM, if you give me a chance, but I need you here, in my game." She holds out her hand, and I realize I have taken out my phone while she's talking.

"So, sweet cheeks," she says, accenting her southern drawl into a painful twang. "Are you willing to accept that we might be ok enough for now and handing me the contraband?"

Pooh - Kevin's Wizard

While I duked it out with the trash faerie, Ixar had gone with Isabella to Hotel du Vin, where he'd done some good old-fashioned investigating. Just like the three of us, Ixar is a wizard. But his power well is deep and evil, in my opinion.

Demons and other summoned beings are meant to stay in their own realm. The Discipline of the Ice Snake would have me blight his abilities from this earth! However, I've no proof that he has done anything wrong, and my best friend, Clint, had brought him into 314 over a year ago. I trust Clint, and begrudgingly the probably evil summoner next to me.

I straighten my seat as Ixar slows his wheezing old car. We turn off the 59 and down a long dirty single-track road. Deep in druid territory, the farm sits in the middle of rolling green and yellow fields. The rich dirt around the old stone building is packed down and full of hoof and boot prints. Based on the location of Teresa's last known location, on the edge of faerie and druid territory, it's not surprising we're here.

"So, we think this guy took her?" I ask as we roll down the drive.

"No," Ixar responds. "There was no sign of violence. The girl's room had already been turned over. The Hotel was a dead end. Teresa seems to have vanished into thin air."

"Then why are we here?" I ask passive-aggressively.

"Farmer Brooks is an old friend," Ixar explains. "He might have more information for us."

Farmer Brooks, I'm assuming, chooses this moment to step out of his sagging barn. His old wrinkled face and large nose stick out from under his Irish cap. Tweed covers him, head to toe, and tucks into mud-coated wellies. I move to open my door, but when it's only partway open, it violently shuts. Something hits the driver's side door shortly after, jostling the vehicle, definitely leaving a dent. We both look at each other as Ixar's window shatters, a hoof just missing the summoners' head.

"Old friend?" I double-check.

"I might have exaggerated," Ixar cautions.

I punch the button to open the sunroof on the car and gracefully leap out of the small space, landing dramatically in a horse stance on either side of the rooftop window. Two sheep are kicking and repeatedly lunging at the doors, their eyes burning an unnatural orange.

With a "keyup," I flip off the car, kicking for the large white ball of wool and anger. I land in a crouch, but the sheep is already charging me. Its head connects with my hip, sending me flying. I manage to flip up just before its hoofs almost connect with my prone form. I can hear Ixar begin chanting, but I have no time to spare him any thought as this crazed sheep is on me once more. Another "keyup" flies from my mouth as I attempt to grab onto the thing's woolly hide, but it's not as thick as it looks, and I find myself on the ground once again.

"You want to dance?" I yell at the sheep as I easily flip back to standing. I grab my shirt, tearing it off and flexing my chest muscles. "Let's dance."

IXAR - JOE'S WIZARD

"Fuknlikra da missers," I finish shouting as my toe completes a magic circle.

A sheep, it's eyes glowing with orange, charges me. But instead of sending me flying, it crashes an immovable magical barrier and stills. I turn, just in time to see shirtless Pooh grab his sheep by the horns and turn its momentum into the ground, flipping it onto its back.

"Well, it was entertaining while it lasted," Farmer Brooks spits. "Ixar, long time no see."

"Farmer Brooks," I acknowledge the old druid with a nod, a demon summoning already on my lips if this goes further south. We eye each other for a moment before the old druid snaps his fingers and both sheep fall lifeless to the ground.

"It's the circle of life, mutton on order tonight. What can I do for you?" Farmer Brooks asks easily, as if he hadn't just tried to have his sheep maul us for his entertainment.

"There's a missing faerie," I state.

Pooh moves, ready to attack the druid, and I shake my head. Farmer Brooks is not a druid to be underestimated.

"With all shifts in magic and the surfacing of relics, you come to me looking for a faerie?" Farmer Brooks scoffs.

"What weirdness?" Pooh asks.

"The energy, the life, souls, my boy," Farmer Brooks explains. "Look around you! England's on the verge of something big, and it starts here. In Yorkshire, the lands of the ancient people who worshiped the true gods."

"I don't understand."

"Really, Kevin?" I interject out of character. "We're just going to put all our cards on the table?"

"You didn't explain your relationship with Farmer Brooks," Kevin points out. "How would Pooh know what the right and wrong thing to say are."

"Then go find yourself a seer," Scrunchy demands in Farmer Brook's voice, cutting off yet another argument between me and Kevin. "I'm not here for your understanding. You need information about a faerie?"

"We do," I manage to take back control of the conversation.

Unfortunately, Pooh's given away our bluff; Farmer Brook's knows we don't know shit now. Anything we get from him is going to cost us.

"Teresa, right?" The old druid confirms when I don't answer right away.

"Yes, what do you want in exchange?" I ask suspiciously.

"Well, my boy. In my advanced years I find myself in need of an apprentice," Farmer Brooks says.

"I'm not looking for an apprenticeship," I respond, finally letting go of my magic. "Is there something, more immediate I can trade you for?"

Farmer Brooks smiles and looks down at the two dead sheep.

"I think information on your missing faerie is worth some blood magic, don't you?"

PAULA LUBELL

When asked by my players what my ultimate goal as a GM is, the answer will always be to kill them. When asked by anyone else, my ultimate goal is to create a fun world and weave together a story that we all enjoy. A part that Joe and Kevin are making incredibly hard for me to do.

"Are you sure you don't have any more questions for the druid?" I double-check.

"He's an evil druid, you even described him as evil, Paul," Kevin snaps. His ability to control the mood in the room is in full effect, his frustration whips around us. "He probably knows exactly where the missing faerie is, and instead of torturing him for information, Joe's helping him with his illegal workings."

"You gave away our hand," Joe defends himself. "The

druid was also described as being three hundred years old and exiled from the druid order for practicing a hybrid form of necromancy; even his order couldn't do anything about him. We wouldn't stand a chance!"

"I don't remember that description," Byron cuts in, always the peacekeeper.

"It was in his private info," I add, motioning to the paper I'd given Joe earlier in the evening.

Most of the time, everyone hears the same thing, but if it's a personal contact or something individual, I pass it to them either in a note or in a private conference in the hall.

"You know sharing that might have made everything easier," Byron scolds.

"I thought Pooh trusted Ixar," Joe adds. "We've been working together for a year."

"All right," I cut in. "I really struggled with where in the timeline to start this campaign because of this exact situation. Assumed trust is difficult to play out."

"How would one go about this?" Ed asks. "I mean, it's an interesting concept. The four of our characters have a history together and an underlying trust that we, as their players, haven't built."

"It gets more fun still," Byron adds. "I'm struggling to trust Pooh because Kevin's last character kept running off on us in the last campaign."

The table laughs – well, all of us but Joe – and tempers cool down. Kevin's last character really was quite shifty, and it's hard to see his new one as the beacon of good he's trying to establish.

"Will you let us retcon it?" Kevin asks me.

"No, we aren't going backwards," I say quickly.

I see this as a bonding experience and will not let them play out the scene again. The room's quiet while we each think, or at least most of us. Joe didn't give me his phone, and he's on it, again. This time, however, he looks up and gives me a sheepish look before turning it upside down on the table. It's a start, I guess.

"This is easy, we're playing a dice game," I declare. "If we're unsure of trust, we will roll on it."

"It's still an interesting moral question," Ed points out. "But that seems reasonable."

"Ixar, as you're harvesting blood magic, all of its going directly into a relic. It looks to be made of bronze and gold, square with thick carved lines at the top, it reminds you of the stones from the fifth element except smaller, maybe six inches tall and two wide. Pooh, as you pace outside the barn, disgusted with Ixar's decisions...did I describe that well?"

"Pretty much," Kevin confirms my description of his character.

"You feel an almost reverent aurora alongside the blood magic," I describe, leaning on the word reverent. Kevin writes a note, hopefully, something helpful, and I turn my attention to Ed and Byron.

"It's not too late in the afternoon," I described. "The wife seems to be on her last errand of the day. She has gone into a spa that the two of you will have no way of following her into without being noticed."

"Can we use magic to see through the walls?" Byron asks.

"Um, a little pervy, but roll?" I respond. "I'm sure Byke has tinkered with something to be able to see through different materials." Dice fly, and with Byron's bonus, his character easily produces spelled binoculars out of his large bag of trinkets.

"All right, it takes you a minute to find where she's gone," I explain. "How closely are you looking? There are a lot of scantily clad female bodies here."

"We're just looking for her. So, a quick glance? We will look closer if we can't find her," Ed says. I have them both roll and then roll a second time to see if they stay focused on finding her or get distracted by all the nudity. They both pass, and neither of them takes me up on my offer of a *FATE* chip to fail.

"You find her on the top floor," I describe. "She's lying naked on a massage table. Do you keep watching?"

"Yes," Byron answers.

"No," Ed states at almost the same time. Ed purses his lips, thinking out loud. "I would say no, but I think Clint would still be watching. Her husband has procured our services after all, and cowboys don't have any sense of propriety."

"All right." I grin and look our token Brit in the eye. "A man comes in from a separate room. He covers her in oils and proceeds to give her a massage that's so good it makes your own muscles seem to relax."

"Is there any magic involved?" Ed asks me.

"Not that you can tell from here," I answer.

I release Ed from my gaze before I make it awkward and then continue. "Although his massage is platonic at first, as the woman relaxes, his hands begin to work in her more personal spaces. Her body flushes as his fingers dip into her most sensitive junction. She moves her legs to give him better access."

Ed has turned beet red at my description, as I knew he would. I look around briefly as all the boys shift uncomfortably. It makes me chuckle.

"The man's hands must be magic, the two of you think," I continue. "As he brings her to climax only touching the outside of her mossy cleft. For a moment, the two of you see a shadow of something, like smoke leaving her body. Then the man leaves, and she slowly stands, dresses, and leaves a fifty- pound note on the massage table before exiting the building. As she gets into her car, you notice her eyes are not clear. She stumbles as she walks reminding you of the people coming out of the gym."

"Um, why were we following this guy's wife again?" Byron asks.

"To see if she is cheating on her husband," I clarify.

"Were those binoculars spelled to take pictures as well?" Clint asks.

"No," Byron says sadly.

I don't want them to get hung up on the wife. The point is that the spa's shady and doing something with magical energy, much like Farmer Brooks. I describe her returning home, a little dazed and tired, to relieve the nanny and put on an apron for her dearest husband's arrival from work. I hope the mundane end will help them focus on the spa.

"Huh," Ed says, stumped.

I feel like I dropped so many hints. Ach! But I will not railroad. If they can't find the story I put in the world for them, then they can make up their own damn story.

SEVEN

Campaign: Reality
Scenario Five: The degrees of nerdiness
Scene: Beers and Zombies.

EDWARD (ED)

"It's lovely, nice grapefruit on the finish," I answer Juan's query about the beer we're currently drinking.

I occasionally go out on Saturday nights for beers. Paul "hosts" her weekly pub crawl with an ever-rotating number of friends. Or maybe acquaintances, though I shouldn't get hung up on semantics.

It's not really my scene, but I'm in the mood tonight. I recognize everyone here. Paul, Kevin, and Joe from our Friday game. Harriet, who's mousey glasses balance precariously on her small nose.

I don't remember ever actually meeting Juan, but he is one of those people you know all about. Not tall, Juan's closer to me in age with long, white-streaked brown hair that he has tied back in a ponytail. A zombie t-shirt with a big blood splatter across the front covers his thin build. He's quite the conspiracy theorist and doomsday prepper. I had to google what that was, though it's exactly what it sounds like. Someone who stockpiles supplies for doomsday.

"It's a little light on the percentage for me," Juan adds. "But it's crisp. It would be better in the summer. Fucking rain."

"The percentage is fine," Joe sticks in from his seat at the end of our small table between Juan and I. "Any more, and it would lose its light citrus."

"If you say so, man," Juan responds. "You playing in Paul's new RP?"

"I am," Joe answers.

"How's that going?" Juan asks.

I look over at Paul, Joe and Juan doing the same. She's seated between Kevin and Harriet and chooses this moment to laugh at something being said. It's swallowed by the sounds bouncing around the cellar of the Little Ale House, but her entire body moves with it.

"I'm enjoying it," Joe says easily.

"Really?" Juan presses. "I've heard Kevin say otherwise."

"I mostly run games," Joe admits. "I struggle a little with some of Paul's core game philosophies."

"Core game philosophies my ass," Kevin suddenly joins our conversation. "This is your first time playing *FATE*. Those chips are meant to be spent and received. It's basic economy. Probably hard to understand through all that muscle."

"I haven't spent or received any either," I quickly add.

Kevin's had too many beers and his tongue is loose. We've seen this before.

"We've all played a system for the first time," Harriot's welsh accent is lovely, attempting to diffuse the tension filling our table. "It's slow learning sometimes."

KATE MESSICK

"Have you read *The Dresden Files?*" I ask Joe changing the topic. Our game's becoming one of Jim Butcher's books. Books that are so popular in the role-playing community that they have spawned their own role-playing system. There's no way Joe hasn't read them.

"No, what does that have to do with our game?" Joe asks.

"Joe, why are you here?" Kevin exclaims loudly.

I duck slightly for making things worse and decide to stay out of it. I can never decide how social I want to be. It's a constant battle. When I'm social and it's good, it's really good. Like game nights. But when I'm social and it's bad, it's really bad. Like right now.

"You are not one of us, clearly." Kevin continues, "You're not interested in gaming or beer. Half-pints – you too worried about your looks to even enjoy that beer? You've spent half this pub crawl on your phone. Maybe you should go find another pack of meatheads and go do whatever it is they do."

Our table goes quiet. I take a small sip of my beer, I know I can't hide with my tall frame, but I would if I could.

"Hey, Ed, mind switching seats with me?" Paul's voice is right behind me, and I hastily stand. She claims my seat with an ungraceful thump, also on beer four or five.

"Kevin, sweetie," she starts. "If you need Joe to go find his people, then maybe I should go find my people too. And maybe Juan, for that matter. Have you ever been in a table-top RPG Juan?"

"Nope. And I'm not starting now," Juan states confidently. "But I stand by Major Tom's – would be our best bet when the zombie apocalypse hits."

"Oh, we haven't been there yet tonight," Paul says, excited. "Joe, do you like zombies?"

"Ah," Joe says.

Before he can answer, Paul gives him a slap on the back.

62

"Of course you do! Everyone likes zombies. To Major Tom's!" Paul cries.

She picks up her drink and finishes it, followed by Joe's. I see the table quickly finishing theirs as well, though I just leave my last bit and look for my coat.

"Anyone who doesn't want me and Joe on their team when the zombies attack can fuck off," Paul adds, looking directly at Kevin.

"Dude," Juan says as we all move into the cold night air. "We have, like, a real team here. Joe and Paul are our brawn. Harriet and Kevin, our brains. I'll blow shit up, and Edward can be our medic."

"Why am I the medic?" I ask.

"You, like, work in hospitals and stuff, right?" Juan confirms.

"I'm an IT manager for a hospital," I correct.

"I heard the word hospital," Juan explains. "So now you're the medic."

I sigh, but it's a happy one as Juan drops back to walk with Joe. I enjoy being included, even if it's misinformed. Harriet and I find ourselves walking on either side of Paul as she leads the way to Major Tom's, our little group following her like baby ducks.

"I had a coffee date," Paul says conspiratorially.

"Is it a secret?" Harriet whispers back.

"Maybe?" Paul admits. "Not really, but I just ended whatever I was doing with Kevin, and I don't want to cause drama."

"Mums the word," Harriet promises.

JOE SMARTIN

I finish reading the new security email and just stare at the black and white of my monitor. The new protocols of a buddy system make sense logically; a secret military base should not be giving anyone an opportunity to be alone and up to no good. But my people are so sparse that there are literally jobs that do not have two people in them. There's no way we can function in teams of two when we need to go into secure spaces. This is going to put us further behind and be virtually impossible to implement. My teams are so overloaded as it is. I lean back in my chair and close my eyes to let my thoughts drift.

To my surprise, they don't drift to my friends in Colorado but to the weekend. I'd been upset at first when Scrunchy spoke before I could answer Kevin during our pub crawl. I don't need anyone, much less a woman, speaking up for me. But the feeling had quickly turned into something different.

No one had ever stood up for me like that. Not in my childhood, and if I'm being honest, not even my close friends. Dillon always challenged me to confront my feelings, which I avoided like the plague. And Sandy. I love Sandy, but I also spent more time helping her heal from her past than she did mine. It wasn't that she didn't care, she just needed things I didn't know how to give. She needed, needs, Dillon. God, she and Dillon are perfect together. They really are. I have been so blind. I'm still blind. I still love her. That doesn't just go away.

"Knock knock," a voice says from behind me.

Right, another thing I don't understand. There are like twenty of us all in the same room with just a few cubicles splitting us into groups. I am a team lead, an officer, and I don't even have an office door.

I stand and turn. To my surprise, Juan is standing with his arms by his sides. The fake bloodstain is in a different place on his zombie shirt today, though a white, opened, short-sleeved button-down hangs off his shoulders so that he looks like he is at least attempting to stick to the dress code.

"Juan," I acknowledge. I step forward and hold out my hand. He gives me a friendly handshake. "I didn't realize you worked in this part of the building."

"Indeed, just a few rooms over," Juan says. "Did you get the email about the new security shit?"

"I just finished reading it."

"Harrison's going to have a hernia," Juan laughs.

"You shouldn't talk about superior officers like that," I respond automatically.

"Dude, remove the stick from your ass," Juan snorts. "It's your military brainwashing that's inserted it. You were cool on Saturday."

"How did you even get a clearance?" I find the words slipping out of my mouth before I can stop them, but Juan grins.

"Better," he says. "Keep your friends close, but your enemies closer, I believe is the saying."

"A time-old trusted saying," I acknowledge. "What can I help you with?"

"It's not really me that needs the help," Juan explains. "Look, no offense but, until Saturday, I really did think you were just another brainless robot coming in to stir up trouble. It's what most of us contractors are used to and honestly expect. And how you're acting."

"Like a brainless robot?" I confirm politely.

"Pretty much except for one rumor, everything else you've done is the same thing every manager has. Stirred shit up to try and leave your mark without dealing with the mess your changes leave behind."

"Except for one rumor?" I point out.

I enjoyed myself on Saturday. In fact, so much so that a group of us are going over to his place this weekend to marathon some zombie movies and eat some sort of questionable freeze-dried food he was raving about. I'm not interested if the guy's just going to start insulting me at work and tell me how to do my job. He's just a contractor, a programmer. He shouldn't feel comfortable lecturing me. This is why the military has fraternization rules. This exact situation!

"You stood up to Harrison when he tried to add more projects to your teams," Juan relates, oblivious to my rising anger. "I thought you would have been kissing his boots and taking everything on."

"My teams are overworked as it is," I say evenly. I should be kissing Harrison's boots. He's the manager for the entire contract I'm working under. "He's asking too much," I tell Juan. "I'm sure your team is overworked as well." I remind myself that Juan is weird and just gave me a compliment in a very backhanded way.

"That's an understatement." Juan whistles. "Anyway, I didn't believe the rumor until I met you. And here's why I came over. Listen to your contractors. If you were escaping a zombie horde, what's the best way?"

"Run really fast?" I answer slowly, scowling.

"No, join it," Juan corrects. "Cover yourself in zombie blood, walk with a limp, and blend in."

"Are you referring to contractors, yourself included, as zombies?" I ask.

I've no idea what to do with this conversation.

"Maybe it's contractors that are blending in," Juan says. "Anyway, dude, I'm headed out for lunch. Take my advice or leave it. Still coming over Saturday?"

"I'll be there," I say after a pause.

As Juan leaves my little space, I sit down slowly and replay our conversation. I think Juan gave me his stamp of approval while telling me to listen to my team and be more flexible. I feel uncomfortable. First, because a contractor waltzed in here to insult me, but second, maybe he isn't wrong. Juan, despite being a contractor, is almost twice my age and has been at Helmwith for years. Maybe I'm the one that needs to adjust my thinking. I shake my head and return to the security email, how on earth are we going to implement this?

EIGHT

Campaign: Where is your god?
Scenario Two: Druids & Disorder
Scene: Mother Shipton's Cave.

BYKE - BYRON'S WIZARD

On the bright side, the husband accepted our flimsy evidence and, both happily and unhappily, paid us for our time. So, we at least accomplished one thing. However, everything else is still clear as mud. Audrey Lakeland herself showed up like a crazy person dumping a pile of trash onto Ixar's desk and demanding we take her faerie problem seriously. Farmer Brooks confirmed that the druids do have Teresa and they have been active on the Rombalds Moor as of late, but he didn't know Teresa's location. However, he added that Teresa was not a pure faerie and he found it odd that the faerie queen wasn't looking for her.

"I'm confused," I finally say into the silent car. "We're not following up on Teresa or Mrs. Lakeland. Instead, we're doing a third thing?"

Clint's driving, and it's his car. The thing is a massive pickup truck, for England. Which is to say the size of a mid-sized four-seater, though it still takes up most of the tiny British roads.

"Farmer Brooks suggested that we find a seer," Ixar explains from his seat next to me. "The only true seer I know is Mother Shipton. By day, her cave is a tourist attraction, but at night her worlds of magic and mortality blend."

"But this doesn't have anything to do with any of the jobs we were hired for," Pooh echoes my confusion, irritably. "Or even following up on Farmer Brooks' intel."

"Mother Shipton will be able to shed some light on the bigger picture, not just the small jobs we've been hired for," Ixar points out. "Magic is moving, my contacts have reported odd lights in the town, what you saw at the spa was not normal. Maybe if we'd worked as a team from the beginning…"

"Don't start with me, summoner," Pooh growls. "A team…"

"Sumthin' straynge is goin' awn," Clint says loudly, cutting Pooh off.

He hits the brakes hard, throwing everyone in the car forward before accelerating again. Cutting off Pooh and Ixar's inevitable argument. Clint adjusts his mirror and continues speaking like nothing happened. "Fuh-auhries end druids gettin' together, magical orgasms, relics an' straynge magic appearin'."

"Farmer Brooks said something about Harrogate being the start of something big," Ixar explains flatly. "I think it's worth getting a point-of-view of someone who's completely neutral."

"I don't think the orgasm was magical," I clarify, a little late to the conversation.

"Just because you've not given a girl one doesn't make it magical," Pooh snickers.

Clint's car slows as we pull into the parking lot for Mother Shipton's Cave at the edge of Knaresborough. It's the dead of night. The ruins of the medieval castle sit framed by the nearly full moon. The market city's ancient buildings slope steeply down, meeting the river below. The cave sits on the opposite side of the river as the town, down a wide dirt path.

We easily slip the barriers. I notice Pooh leave cash for the entry fee at the empty dark ticket booth. I absently finger the straps of the pack on my back. I'm not like Clint, guns and knives strapped all over him. Or Ixar with his fancy duster filled with potions and tools of his trade. Everything I need is in my pack, my sturdy green waterproof backpacking pack to be precise, the twenty-seven different pockets filled with all my gadgets and toys.

"Pooh, Clint, we need to work together," I hear Ixar call in vain, as the two wizards peel off into the moonlit path. I don't remember planning. In fact, I don't know anything about this place. Pooh might. He's been around for a while, but Clint probably doesn't. He's most definitely not local.

"Shit," Ixar curses.

"How loud do you say that?" Paul asks.

"Very quietly," Joe answers, frustrated.

I shake my head. Obviously, our team communication has not improved from last week.

I hurry to keep up with the tall summoner as he chooses the branch to the right. As we come around the corner, the tinkle of water tickles my ears and an unnaturally bright fog mutes my hearing and limits my vision. I jump at the sound of two quickly fired bullets.

Something large hits my side, sending me flying. A hard, rough surface stops my flight forcing all the air out of my lungs. Water splash on the back of my neck as the sound of breaking clay comes from somewhere nearby. One of my small bombs is already in my hand as I push myself up.

"Ursula Southeil, we come seeking a reading, your expertise," Ixar's voice booms all around us.

"You'll have to find me first," a voice cackles.

I feel more than see whatever hit me the first time come at me again, and I dive to the side. Something bumps into me, and I raise the bomb in my hand, ready to throw. Fortunately, Pooh's hand catches my wrist.

"We need to lift the fog," Pooh whispers.

I nod vigorously. "Heat evaporates fog," I point out. "Assuming it's real fog."

"My ice magic can feel the water. It's real," Pooh assures me. The fog in front of us swirls, and Pooh lunges forward, disappearing into the dark, muted world.

"Ixar, we need heat, lots of it," I yell into the grey.

"It's going to get really, really warm," Ixar bellows before he begins chanting.

Off to my left, a ball of orange stains the thick white world. The orange grows into red, the heat begins to burn my face as Ixar's hellfire moves through it, evaporating the moisture. A small pool of water appears out of the fog behind me, and I jump in. The heat from Ixar's spell passing over me harmlessly.

As I come up for air a few seconds later, the night sky's once again black, stars twinkling happily down at me. I'm in a shallow pool, its sides covered in white minerals. I wince as my shoes put deep scratches in buildup that probably took thousands of years to shape.

Mother Shipton's Cave looms before me. It's bathed in shadow, despite the night. There's some sort of magical glow outlining its mouth and the woman that stands in it.

She's dressed in brown linen pants. Her top, layers of

bright colorful cotton that give you the sense of a dirty rainbow. Her face is a twisted mess of flesh and burn scars. Long blond and white hair curls widely around her head. Two giant moths rest along her biceps, their antennae are easily as long as her arm.

"My wisdom is never free, never wanted, and never precise," Mother Shipton cackles. "As you knew my true name, managed to clear my fog, and provided me an offering, I will give you one reading. One question only."

"What done we offer?" Clint calls out.

Mother Shipton cackles again. Her eyes begin to fill with white as her arms rise. The two moths' wings come to a point, their markings almost look like hands reaching into the seer's mind.

"No, that wasn't our question," Kevin says, quickly breaking character.

"She said one question only," Paul reiterates. "She literally just specifically said, ONE QUESTION."

"But then this entire evening was a waist!" Kevin exclaims. "Joe talked us into doing what he wanted, instead of any of the jobs we were given, and now we don't have shit to show for it!"

"I'm sorry, but it's what Clint would have asked," Ed apologies standing up for his actions.

I give Ed a supportive nod and frown at Kevin. His face turns red as he clamps his mouth shut, glaring daggers at Joe.

"Does anyone know what we offered?" Ed asks again, not in character this time.

"Don't apologize," Paul says quickly. "In fact, here's your FATE chip for good role-playing. Now, what you offered..."

PAULA LUBELL

"It's me or him," Kevin hisses.

We're alone in the middle of Byron's cluttered 3D printing studio. The slight chemical smell in the air matches the cacophony of colors around us.

"Just calm down," I say to Kevin, holding my hands out in front of me.

"I don't need to calm down," Kevin states. "I've been playing in Byron's games before you even arrived in England. And if one of us has to go, it should be him."

"Neither of you need to go," I try again.

"He's an ass," Kevin barley manages to keep his voice down. "He's trying to tell us what to do and how to play."

"He's the only one of you that actually put Rapport and Contacts into their character build," I point out logically. "He's just playing his character."

"You're so blind," Kevin states. "He waltzes in here all muscles and confidence and you just follow him like a fucking lemming."

"Kevin, give me some credit," I respond, clenching my jaw.

Kevin deflates slightly, "I'll give it another chance, but know that I'm not having fun."

"Yeah, you made that pretty clear," I let him know.

Kevin dramatically stomps up the stairs and out of Byron's house and I shake my head. It's not all his fault. He just needs to cool off, or he and Joe need to have a heart to heart. Kevin got picked on a lot in school, by kids that look and act a lot like Joe. And it really doesn't help that I solidly turned him down around the same time Joe came into the picture. Women make everything worse.

Byron's still looking at me, his eyes filled with betrayal, when I walk back into THE CAVE. I think I even see his handlebar mustache drooping. If it wasn't so entertaining, I would feel bad, but life must go on, even for made-up characters.

"Kevin still upset?" Ed asks.

"Yup," I say simply not waiting to get into it.

"I can't believe you enslaved Byke on the third session," Byron almost cries. He picks up the goblin miniature with a big backpack he just printed. He hadn't even sanded the mold lines off it yet.

"Enslaved is so not PC these days," I add. "Think of it as an unpaid internship."

"Still not cool," Byron mumbles.

"Then maybe the group should communicate and make a plan," I suggest.

"You didn't really provide a situation for us to do that," Joe points out.

"It's not my job to make you work together! I'm merely your guide, your god, and your taskmaster. Fuck if I care if you do it the hard way or the easy way."

"You should care, you're the GM," Joe insists.

"I think we're just going to have to agree to disagree on this one," I quip. "I'm not your manager."

"Does enslavement come with anything?" Byron asks, a little hopeful this time.

"It comes with a giant moth," I giggle, focusing on Byron. "But really, google Mother Shipton's Moth. Those are some interesting patterns."

"They're real moths?" Joe asks.

"They are," I respond. "Mother Shipton's cave is a real cave, too, as is her legend, though I tweaked it to fit my story."

"Where is it?" Joe asks.

"Knaresborough," Ed answers. "Just like in the game."

I see Joe reach for his phone and frown. I pull it out of my bag and hand it over. He didn't let me take it last week, but this week, he turned it over before I even started. I hope it helped him. I really do.

"It's a fifteen-minute train ride away," Joe says after a moment. "Has anyone been?"

"Only to the town," I answer. "I haven't visited the cave. I actually was hoping that some of this campaign would help motivate me to explore more. This weather just kills my mood."

"The cave is pretty touristy," Byron begins.

As far as I can tell, Byron has been everywhere. He launches into a story about his kids. I glance over at Joe, who is giving me an odd look. I try to mimic it and end up just crossing my eyes awkwardly. I'm just not great socially. I'm really not. Especially when I have a crush on someone who doesn't even know I exist.

"Anyone interested in checking out Mother Shipton's Cave?" Joe asks the table when Byron runs out of words.

"I checked on this one," I say sadly as I gather my stuff. "It's closed for the winter season, opens back up in March. But, if anyone else is down," I look directly at Joe, who meets my eyes. "Not to give anything away, but there might be other locations to explore."

"Sounds like fun." Joe smiles.

I feel a little thrill of excitement.

"If you don't mind me bringing the kids and the weather is good," Byron adds to our moment.

"If you can convince your teenagers to go," I answer Byron. "Then you're truly magical. We'll just have to see what you find in my game."

I direct my words at Joe again, but he's looking down at his phone. Right. Joe's hung up on Sandy, a short, adorable, thin, Asian. The opposite of me. He's not my prince charming, we're just friends. Besides, I already have a second date with Luis all set up. I shouldn't be interested in Joe at all.

NINE

Campaign: Reality
Scenario One: Moving on.
Scene: The dating game.

Paula Lubell

I'd chickened out. After a lovely, but very short coffee date with Luis, I'd realized he was outside of my normal dating world. Not that there was anything wrong with that, but I needed help. Most of my social circle was nerdy and most of the guys I dated in the same spectrum. Luis is a different beast. Defiantly a few years older than me, he had been charming, very well spoken and not nerdy, at all. I'd quickly clammed up about my hobbies not wanting to scare him off.

"Every man is nerdy, just about different things," Ericka reminds me as we freshened up in the bathroom. Ericka's one of my gym buddies, actually this is the first time we'd done anything outside of the gym together and she'd been the perfect choice for a double date.

"Women are nerdy too," I add looking in the mirror and adjusting my curled locks.

Ericka had even met me in advance to help me put on some make-up and choose an outfit that toned down my square shoulders and extra pounds around my hips. Dressed in purple and a leather mini skirt, I didn't much looked like myself, but I looked good. And Luis' approving gaze had been worth it.

"You need to engage Luis more," Ericka reminds me. "I hadn't realized, he's pretty high up the chain of command, quite the catch."

"That kind of thing really doesn't matter to me," I point out.

"And don't talk about that stupid game you play," Ericka continues as if I hadn't spoken.

"Tabletop is not stupid," I snap. "And I'm not going to stop playing it for some guy."

"Sorry," Ericka says, clearly not sorry. "I'm not trying to dictate your life, but you asked me for help and that's my advice."

"I'm sorry I snapped," I apologize immediately.

"Anyway, good luck," Ericka finishes as we leave the bathroom, "You're going to need it."

She gives me a hug, before linking arms with her own date and heading for the exit. I take a deep breath and find Luis at our now private table.

"You don't look like you're having fun," Luis says to me as I sit.

He puts both his elbows on the table and links his hands together before resting his chin on them. Not knowing what else to do, I copy him.

"I'm not *not* having fun," I answer.

It's true, but Ericka spent most of the night steering the conversation. I feel like Luis is a series of hobbies and facts, not a person. I know that he loves historical fiction, especially books about boats – sorry, ships. That he's training for a marathon. It will be his fifth. He works on base but isn't military, a govie, and has another year before his contract's up.

"You have amazing blue eyes," Luis says. I flush at the sudden compliment. "Almost turquoise with the lighting in here."

"You do, too," I say back lamely.

"And you're stunning," he adds. "I apologize if this is too forward, but I really admire your inner strength."

"That's laying it on a little thick," I manage to say.

My entire body flushes with the compliments. Luis has a nice voice, not quite as low as Joe's, but it lilts with color, no real hint of any accent.

"Is there anything I can do to make this night more fun for you?" Luis asks me.

"Honestly, I'm just a little uncomfortable. All dressed up like this, it's just not me. The compliments help, though."

"Then I shall keep them coming. There's no shortage of source material for me to find."

"Hey, are you up for an adventure?" I suddenly say, having an idea.

"Do I get to know what it is first?" Luis asks, taking his chin off his hands and sitting up.

"Well, I'll give you some hints," I laugh. "I'm uncharacteristically dressed up, fancy shoes and all. I have a handsome man on my arm. There's something walking distance from here I have always wanted to try."

"That doesn't give me much to go on," Luis chuckles. "But let's go."

I stumble a little and laugh as we leave the Cuban restaurant a few hours later. The two-tiered place is decorated with wood, wrought-iron, and fake plants, the bar area on the second floor cleared for their free salsa dancing class. It had been packed.

"You're really, really bad at not leading," Luis laughs.

His hand comes around my waist to steady me. We start walking towards the taxi stand in the middle of town, the date coming to a close. What had started as an uncomfortable evening has turned out amazingly well.

"I've always wanted to try salsa dancing," I laugh. "I don't think there was a person there that I didn't stomp on their toes, though. I'm not super coordinated."

"My favorite was the guy that physically grabbed your hand and shook you like a miss behaving toddler when you tried to lead," Luis recalls.

"You were watching?" I say, falsely scandalized.

"How could I not?" He pulls me into him. "You were the best looking woman in the room."

"Ok, I know I said I like compliments. But you're going to blow up my ego if you keep this up." I feel Luis's arm tighten around my waist and he draws me into his chest. I lean into him as his beard tickles my nose and our lips meet. Luis is a gentleman and doesn't push his luck, keeping it clean and his hands to himself. I break the kiss and move my own arm around his waist. We walk quietly together. It's magically not raining, though the night's bitter cold with wisps of fog diffusing the street lamps.

"Are you sure I can't walk you home?" Luis double checks.

"I don't live far," I say. "I don't usually even kiss on a first date."

"I'm in no rush," Luis says. "The best things in life are worth waiting for."

I flush, butterflies filling my stomach. We part at the taxi stand, and I feel my phone go off in my pocket moments later.

Luis: I had a great time. Run with me Sunday?

I hate running and I'm usually hung over on Sunday, but I would like to see Luis again.

Paula: I did too. What time?

TEN

Campaign: Where is your god?
Scenario Two: Druids & Disorder
Scene: Mother Shipton's magic potion

The Office Cat

"At least we managed to get something out of it," Pooh admits. "Although we don't know what the potion does."

"Something out of it?" Byke's voice goes up an octave. "I'm tethered, for life, to an immortal creepy seer."

"But she done let ya gitty-up," Clint states.

"Gitty-up?" Byke repeats Clint's last word.

"Cut a path," Clint elaborates. "Exit thuh building, er, cave."

"This cowboy talk translator is quite amusing," Ed laughs.

"You do know that no one in America actually talks like that," Byron points out.

"That's too bad. They do in all the Westerns," Ed adds, disappointed.

Ixar's leaning against Byke's desk, looking darkly at Pooh. Byke's nervously fiddling with something. But Clint, my favorite, has set a bottle of something purple on his desk and is now ignoring it. I easily stealth my way over to it and take a sniff. It's a magical signature transfiguration potion. They just need to add a little bit of a person into the bottle and drink it, and they will mimic that person's magic. Based on the turn in conversation, they don't seem to know that.

"Mother Shipton said, 'To live in another's shoes is to embody their very being,' when she gave it to us," Ixar quotes.

I slowly reach out a paw and gently swat at the bottle. It wobbles. Encouraged, I swat it harder, and it moves toward the edge of the table. When no one notices, I slink closer and give it a good bap. The bottle tips.

"Clint, that stupid cat," Ixar barks. Clint grabs his potion bottle before I can knock it again. I sit and meow pitifully at him for taking my new toy.

Paula Lubell

"Ixar would know what this is," Joe insists. "Despite my roll."

"Well, you can use a *FATE* chip to roll again," I remind him.

It was a really bad roll, three negatives, even with his feat, that gives him bonuses. "And you can tag your back story. But even in your back story, you admit that you've very little practical experience with potions, having been on the move most of your life."

"You read my back story," Joe says, I can hear the surprised pleasure in his voice, and I give him a small nod.

"Yeah, five paragraphs," I say, keeping it light. "I almost died. Next time I'm going to make you read it onto a recording so I have a book on tape. I did print it out. Mind if I pass it around, or is it a secret?"

"No, I think the group would know," Joe says.

I nod and pass the paper around. Everyone takes a moment to read it over.

Ixar was orphaned at a young age. Conjuring the demon of envy Leviathan by accident, Ixar was tricked into binding his soul with the demon giving it access to the material plane. Joe spent his childhood learning, by trial and error, how to balance evil magics, summon lower demons, and control Leviathan. However, something odd happened. Normally demons ruthlessly used their hosts, gaining enough control to kill them. Instead, Leviathan's nature softened toward her human. The two of them created a bond closer than any family.

The pact between a demon and a wizard's not looked upon favorably. It made Ixar an outcast from the magical world, so he stayed on the move. Good looking and charismatic, he never stayed in the same place long. Building his network of mostly unsavory contacts and a name for himself as someone who could get you anything you needed.

His friendships with his fellow wizards at 314 PI are the first ones he has ever had outside of his demon. And he cherishes them, a huge part of his obsession with teamwork and doing everything together.

"Great touch there," Byron comments after reading Joe's backstory.

"I'll actually give you a *FATE* chip for that," I add, passing over one of my little poker chips. "Writing your own stubbornness into your character so you can roleplay out being stubborn has to break a law of physics or something."

Joe gives me a cheeky grin. He'd been toying with me from the beginning.

"I think we should go clear out the trash faerie," Kevin states.

He passes me Joe's backstory, his nose turned up like he's smelled something bad.

"I agree," Joe adds.

Kevin and Joe eye each other.

"We could use a win," Byron adds.

I chuckle at their assumption that she will be an easy win. If they only knew.

"Alright, new scene," I declare.

My players shuffle. Byron refills drinks and returns to the table as I organize myself and try to think up a name that they can tag to use their *FATE* chips, but that doesn't give away my game.

"The Easy Trash Faerie," I finally steel Kevin's words with a grin. He gives me a worried half-smile back. "What's your plan?"

I hold my breath as Kevin and Joe actually talk. It's like watching two people dance at a rave. They are keeping their own space and don't look remotely similar, but they are both in the same room, the bass booming. My thoughts briefly wander to Luis.

In the end, I hadn't told him about my role-play habits. Not that I'm ashamed or anything, but Luis didn't give off much of the nerdy vibe. I wonder if he would ever be open to trying. Shit, we had one date. It was a good date though, maybe I like him a little more than I want to admit.

"Um, Paul," Kevin says. "We have our plan."

"Sorry, say it again," I respond, ducking a bit for spacing out. After the brief recap, I nod.

"You arrive at the alley in between the little boutique and Mrs. Lakeland's store..." I start to describe. The potion, completely forgotten for now.

ELEVEN

Campaign: Reality
Scenario Six: Moving on
Scene: Being social is weird.

JOE SMARTIN

S crunchy comes in from her cardio, with a slight limp on her left leg.

"You ok?" I ask her immediately.

"Yes, my ass just hurts," she says. "It's really tight."

"We should stretch before we get started anyway," I say evenly, equally annoyed and worried. "Did you work out on Sunday?" The question comes out more accusatory than I meant.

We'd agreed to start with back and shoulders on Monday. I'd shifted my workouts accordingly, as Scrunchy had agreed to do. I'd been looking forward to this all weekend.

"No," Scrunchy says quickly. "I got invited to go for a run, and like an idiot, I agreed. Oh my fucking god, Joe, I hate running. And now my butt hurts, and my calves. I thought those were pretty strong."

"I'm not much of a runner myself," I add. "Why did you go if you hate it?"

"Because I wanted to spend time with the guy," Scrunchy answers sheepishly.

Patches of color appear on her cheeks. I suddenly remembered that she'd gone light on her beers Saturday because she had a date the next day. The group had teased her mercilessly, especially when someone mentioned that it was probably with another woman. She'd taken it in stride and neither confirmed nor denied anything, letting the drama run its entertaining course for the night.

"Was it fun, at least?" I ask.

A weird uneasiness tries to curl in my stomach, and I ignore it.

"It was running, Joe," Scrunchy says dramatically.

I pull two padded mats off the wall and put them on the floor.

"Here on your back," I gesture to the mats.

Scrunchy flushes and then hurries to do as I ask. I get her to bend her left knee before crossing it over her right straight one. With practiced ease, I gently press down on her shoulder and knee at the same time, forcing her back to stay on the ground while her leg stretches out her back, butt, and hamstrings.

She groans, and I can feel the tension in her body lesson as I put a little more weight on her stretch. Her groan makes the blood from my brain attempt to descend lower than it should. I notice the swell of her breasts, her ample cleavage, sweat still dripping into the crevice.

"This feels really good," Scrunchy whispers.

I grunt, unsure what else to say, and look away from her chest before she notices. I have her switch sides, and together, we do a few more stretches before we head over to the free weights for shoulders.

"Are you going to see him again?" I ask.

I'm not sure why I'm asking. I'm not one for girl talk.

Scrunchy gives me a look like she knows it, "Probably. Let's lift."

EDWARD (ED)

"Ed!" I look around at hearing my name and find Paul waving at me.

She's seated alone at the bar in Harrogate's swanky cinema. I meander over to her and join her on the posh leather seats.

"Seeing a movie?" I ask the obvious.

"*Old Man and the Sea*," she answers.

I raise an eyebrow at her, although I never miss the cinema's evening reshowing's of historical gems, I've never seen Paul here.

"I didn't know you were interested in ships, or Hemingway."

"I'm not."

"Oh."

"Who's your friend?" a man asks.

He comes up behind Paul, giving me a hard look. Paul turns and greets him.

"This is Ed, um, Edward, a friend." Paul introduces us. "Ed, this is Luis, my date."

"Nice to meet you," I say politely.

"Are you waiting on someone?" Luis asks me.

"No," I answer.

"I was just about to ask Ed if he wanted to join us," Paul explains.

"There's really no need," I tell them.

Paul nods, probably expecting the answer. She knows my social patterns by now. Although I enjoy my friends, new people can put me off.

"Would you entertain Luis while I go freshen up?" she asks.

Blast, she apparently doesn't know them as well as I thought. Before I can react, Paul's walking away from us. I blink, trying to understand how I got into this situation.

"So, how do you know Paula?" Luis asks me.

"Mutual friends through gaming," I respond. "How did you and Paul meet?"

"She dropped dice on my head," Luis laughs.

The laughter releases some of the tension in his body. I have this odd feeling that my answer put him at ease. "I didn't even know there was such a thing as a twenty-sided dice, but I'm glad she dropped it. We've only been on a few dates, but she's something special. You know what dating's like as you get older."

"I do," I say to keep Luis talking so I won't have too.

I don't actually understand dating at all. I never married. I've had a few girlfriends off and on in my adult life, more because society said I should want a relationship, but I've never really gravitated to another person. I'm a very happy bachelor who enjoys his hobbies.

"You just know what you want," Luis continues. "Looks and personality start mattering less, it's more about finding someone that can fit into your lifestyle."

"I see," I comment.

On some level, he isn't wrong, but it seems like a rather ruthless way to view it.

He orders drinks, and my eyes slightly widen as a £150

bottle of wine and two glasses appear in front of him. I know I accuse my American friends of blowing money on travel. And Byron and I both get into trouble on miniatures, but this takes it to a new level.

"Ready?" Paul asks as she returns. I shake off my surprise as the three of us head toward our movie.

TWELVE

Campaign: Where is your god?
Scenario Three: Rombald the Giant.
Scene: A traveling we go.

Joe Smartin

Kevin and I eye each other across the table. Scrunchy's late, even late for her. Kevin and I seem to have reached an unspoken truce, but without Scrunchy around it teeters.

"How'd the security meeting go? How are they planning on buddying up people in isolated jobs?" Byron asks me, trying to break Kevin and my staring contest.

"Should we be talking about work here?" I respond, glancing over at Ed.

"It's fine," Byron reassures me. "My cellar's clean of bugs, at least electronic ones."

I narrow my eyes at Byron, he's laughing at me.

"For now, they're putting a bandage on it," I answer. "Mangers are covering when a buddy can't be found."

"Which is going to be all the time," Kevin adds.

"I don't want to speculate," I sigh, already seeing my workload at least triple.

"It'll work out," Kevin says flippantly. "It's not like managers actually do anything anyway."

"You've no idea, Kevin, you wouldn't last a day in my shoes," I say shaking my head.

"Do you even know what I do?" Kevin asks narrowing his eyes.

"Kids," Byron interrupts us. "Remember work stays at work."

"You started it," Kevin shoots at Byron.

"Juan tells me you have a stick up your bum at work," Ed interjects.

THE CAVE momentarily goes quiet in the wake of the Brit's words. Kevin barks out a laugh and I look at Ed, taken aback.

"It's the only thing I have to add to this conversation," Ed points out. "I can't even get onto your base to get a frame of reference."

"Fair. Juan told me that too," I admit, still scowling at our token Brit.

"So, the trash faerie was a disaster," Byron changes the topic of conversation.

That was an understatement. If we hadn't broken the rock at the top of her staff, we would all be rolling new characters this evening. As it is, breaking the rock forced a stalemate, but not before she cursed me...er Ixar.

"Yes, we should've picked up on that possibility when Paul named the scene 'The Easy Trash Faerie,'" Ed points out.

We hear steps coming down the cellar stairs, and a few seconds later, Scrunchy appears, her head lost in a sea of helium balloons.

"Only thirty minutes late," Byron chastises, standing to get her a drink.

"I had to pick up balloons," Scrunchy says with a grin.

Static electricity is making pieces of her messy hair stick to some of the balloons. The excitement in her eyes makes her look a little crazy as she looks right at me.

"Why?" I ask hesitantly.

POOH - KEVIN'S WIZARD

I'm shaking because I'm laughing so hard. Even if I wanted to, I can't stop.

"It's not funny," a small high-pitched voice says from next to me, perfectly matching the tiny three-foot shrunken Ixar it came out of.

"The helium balloons are the perfect touch," I praise Paul.

"I better not be losing brain cells from breathing this," Joe says darkly.

He has an untied balloon in his hand. Before he can talk in character, he has to take a hit off it. Best start to any game ever. As much as I dislike Joe, I love Paul's game.

"Anyway, all right, you're all loaded into Clint's massive red truck following the trash faerie's directions into the Ilkley Moors. The dark brown leather interior has gone from pristine to dotted with mud as you've not had time to clean it between fights. Ixar's tiny, faerie-cursed body is the size of a toddler's, his tiny green slacks peek out of his now adorable little duster and swing, unable to touch the floor of the truck."

I start laughing again as Joe grumbles.

"Why do faeries have pet rocks at all?" Byke asks from the passenger's seat, wiping a tear out of his eye.

"They use them to store magic," I explain. "I do the same, but the only medium that holds ice is diamonds."

"Jus' a lidl rich for mah blood," Clint says.

"Let's just find her a new pet rock so she will lift this stupid curse," Ixar's high-pitched little voice says. I laugh again, it will never not be funny.

———

Ilkley Moor is located just south of the Yorkshire Dales National Park. Low green bushes mix with the light purple shrubs of heather that bloom in late summer. A few of their buds have come to life early this year. The moors are not flat. Rolling hills meet with bright blue skies, and large rocks scatter across the landscape. We arrive at the trailhead for Cow and Calf Rocks. Legends say that giants sculpted the grounds. Most legends are based in fact.

"On the fields of Ilkley, when no husband can speak falsely and no wife can hear, a question will be asked. A question that needs no answer," Byke says, his voice ethereal.

I turn just in time to see a tiny Ixar attempt to steady his friend as Byke eyes return to normal. I shiver – Mother Shipton.

"Did it happen again?" Byke asks.

Ixar pats his knee cap.

"It did, my friend," Ixar squeaks.

Second time, given the first prophecy had predicted we would stop for gas. And we had. Byke has no memory when Mother Shipton's magic uses him as a conduit. We just hope it stays harmless.

Halfway up the trail to Cow and Calf Rocks, I take pity on Ixar's tiny legs pumping hard to keep up with us and place him on my shoulders. We follow the trash faerie's directions precisely.

Two pillar like rocks come into view, and we leave the trail to go between them. It takes some looking, but we eventually find the two lines of stone, five on one side and four on the other. The two largest are about a foot apart and a foot tall, the stones getting smaller in an unnaturally straight line.

"Should we bring her a bigger stone?" Byke asks. "Bigger is always better, right?"

"I don't want her to have more power," Ixar squeaks. I set him down, and he moves, examining the rows of stone. "She's already unnaturally powerful."

"That sher is," Clint agrees, obviously just as puzzled.

With a swagger, the wanna-be cowboy joins Ixar and attempts to pluck the smallest rock from the ground. To no one's surprise, it's stuck fast. We try the simple stuff to dislodge it first, but it seems to be connected to something bigger underneath.

Byke procures a magical hatchet from his pack, and I, being the strongest, sit down to chip away at it. Upon my first whack, I sense a jolt of energy into my arm, but the stone remains smooth. My second good chop seems to make the ground shake, but still no change in the stone.

"Stop," Ixar warns.

But his warning's too late. I've already let my most powerful swing drive the hatchet forward, and it sinks, not far, but into the stone. As I pull the hatchet out, the ground around me shakes violently. I don't get a chance to examine it as I'm suddenly thrust up and then tumble down a steep surface, rocks and dirt raining down. Something massive rises from just below the surface of the earth. The humanoid form stands uncertainly and gazes at us.

ROMBALD THE GIANT

Character description: Three stories tall, with gray skin, giant sky-blue eyes, and a face like Quasimodo. Rombald is bald, naked, and confused. He speaks giant and some Gaelic. Non-magical, other than being a giant.

I'm awoken from my sleep by pain in my toe. I heave my slumbering body up. I can feel roots and dirt of years of sleep slide off of me. I take a gulping breath of air, not quite as sweet as I remember, and reach for my toe to see what's wrong. I can't remember if I was dreaming. How long had I been sleeping? As I'm trying to orient myself, something cold hits me in the back. I absently bat at it but don't stop my examination of my toe. It has a chip in it!

"Oguwage, nig gady!" I hear a voice yell. I turn and find myself facing a little human. His broad hat looks ridiculous on him, and he has a little metal thing in his hand. There's a sudden bang, and something grazes my eye, annoyingly.

"What's going on?" I bellow in Gaelic as I rub my eye.

Something explodes on my side. This time, pain blossoms. With a roar, I stand and attempt to crush the being in front of me. He dodges out of the way, and the momentum of my swing turns me toward another one. This one looks human, but smells like a goblin. Filthy little things, but smart.

"Why are you attacking me?" I ask him.

But he yells gibberish I can't understand and another projectile comes flying at me. I catch this one, but it blows up in my hand. Green blood, along with part of one of my fingers, goes flying off. I feel my anger rise as all thoughts of trying to understand what's going on leave my head.

"I will grind up your bones to make my bread!" I bellow and charge.

PAULA LUBELL

They are murderers and rolling really well. All of them, but
Byron turn in a *FATE* chip during battle. I bet Byron would
have, too, if he wasn't out at the moment. They've come up
with a ridiculously crazy finishing move to kill my giant. I
just pray they fail epically to salvage my entire storyline with
Rombald...hours of planning. I have jokes already written
out. I even made Byke a prophecy, just for this moment, so
they would talk to him, and they're ignoring it!

"Really?" I say as Byron rolls three pulse signs for Byke's
Athletics. "Um, Kevin, roll me Athletics and Shoot."

Dice fly. Kevin actually jumps up and whoops. That's a +5
and a +6, respectively, literally the highest he could have
rolled. I sigh, and my brain immediately tries to think of
ways to salvage the situation. Maybe Rombald had a brother.

"We need to go to Vegas," Byron states.

"Is there a British Vegas?" Joe asks, looking at Ed.

"Blackpool?" Ed laughs.

The Americans give him a funny look, and Ed takes a
long, suffering breath.

"Pooh picks up Byke and the two of them charge the
unsteady giant, head-on," I describe. "With a yell, Pooh
launches Byke into the air and between momentum and
magic, Byke lands directly on the roaring giant's face, where
he shoves his remaining bomb up the giant's nose." I pause
before adding, "I hate you guys," and then continue. "With a
cry, Byke casts a hover spell and manages to float, unharmed
to the ground just as the bomb explodes. Green and gray
ooze sprays everywhere. The substance is a concoction of
brains, boogers, and giant blood. Everyone has a mild
condition of sticky and grossed out."

"That was epic," Byron whoops.

I let them all chat about their victory as I contemplate my next move. The giant was intended to be unbeatable, he was their introduction to the third faction in town, their hint to the druid that's pulling the strings behind the scene. Depending on how the conversation went, he had things for them they needed for the end plot. But no, they decided he needed to die and just would not get past it. If I told them just to move on, it would take away their characters' free will. There was no way I was going to do that. I start doodling his body on the ground as they talk excitedly of their victory.

"I just thought of something," Kevin interjects. "If just his toe gave the faerie that much power. Well, we now have a small boulder field of his body parts."

"Uh," Byron says.

They all look at me, and I feel myself start to smile. Ok, I can salvage this.

"The stone also looks pretty humanoid to be a boulder field," Joe points out my doodle.

I forgot that when I doodled, everything I did was projected onto the table. I sit up straighter. Yes, totally meant to draw that. "Would people know the properties of the stone? Does his entire body have the same magical properties as his toe?"

"Roll me lore, Joe," I tell Joe to stall him.

He rolls while I make up facts in my head and reach for the *FATE* rule book.

"Yes," I say confidently after double checking something. "Magical people will know exactly what happened here. Maybe not the average wizard, but definitely anyone in touch with Earth magic or who knew Rombald. So, druids, faeries, and other giants or creatures that live underground. Trolls, for example," I stress the word trolls. "And you don't know, but, obviously, parts of Rombald were flesh like, but some stone. Your best guess is the parts that are only stone have magical properties, and with a few exceptions, the rest don't."

"We can't let the magic fall into the wrong hands," Kevin declares.

"You proposin' that we butcher ourselves a giant?" Ed says in Clint's voice.

Four heads turn to me, and I just shrug.

"You killed him," I say. "What do you want to do now?"

THIRTEEN

Campaign: Reality
Scenario Seven: All up in each other's business.
Scene One: All things change.

JOE SMARTIN

I wave Kevin over as he comes down the stairs to the cellar of The Little Ale House. The place is packed. It feels weird not saving Scrunchy a seat, but I move my coats, giving away her coveted spot by my side.

"No Paul?" Kevin asks as he sits.

"No Paul," I confirm.

"We need to find out who this fucker is," Juan snaps.

A few heads turn toward his raised voice.

"What?" Kevin asks, having missed the beginning of the conversation.

"She's on a date," I say simply, unsure why I don't want to say it.

Scrunchy and I had spent the day hiking Cow and Calf

Rocks. She hadn't mentioned her date until she'd dropped me off at my flat telling me to pass on her apologies.

"Same guy," Juan points out.

"How would you know it's the same guy?" I ask.

"My wife talked to someone in her walking group who talked to her friend who talked to whomever. I lost interest. My wife talks a lot. Unless Paul's traveling, she hasn't missed beers since we started them. So, it can't be a first date."

"She's backed out of our Wednesday game next week," Kevin adds, sadly.

"I'm assuming that's unusual?" Little conspiracy theory gears visibly turn in Juan's eyes.

"It is," Kevin confirms.

"Look," Juan interjects. "When the apocalypse comes, we have our core team. Much like any team, there are key people, and Paul is one of them. We won't survive without her."

"That's a little dramatic," I add, although I don't like the idea that someone is pulling her away from her hobbies either.

"He can't be a nerd," Kevin says.

He looks at me expectantly as we dive into Juan's crazy. "It can't be one of us."

"I thought I wasn't one of you," I point out bluntly.

"You're not," Kevin says automatically. He takes a deep breath. "I don't like to be wrong. You're some half-breed. I will never forgive your other half for being what it is. But, well, I told Paul I would leave our game if she didn't kick you out, and not only did she *not* kick you out, she didn't hold it against me or bring it up again. I'm also still laughing at the balloons. Allies, if not friends?"

Kevin holds out his hand. It's a little awkward as we're already virtually bumping elbows, all crammed around the small table.

I take a sip of his half-pint and then shake Kevin's hand. "Allies," I agree. "Just like shrunken Ixar and Pooh."

"Jesus Christ," Juan exclaims. "I don't know what a shrunken Ixar is, but I sure as shit don't want to know why anyone would poo on it."

"No, it's…" Kevin quickly tries to explain.

"Hey, Ed," Juan yells to the other end of the table before Kevin can finish.

I give Kevin a grin and pick up my glass for a clink.

"Like shrunken Ixar and Pooh," Kevin says quietly and presses his glass against mine.

PAULA LUBELL

"I'm literally the last person on Earth you want work advice from, Joe," I laugh.

Joe and I are trying out a new independent restaurant that opened up. The interior's understated. The blue and light wood soothing, a few pictures of white buildings with blue roofs dot the walls.

I'm grateful we're eating late. I got a chance to shower and change out of my work clothing. My choice of tight jeans and a long flannel V-neck button-down is perfect. I even matched it with some jewelry. I've been wearing more of it recently. Luis has gotten me a few extremely nice pieces. I'd no idea government employees' jobs paid so well. All the compliments from Luis are honestly making me feel rather feminine and sexy. I'm starting to look for ways to keep those compliments coming. The pleaser in me coming out.

"That can't be true," Joe exclaims.

Our plates are half clean. The decor might be

understated, but the food's amazing, probably the best Greek food I've ever had.

"It is," I say forlornly. "My management skills are so bad, they are legendary. Ask anyone and I bet they'll agree."

"I won't ask," Joe says. "I can't imagine you being bad at your job."

"I'm not bad at my job," I say quickly. "I'm bad at management. I'm very good at what I do."

"I thought you managed a radome team," Joe points out.

"I do."

"But you're not a manager?" Joe asks, confused.

I take a deep breath. Men are so dense. A piece of me wonders if I'm in denial, but I don't let it take root. Men are dense.

"I'm an amazing radome tech," I say slowly. "Which is what I do. I'm bad at managing people. Hence, you don't want my advice."

"I think you're great at time management in your game," Joe answers. "And if you're managing, you're not a tech anymore."

"I'm going to cling onto the part of that where you said I was great at something not job-related," I laugh. "So, what did you want to ask me?"

Joe's body language wilts a little and he scrubs his hands through his hair. Even in the low lighting I can see a few new white strands appearing in the mix.

"Are the new security protocols that bad?" I ask.

"I worked twelve hours on Sunday just to get my own work done," Joe admits. "And it's not just me. I'm salary, there's not even overtime pay involved in this. At least the contractors get a bonus when they need to come in. Bloody contractors."

"No pay is not ok," I snort. Joe rolls his eyes, and I focus. "I feel like everything you're telling me is why the security escort office exists. I know it's only above ground, but the staff is good. They're literally trained to watch people do their jobs and make sure they don't break security protocols, assuming you remembered to fill out the correct escort request form."

"A personal experience there?" Joe asks.

"A lot of personal experiences there," I add.

"But you learned from them," Joe assumes, his smile radiating. "And figured out the correct paperwork for next time."

I give him a flat look. "Har, har. All right. I don't have much to do with the stuff that goes on underground, but above ground, we use the escort office constantly so our contractors can move around freely. Just like what you need in the new buddy system. I don't know if it would work, but I can set up a meeting with you and Deb, Debora. She runs the office. I might not have my shit together, but she's very good at what she does."

"You have your shit together," Joe insists.

"Joe, you don't even know me," I caution. "It might feel like it because we spend all this time together and I know so much about you," I can hear the anger tinge my voice as it picks up speed. "But you still spend half our time together on your phone. You don't ask me questions about me or my life. I'm not saying that needs to change. I know you have a lot going on, and I respect that, but don't presume to make assumptions about me."

Joe just looks at me, and I feel myself flush, the anger from my outburst quickly draining. Though it felt good. God, it felt good. I want to take Joe back to my flat and really yell at him. Tell him what an idiot he's being and to just get over Sandy. That there are other fish in the sea. And then, in my little fantasy, he would magically get over her and carry my heavy ass into the bedroom...right, there, that's what I needed. Even Joe couldn't carry my heavy ass. I lock my crush back up.

"Sorry," I mumble. "Well, sorry, not sorry," I amend. "Whatever."

Joe's still just watching me, and I realize I'm pretty much just having a conversation with myself. I pick up my water and finish it.

"Anyway," I continue my voice back to normal. "When's the best time for you to meet with Deb? I think she's on the same contract as Gate D and security. Do you want to meet with all of them?"

"Ah, yes," Joe says.

I can see he's struggling with the abrupt change in topic, but also grateful. I give him a few moments.

"I need all of this to stay on the down-low," Joe tells me as we look at schedules.

"Oh, office drama?"

"More like, it's easier to say sorry than ask for permission," Joe admits.

"Breaking the rules?" I say in mock horror. "What is our little soldier coming to?"

FOURTEEN

Campaign: Where is your god?
Scenario Three Point Five: Rombald the dead Giant.
Scene: Giveth and Receiveth.

THE OFFICE CAT

I scamper through the door to the front room as tiny Ixar opens it. Though most of the troll's fluids were on his duster left in the back room, I can still see green snot and smell something lovely on his shoes and the hem of his tiny pants. I dart in to get a better smell, and he shoes me away.

The buzzer for their door has been going crazy, and the door's release is just out of reach for his new stature. I watch amused as he jumps up and down. He finally hits it before turning to his next challenge, where to stand, quickly deciding to climb up on the desk. I gracefully jump up myself, still sniffing.

"Cat..." Ixar starts to say before the door to the room bursts open. I jump and hide behind Ixar at the sudden noise.

Two women fight to be the first one through the door. I

recognize Cercia's scent, much too familiar. Her witch Halloween costume made of pink and orange floral prints makes me dizzy. A part-troll muscles her way past the pale petite necromancer, her comically large feet interest me.

"Ah, Isabella," Ixar squeaks. "And Cercia."

The two women give Ixar a disbelieving glance before eyeing each other. I crouch down, eyeing Isabella's exceptionally large feet, Ixar's shoes forgotten. They are so long? Do they wiggle?

"Now you're just rubbing it in. She's part troll. I get it," Joe grumbles.

"I wiggle my butt," I continue describing the cat. *"Ready to spring if she even wiggles a toe."*

"Ladies," Ixar's high voice tries to placate them both.

"I don't know what she wants," Isabella turns to Ixar, livid. "But know that WE know what you did. I trusted you to help. I paid you to look for her." Isabella clenches her fists. "You won't see me again, but know that Pebbles is out for vengeance."

Before I can respond to Isabella she dramatically exits the room.

"We can hear all of this from the back room, right?" Kevin interrupts me to ask.

"Um, yes? I see no reason for you not to be able to," I answer looking at Joe and Byron. They just shrug.

"Clint and I follow Isabella," Kevin tells me. *"Carefully."*

"Oh, do you now," I say, flipping through a few of my notes. *"All right, both of you roll me Stealth."* I roll Isabella's Notice and force my face to stay neutral. *"We will come back to that."* I tell Kevin and Ed moving my attention back to Joe in the front room.

"Well, that was exciting," Cercia comments.

"What can I do for you, Cercia?" Ixar asks the young necromancer tiredly.

Cercia slinks up to the desk and sits down, exposing quite

a bit of skin. "Well," Her voice is light, almost whimsical. "I'm in the market for some giant parts."

"What makes you think I have access to giant parts?"

"Don't be dumb," Cercia chastises. "The trolls are livid. Clint's truck was seen leaving Cow and Calf Rocks and you still have his guts on your shoes."

"I see," Ixar squeaks.

"Rombald was very well known and well-liked during his time...you did realize the Ilkley Moor is part of Rombalds Moor, right? He'd even traded his toe to the faerie queen so he could sleep instead of feeling the pain of his wife's loss upon her death. It's tragically romantic if I'm being honest."

"I see," Ixar squeaks again.

"Really? Is there a powerful NPC in this game we can't piss off?" Kevin complains.

"Farmer Brooks likes you," I point out.

Kevin looks at me with murder in his eyes, and I turn my attention back to Joe.

"A man of few words," Cercia chides Ixar.

I absently paw at the busy pattern on her skirt as she stands, shooing me away.

"Well, Ixar, I'm in the market to procure some of those rocks, body parts, whatever you consider them. Midnight. That should give you enough time to get things sorted. I'm willing to pay extra for his family jewels, in more ways than one."

I dangle a FATE chip in front of Joe's face.

"You know this woman, intimately," I tell him, nodding as if he's already agreed. "Your history is recent and deep. In fact, the necromancer is envious of your power and is easily made jealous when you lavish attention upon other women. You've multiple times let Leviathan feed off her. She knows it, you know it. You ended it. I can make up why or you can, as long as it's because of something bad she did."

Joe eyes the FATE chip. I give him an encouraging nod and squeal like a teenage girl when he takes it from me.

"This evening, 10,000 pounds cash, you know the drill," Ixar instructs Cercia.

Paula Lubell

"There's nothing we can roll to get out of this," Kevin double checks.

"Nope," I say. "You split the party and followed a troll, who just warned you that the trolls were out for blood, into troll territory. You were ambushed by twelve magically resistant hulking trolls and now find yourselves locked in what looks like a beer cellar. Three trolls are locked in the cellar with you, watching your every move angry as shit."

Kevin huffs and takes out his phone. Ed quietly does the same. Their postures too closely mimic their wizards in my game as they deflate and wait.

"Don't split the party," a voice whispers.

I'm not sure who whispered it, but it gives me the chills.

"Now, Ixar and Byke," I explain. "You're at the MPD library of magical books. Byke has a library card and you've been escorted to a single section. Magical knowledge is tightly controlled here. Ixar you're along as his non-magical assistant as you've done once or twice in the past, being unregistered and all. You've not been their long before Ixar gets a phone call from an unknown number."

"I answer it," Joe tells me.

"You get some dirty looks for answering a phone in a library," I continue. "But a very gravelly voice tells you that your murdering friends are in their possession. You must bring ALL of Rombald's body parts to the cenotaph at midnight or they will kill them and come for you next, supernatural borders be damned."

"Right," Joe says. "I tell, I'm assuming it's a troll, that we'll be there."

"Good," I say in my best gravelly troll voice.

Unwilling to face the possible faerie queen with only two people and Clint and Pooh's jail location only being know to me, I let Ixar and Byke roll, searching the library. The watchful eyes of the MPD follow their movements. As midnight approaches, Ixar pockets the toe and Rombald's family jewels without telling Byke, putting the rest of the rocks in a bag of holding as instructed.

I've an epic battle set up around the cenotaph in the middle of Harrogate. Cercia even joins Ixar and Byke as they are scouting for possible traps, just a few minutes before the clock strikes.

Is it a trap? Of course it's a trap! They have a few mediocre rolls and spot a druid containment spell, triggered by stepping on the grass that surrounds cenotaph.

"Do you want to do anything else before midnight strikes?" I double check.

"Is there any way to send Cercia packing?" Kevin asks me, again.

"Pooh doesn't even know this is happening," I remind him. "You're stuck in a cellar. Stop meta gaming, and no. Short of incapacitating her, Ixar promised her Rombald's balls and now seems to be reneging on the deal. She's glued to his side until she gets what she wants."

"I guess we're good to go then," Byron says hesitantly.

I confirm where their miniatures are standing, waiting in the shadows, and then smile evilly. "Pebbles, the troll representative, walks confidently onto the grass," I announce.

"No, wait!" Joe yells in Ixar's voice, but too late as my NPC triggers the druid's spell.

"Double-cross!" I bellow in my horrible low troll voice.

IXAR - JOE'S WIZARD

An explosion nearby makes me lose my balance, and my tiny body bounces as I hit the ground. Acid flies through the air where my head would have been, spit from a giant faerie flower brought to life. Stuck in the druid's magic, Pebble's giant club is slowly chipping away at the druid's containment spell. The area around the cenotaph has devolved into chaos as every magical faction seems to have turned up for our apparently not-so-secret exchange.

"We need to free Pebbles," I reiterate, thinking of our captured friends.

I start to sink into the ground, an unseen enemy attempting to trap me. It's partially successful. I manage to pull one foot out of the ground before the other gets stuck fast. I roll, just missing another spit from a flower and start to tug at my ankle.

"Need something, sugar?" Cercia asks me.

I can see black magic dripping off her fingers and dark purple fire in her eyes. Before I can answer, the skeleton of some small creature bursts from the ground next to me and begins to dig at my trapped foot.

"MPD! Stop all magic, and freeze," A voice booms over a megaphone.

The sounds of a helicopter take over the sounds of battle as lights suddenly beam down on the area. I roll onto my back as the little undead rodent frees my foot. My feet now under me, I leap for the flower, directing it's spitting face toward the druid's containment spells still holding Pebbles.

With the arrival of the MPD, the chaos changes from

violence to fleeing. I can't use my magic now. I direct every ounce of strength and bodyweight I have to keep the flower aimed at Pebbles, the acid helping burn away the druid's magic to free the troll.

"Ixar, we need to run," Cercia yells.

"The trolls have my friends," my little voice screams.

The flower bucks against my attempt to control it and lifts me off my tiny feet. I hear Cercia growl something and run for it, leaving me on my own. As I'm about to be thrown off, Byke's hands grip my legs and the two of us are able to aim the flower. It only takes a few focused spits, and the soft glow of the spell vanishes

"We need to go!" Byke exclaims as he places a bomb at the bottom of the flower. The two of us leap toward Pebbles as dirt and flower bits rain down on our backs.

"How dare traitors save Pebbles," Pebbles bellows, now right in front of us.

He moves his club above his head. For a minute, I think he's going to try and squish me. I feel Leviathan tense inside me. She can only come when summoned unless my body is in mortal danger.

"You three, in the middle. Drop your items and put your hands up," an MPD officer demands. Pebbles narrows his eyes and then steps back from us. He bends his knees and turns his body in a wide circle. Both arms holding the club, he spins. And spins again, faster, the club now angled up. With a bellow, he releases his club at the top. Sparks decorate the sky as his club collides with the helicopter.

"Don't make me regret this," Pebbles warns.

He turns and motions for us to follow. I spare a glance behind me. Cercia's glaring daggers at my back from her unhappy position between two MPD officers, her wrists already cuffed. I leap onto Pebbles back as the troll turns to run.

"Really?" Scrunchy asks. "You leap onto an unsuspecting troll's back with no warning?"

"I'm like three feet tall," I chuckle. "There's no way I'm out running anyone, and Byke's a fat goblin. He can't carry me."

"I'll give you a FATE chip to fail on purpose," Paul tempts me.

"I'll take my chances with a roll. Thank you very much." I worry when Paul also rolls behind her GM screen. I have two plus signs showing Paul grimaces. Probably good for me.

I leap for Pebbles' back. The troll doesn't even seem to notice my weight as we sprint toward the thrumming nightlife that is troll territory.

———————

PAULA LUBELL

"This way," Pooh motions to Clint. His ice magic prying up a hidden door under one of the kegs. "I've no idea why the trolls ran off, but let's not look a gift horse in the mouth."

"The two of you drop into a pitch-black tunnel," I describe. "Goosebumps cover your skin as the temperature drops. Kevin, I'm not even going to make you roll your wizard trance. Above you and to the south east, magic is being thrown around like there is a war raging. Below you and to the north however, you feel that same "revenant" energy tickling your senses. A relic."

"I grab Clint's arm and we book it toward the relic," Kevin said.

"Roll Athletics, both of you," I direct.

They do and they both roll well enough that Pooh easily and quickly guides them through the dark. They jump down a deep hole with deep water at its bottom.

"I shoot up to the surface much too fast," Ed sticks in, not bothering with the accent. He starts laughing. "I feel that cowboys don't learn how to swim. Clint would not have learned to swim. However, Clint, like all cowboys, is prepared for anything. As such, he has a set of arm floaters that he keeps under his shirt at all times."

"They totally rip apart your nice cowboy sleeves as you activate them," I add as I hand him a *FATE chip*. "And they are bright fucking yellow with an emergency whistle attached."

"It's bedder the-yn drownin'," Ed switches to his cowboy accent.

"The two of you dry off and quickly discover this is an underground lake in a massive cave. One long tunnel leads even further north, a dock with a raised hatch sits on the other end. Oddly, your water-logged Nokia phone survived Clint, and somehow has service down here. It beeps with a message."

"Well, what does the message say?" Ed asks.

"It's spam for Just-Eat," I respond. "But at least you know it's working so you-all can regroup in two weeks. We will end here for the night."

"It's only 10:45," Kevin points out. "I've got a few more minutes."

"Sorry," I say. "It's a good place to stop. And just a reminder, no game next week."

"You're not canceling for him?" Kevin whines immediately.

I roll my eyes. "No, I told you about this when I booked it, like three months ago. I'm going to Italy for a few days. I need to see the sun."

"Oh, right," Kevin mumbles, his own phone out.

Byron's ritual of gathering our dirty glasses and cleaning his bar commences. Ed looks down though his bifocals at his new paint job on his miniature for Clint.

"Very nice," Joe says. "Where in Italy?"

"A little island called Ischia. Just above the Amalfi Coast,"

I answer handing Joe his phone. "It's off-season," I continue gathering my stuff as Joe's attention goes to his phone. "Everything's super cheap. Lots of things aren't open, but the island has natural hot springs. I hear dinosaurs still soak in them."

No one says anything, why am I still talking?

"Are you going to drive the coast?" Joe asks, not looking up from his phone.

I smile, ok, maybe not listening, but maybe not focusing on Sandy. I move to peak over his shoulder, he's googling my trip.

"Maybe," I say, those stupid butter flies returning to my stomach. "I rented a car. But it depends on the weather and how much I drink."

Joe grunts in response.

"Are there any markings on the raised hatch?" Kevin asks. "I hate cliff hangers."

I just grin and keep my mouth shut.

FIFTEEN

Campaign: Reality
Scenario Seven: All up in each other's business.
Scene: A meeting of minds.

PAULA LUBELL

"That poor girl is going to take shit for the rest of her career," I finish my story with a laugh as Luis and I stroll through lively streets of Harrogate's nightlife.

"If she has a career," Luis adds.

"A little dark there," I immediately defend the woman in my story. "It was an honest mistake, she didn't remember how tall her vehicle was, and no one got hurt."

"Paula, she ran a police van into the basket of a stopped cherry picker...with someone in it!"

"Everyone makes mistakes, relax," I placate.

I pick up Luis's hand and give it a squeeze. I told him this story because I thought it was funny. I didn't think he would get upset about it. We're walking toward the taxi stand, once again, after a lovely evening of food, wine, and entertainment. Classical music this time, Luis ever broadening my horizons.

"It's not her fault," Luis relents. "It's those idiots at the escort office. They should've had a person stopping traffic on the blind curve."

"I didn't bring this up with you to discuss health and safety policy," I groan, distinctly aware of the three new meetings that had been scheduled by health and safety to discuss just that. "And the escort office is not full of idiots."

"You're so loyal," Luis stops walking and pulls me to him for a quick kiss. "I love it."

I flush at the compliment as Luis tucks me into his arm and we begin walking again.

"The escort office might be able to help implement the new buddy system," I add, trying to get Luis to see them in a better light. "I mean, it's literally their function to enable people to do their jobs."

"Paula, that will never happen. What we do below ground is too complicated and too important."

"It may be more complicated, but it's not more important than anything else," I insist, thinking selfishly of my own job. If one of the radomes breaks, it exposes the radar to weather. And if the radar breaks, no one underground will have any data to do whatever it is they do with it.

"Let's say I agree with your foolish idealism and everyone is equally important," Luis responds. "Even if it wasn't, there's no way the escort office can even work underground, they don't have contracts there."

"Where there's a will, there's a way," I declare.

"Your enthusiasm is refreshing," Luis laughs. "But ultimately wrong. Let's get off this serious topic, what did you think of the music tonight?"

Luis squeezes the arm still around my waist, and I relax slightly. He finds my enthusiasm refreshing? What a derogatory way to brush me off. Actually, a lot of what just came out of his mouth was pretty demeaning. I take a few breaths. I'm sure Luis didn't realize his words came across that way. We're still feeling each other out.

Never as good at defending myself as I am other people, I smile at Luis and dive back into the romance of the evening. Romantic it had been, and in love I will be!

Joe Smartin

"What's this bullshit, Smartin?" My boss, the man in control of my entire section doesn't even wait until I have his office door closed before he starts yelling.

Harrison's shorter than me and not as built. Intricate sleeves are tattooed up his arms. Like every day, he's dressed to impress, slacks and a crisp white button-down cover his person. His suit jacket rests on the back of his fancy desk chair. I don't let anything show on my face. I'm dressed impeccably as always. My fatigues pressed and shoes shined. My badge hangs around my neck on a boring standard-issue lanyard. I refuse to let Harrison or this place intimidate me, and that starts with how I present myself.

"I'm sorry, sir, you're going to have to be more specific," I say.

I know exactly what has set him off, but this needs to be handled delicately.

"I have a request for a verification of work adjustment sitting in my in-box," He growls.

I swallow my smile.

Scrunchy's idea to meet with the escort office had been excellent Deb had been very open to expanding her army of escorts underground. Although I'm not entirely sure how we're going to make it happen. Before we make any plans, I need to make sure it's even possible. I'd skipped a few steps and contacted the Director of Helmwith herself. Not unaware of the issues with the new buddy system, she'd liked the concept but needed more information hence "verification of work adjustment."

"There hasn't even been a Request For Proposal for this base yet," Harrison fumes, referring to the document I'd skipped by talking to the Director. I realize I've started smiling and school my face back to neutral. Although Harrison and I have butted heads from the beginning, his reaction today seems a little over the top.

"And there doesn't need to be!" he bellows. "Contracts are sorting themselves out. Lockheed and Northgruben have just asked for contract adjustments to increase personnel. There's no reason anything needs to change, contracting companies are benefiting."

"But contractors are suffering, all of us are suffering, it's too big a workload," I counter. I'd worked Saturday and Sunday last weekend and was still not caught up. "Getting a few more people might help in six months but doesn't fix our security problem now," I state evenly. "It will just make them more money in the end and leave us with the same problem."

"Smartin, did I say you were welcome to speak your mind?" Harrison barks.

I close my mouth. The contractors are rubbing off on me. I'm surprised I had just shared my opinion like that, very out of character for me.

"It might not fix security," Harrison explains. "But we need to keep the contracting companies happy. Give the teams we have a chance before we try to change things."

I have to blink a few times, keep the contracting companies happy? Contracting companies fought over these contracts like cats and dogs, they are lucrative. It's the companies that go to all kinds of extremes to please the government, not the other way around.

"I heard a rumor that there was a security meeting with the escort office. The escort office, Smartin. Those idiots couldn't change a light bulb if we stuck them on a ladder with it right in front of their faces."

"Sir, I set up that meeting." I have to be honest at this point.

Harrison gets really quiet; I see his lips flex a few times. "You set up that meeting."

"Yes, sir. It needed to be done. They're a tool that's being underutilized."

"And why didn't you come to me with this idea?" Harrison demands quietly.

I think for a moment. I can't tell him the truth, that he's ignored my ideas since I got here and done nothing but overwork his teams. If he hadn't been open to my feedback before, he certainly won't be now.

"I didn't know who to bring it to, sir," I half-lie. "I know how busy everyone is. I pursued it in my own time and was only going to tell you if it worked."

"I know horse shit when I see it," Harrison barks.

There's quiet tension between us. I should fill it with flattery or some self-deprecating comment to put him at ease. He's my superior, but I just don't have it in me. I don't know who's to blame for this mess, but I know who's not helping to clean it up. Harrison. I've spent my life being loyal to my superiors, to kissing their boots because I believe in our system. But Harrison's using our people like they are an expendable resource, and I can't stand by and watch it.

"You're dismissed," Harrison threatens. "And if I even catch a whiff of this happening again, it will be your career."

"Yes, sir," I say tightly.

As I come out of Harrison's office, Juan pushes off the

wall. I give him a warning look, and he ignores it, falling into step with me.

"That went well," Juan deadpans.

"Shut up and get back to work," I say gruffly.

Juan winks at me and puts his hands behind his head, strolling back to his office.

PAULA LUBELL

"Son of a bitch," I exclaim. I pick up my dice and rub them between my fingers. I should have brought my yellow dice to Ethan's game tonight, my orange ones have betrayed me so many times!

"You can do this, Paul," Harriet says next to me, her mousey glasses bobbing.

I nod, not looking away from my dice tray. Gonk is going to die, my massive fluffy white Bugbear is going to die...and I was having such a good week too!

"Yo, relax, and roll," Kevin tells me. With a nervous release, my die misses the dice tray but lands on an eleven. Thank god, anything lower and I would be dead. Or, I mean, Gonk would be dead.

"Ok, your stable," Ethan says, his smooth midwestern accent is easy on the ears. "But still unconscious."

I listen and laugh as our party manages to construct a type of sled to pull Gonk in. Ethan gets us to a safe enough spot, and we end the session starting a long rest.

"Are you bringing him to your game or our game?" Harriet asks me.

"What?" I ask.

"Your man." Harriet grins.

"Harriet!" I exclaim.

"It's ok, Kevin filled us all in while we were waiting for you," Harriet admits.

I shoot Kevin a dirty look.

"I was showing off mine, too," Kevin admits defensively.

"You have a new man?" I ask, one eyebrow raised. "It can't be Joe, Joe's my bromance."

"Very funny," Kevin laughs. "I met her online, like two weeks ago."

"That's great," I say. "You know you can tell me these things, right?"

"Yeah, you helped me set up my dating profile, but your never around anymore for me to tell you things," Kevin whines.

"That's not true." Though now that I'm thinking about it, I have missed a game and two beer nights. "Maybe a little true," I amend.

Luis is so good about planning activities for us, but they often conflict with my big social nights. I love the feeling of being wanted though. Hopefully when his work frees up our dates will stop conflicting with my hobbies.

"He needs to get involved in your hobbies, too," Harriet states. "I mean, maybe needs is a strong word..."

"No," Kevin says. "Listen to the Brit. The British accent makes every idea they have a good one."

"It's a Welsh accent and it certainly does not," Ethan laughs. "Just because you're dating a Brit doesn't mean you have to kiss up when she isn't even here. Paul, it's a good idea to share hobbies, but it's also fine to not share hobbies as long you respect each other's choices."

"I think that's key," Ed speaks up for the first time. "I'm not one for relationship advice, seeing as I'm not in one nor looking for one, but I'm really happy with my social group at the minute because all of you respect my choices even when we disagree."

"We never disagree," Kevin disagrees dramatically.

Ed gives Kevin an exasperated look.

"Sorry, I get it," Kevin placates.

"How are you going to know if Luis respects your hobbies if you don't even talk to him about them," Harriet asks, turning the conversation back to my dating life. It's a good point, one I'd just been pondering. I need to just get over my fear. If Louis really likes me, he will like my hobbies too.

"Let's get some dates on the books. Kevin you can bring your new romance?" Harriet asks.

"Lyla," Kevin fills in her name. "And no, long distance. You will just have to hear about her for now. We're looking into an online campaign, but I would still be happy to play in a one-shot. I bet Joe would join us."

"I'd run it for you," Ethan offers. "I've only met Joe at beers, but he seems cool…for a military robot."

"He's a meathead," Kevin says quickly.

"He's not," I defend.

"Then have Ethan run a game for us so he can make his own judgment," Kevin answers. There's a moment of quiet.

"I see what you did there," I say, narrowing my eyes at Kevin. "That was quite manipulative."

"I'd offer you a *FATE* chip to go with it, but…" Kevin grins.

"All right, fine," I relent. "I'll talk to him." We sit down and go over calendars and come up with a few free Saturdays and Sundays that might work. I'm both excited and nervous. Ethan's a great Game Master, especially for new players. But I'm terrified that Luis won't get into it. And then what?

"You want to come to Italy with me?" I repeat what Joe said.

It's back and shoulder day, my favorite. I wonder if Joe knows it always puts me in a good mood and picked today to ask.

"Well, it doesn't have to be with you," Joe amends. "I could use a break, and your trip sounds fun. We could do a few things together, and then explore on our own."

"So, you don't want to go to Italy with me?" I ask, keeping my voice flat.

"No, that's not what I meant," Joe says, all flustered. I love making men uncomfortable. It's so easy. "It's more fun to travel with another person. I know I don't like traveling alone. It's not safe for a woman…" I let him dig his hole in the ground a little deeper as words just come out of his mouth, each one more terrible than the last as he tries to find reasons that aren't reasons for us to travel together. I punch him in the shoulder.

"Joe, shut up," I say. "This isn't going to be like Ireland. I have goals, I have massages scheduled, and I'm staying at a nice resort where I plan on paying a cute Italian waiter to bring me drinks while I turn into a prune in mineral water."

"I won't get in the way of that," Joe promises.

"And I'm not lifting or running," I say again. "My goal is to gain at least a pound a day on pasta."

"We can work it off when we get back," Joe tells me.

"Maybe," I say darkly. "Maybe I want to keep those pounds."

"You're looking thin," Joe tells me. I go to punch him in the arm again, but he catches my fist this time. "I wasn't joking."

"Ugh, I've lost six pounds, Joe," I wail dramatically. Not that I didn't have them to lose, but I love food. I don't like to lose weight, I just like being me.

"Isn't that a good thing?" Joe asks.

"Are you calling me fat, Joe?" I ask seriously.

What the fuck kind of question is that? Why do people just assume losing weight is a good thing? Life is fucking short, eat dessert first. Joe goes white and puts his hands out.

"No, that's not at all what I was saying," Joe objects.

"Seriously?" I ask, all the humor out of my voice. "Do I look that much better six pounds lighter that it's a good thing?"

Joe runs his hands through his sweaty hair a few times and then down his face. I'm not trying to fluster anyone now. I'm honestly curious. Luis had made a comment as well. Several, actually. I wouldn't say I'm trying to lose weight, but he has me trying some food diet he's doing, and with that, combined with the extra running, weight has just come off me in the last few weeks. Personally, I'm a little mad. My pants don't fit now, but Luis seems to think I look better, too. And I'm starting to crave his compliments. I can feel body image insecurities I thought I were long over creeping back into my brain. I do not like it.

"I don't know the right answer to this," Joe says after too long a silence.

"All right," I deadpan. "If you don't know the right answer, that means you do think I look better six pounds lighter and just don't want to say it."

"No," Joe counters. "It could mean you don't look better six pounds lighter, and I don't want to make you feel uncomfortable."

"I look so bad I should feel uncomfortable?" I say incredulously.

"Scrunchy," Joe sputters. "No. Not at all. I don't see you like that. You're my friend. I mean, it doesn't matter what you look like because you're you. And you're amazing. Weight really doesn't mean anything."

I blink at Joe a few times. Wow, there's a lot to unpack in

that. Joe doesn't see me like that. Ouch, but not new news. However, he called me amazing.

"Take off your shirt," I demand.

Joe raises an eyebrow and looks around at the usual morning crew, but does as I ask. I try not to drool as I search his figure. All bulky muscles, his chest is covered in the perfect amount of man fuzz that goes down to his belly button. I find what I'm looking for and poke the world's smallest beer pouch he now has over what were his perfectly chiseled abs.

"Hey," Joe says, warily.

"Does that bother you?"

"Yes, you poking me does. You hit hard, and I think even your finger has muscles in it."

"Thank you," I say with a grin. I hope my finger has muscles in it. Muscles everywhere! "Now answer the real question."

"Well." He puts his shirt back on. "I'm of two minds on that. I don't like it. I'm used to enjoying things in a bit more moderation than I have been here, but I'm also getting older. My metabolism is slowing down and all. I find that I'm enjoying the company that I'm keeping while shaping this particular body part more than the need to stop its growth."

"Joe," I draw out his name dramatically. "Are you flirting with me?"

"Um, maybe, a little bit. Is that weird?"

"Yes," I state, but it also turns my insides all gooey, which it shouldn't. I'm with Luis. We even had a good talk about how it's his turn to try my hobbies. He agreed to play in Ethan's one-shot when I'm back in town.

"Now, let's super set to try and make up lost time," I say to change the subject. Joe seems just as happy to move on, but before we pick up another weight, he grabs my attention.

"And Italy?" Joe presses.

"I'll send you my itinerary, travel buddy," I coo. I make the voice I hear mothers using when they talk to babies. "Since I know how scary it can be to travel alone. Especially for a delicate woman, like yourself."

Joe rolls his eyes as we jump back into it. It isn't until much later in the day that I realize he called me Scrunchy, I wonder where he got that from?

SIXTEEN

Campaign: Reality
Scenario Eight: Ischia, Italy
Scene Eleven: Emotions never line up at convenient times.

P A U L A   L U B E L L

For better or worse, I decide not to tell Luis that Joe's joining me. I'd booked the trip long before I knew Luis even existed, originally planning to go by myself. I'd even asked Luis if he wanted to join me last week. Like most things that weren't his idea, he hadn't really been interested. Telling him I found someone else, after he turned me down, just seemed like a recipe for drama. And technically, I didn't find someone, Joe invited himself. The time apart from Luis's overwhelming presents will be good for me, maybe help me sort my emotions.

Traveling with Joe is frighteningly easy and relaxed. We both have similar mind sets and energy levels. It's refreshing. Joe, like me, doesn't pack much. He doesn't stress, though he wanted to get to the airport two hours early, an hour earlier than I like to. However, he has access to the premier lounge, and my holiday ends up starting with "free" bottomless mimosas before we even get out of England.

The weather in Italy is unseasonably warm and sunny. We pay extra to both be able to drive the rental car, and as promised, Joe joins me on my plans to scale Mount Vesuvius. The volcano that erupted and preserved most of this area's Roman population in ash. Although a sleeping volcano now, our view from the top could have easily been ash, it was so full of haze and pollution. I'd no idea just how populated and dirty this part of Naples is. I wonder what will happen if the volcano ever erupts again.

The point is pushed as we explore Pompeii, buried for thousands of years. The massive archeological dig is incredible and so well preserved. I can picture the people that lived here. Joe and I wander restored courtyards, mosaics, and peek into the ancient Roman world. Injecting ourselves into a few of the many pictures we take.

On the way out, Joe stops to use the facilities and I take the moments to send Luis a few pictures. He immediately responds with a book recommendation on Roman history. I'm reading the book's very dry description when Joe's voice, thankfully, gives me something else to focus on.

"Pompeii would make an amazing setting for a horror role-playing game," Joe comments. I feel myself bounce up and down on the balls of my feet. My interest in my phone is lost as Joe runs a hand through his hair and motions toward the parking lot.

"Any theme," I agree as we start to walk. "It doesn't have to be horror just because it's old and probably haunted. You could give it an urban fantasy bend and breathe new life into it as a hidden vampire world. Or post-apocalyptic! Survival of the fittest after another eruption."

"I think if it blows, not much will be left of anything," Joe responds practically. "I see why you went vampire, but if we're not going horror, maybe druid," Joe counters. "The volcano left the city steeped in powerful nature magic..."

It takes every bit of self-control I have not to skip and latch onto Joe's arm as we discuss possible alternate realities for Pompeii. Like all good discussions do, the topic morphs and changes, soon we're on and then off our ferry to our final destination, the little Italian island of Ischia.

I wake up late the next day and spend most of it either sitting in mineral water or getting my body rubbed down by hot rocks. Joe reappears in my very relaxed and happy presence for dinner, even enjoying his own evening massage. He has lots of pictures from his daytime exploration, and they make me bummed I missed it. I refuse to acknowledge it wasn't the adventure I missed, but him.

The next morning, I let Joe talk me into leaving the hotel and taking the ferry back to the mainland to drive the Amalfi Coast. The weather was perfect, and we stopped often for pictures of the cliffs and adorable little seaside villages. I was pleasantly surprised when Joe started telling me stories about his early military career. I felt bad laughing a few times. Several of his stories ended up with his scrubbing floors and trying to learn to be a nicer person.

"You know you're still kind of a dick," I laugh. Joe glances at me. We've been switching off drivers and he's driving at the moment. "I mean, bless your heart, you're trying. We all love you anyways. I can't imagine how bad you were before your old friends clued you in," I add to soften the blow. Joe's next glance is accompanied by a grin that says he knows that I'm backpedaling. I stick my tongue out at him.

"I don't know why I'm thinking of my early twenties today, maybe it's the sun that has got me feeling nostalgic. I haven't seen most of those guys in years," Joe admits before jumping into another story, this one his first *D&D* game ever. The story brings back memories and feelings of my childhood, adding to my delight.

A little later, we've switched drivers again, and I want to walk on the beach. With Joe unable to stop my whims from the passenger seat, we follow some questionable signs to what I hope is a parking lot. I still don't know if it is or not, but we leave the rental and walk below a steep cliff. The warm golden sand pushes between my toes. The salt kisses my face as a cool breeze plays with my hair. We stumble upon a little restaurant made of wood and cut into the cliffside. It looks very closed. Despite Joe's pleas to leave it be, I knock, curious. Joe shakes his head, and we both jump when an older woman opens the door.

After an exchange in half-English, half-Italian, and a lot of hand signals, the woman lets us in. We're greeted a second time by the owner's granddaughter, in English this time. She's visiting, and we're welcome to stay for pasta if we speak in English with her. It's literally the best pasta I've ever had.

Joe is amazing with the little girl. Patient, sweet, it's a side of him I didn't know he had. Even his face softens. I can see stars in the little girl's eyes as she learns from him. I'm pretty sure I have them too, and I have a sudden longing to see my own family. God, to have my own family, honestly, not that I'm anywhere close to that. I shouldn't have said yes to letting Joe be my travel buddy. This is not helping my "just friends" mentality. I must be a glutton for punishment, my stupid crush is just getting worse, not better.

Our drive and ferry back to Ischia is quiet. I let Joe do most of the driving and send a few messages to my neglected family group chat. The action helps relieve my wave of homesickness, and even though he doesn't ask, I brutally use Joe to lift my spirits with a story or two about my childhood.

By the time we're back at the resort, I have managed to bring my mood back around. Now Joe is floating next to me. Both of us have our arms crossed over the side of the mineral pool, the hot water steaming around us as we gaze at the stunning sunset blooming over the ocean. This has to be one of the most romantic set of days I've ever been a part of. And I had it with Joe, who probably doesn't even realize how romantic it is. He's probably thinking about Sandy.

"Più vino?" the waiter asks, interrupting my thoughts.

JOE SMARTIN

"Più vino?" the waiter asks.

"Yes, please," Scrunchy gushes. The man refills both our wine glasses.

"You want picture?" the waiter asks in broken English. He's already picking up Scrunchy's phone that she left with her towel on a lounger nearby, not that it's warm enough to lounge outside of the water.

"Oh, no…" Scrunchy starts to say.

"Very romantic, foto perfetta," the waiter interrupts, motioning for us to move together.

"He'll be gone faster if we just do it," I say in Scrunchy's ear.

She nods, and I feel her arm snake around my waist under the water. I put mine around hers as well and pull her into me as we smile.

"Kissing picture?" the waiter asks.

"No," Scrunchy says, quickly swimming forward. "Thank you, that was great." The waiter nods and picks up his serving tray again, scooting off.

We resume our original spots, and I take another sip of

the wine. Scrunchy's waist felt good under my fingers. She's wearing a bikini top and board shorts. They both accent her figure beautifully, though they don't give her much of an ass. I wonder if she ever wears the matching bikini bottoms. That's a thing, right?

"Did you and Dillon ever do stuff together?" Scrunchy asks. I feel my eyebrows lift, and I cock my head to one side.

"Are you seriously thinking about my sex life right now?" I ask stupidly.

"Yeah, I guess I am," Scrunchy giggles awkwardly. "I don't have much of one, and I was just curious."

"What about your boyfriend?" I can't stop from asking.

"Eh," Scrunchy says. "Honestly, there are very few things a man can do that a vibrator can't do better. I'm holding out for something special."

"Cold," I say, really unsure how to respond. "And I think you're very wrong about men's abilities."

"So, you and Dillon?" Scrunchy prompts.

"Ah," I say a little awkwardly. Scrunchy sips her wine, still not looking away from the sunset.

"I mean, I would be lying if I said no," I say honestly. "I'm not really comfortable going into details, but men just aren't really a thing for me. Most of what we did was driven by what Sandy wanted, not that I didn't enjoy it, but we wanted Sandy to be happy."

"Wanted?" Scrunchy says.

"Want," I amend. "Even if everything is different now. I still want her to be happy."

"You're such a good man, Joe," Scrunchy says. "You were amazing with that little girl today."

"I love kids," I say. "My parents were not really there for me. I really want to have kids of my own to give them what I never had."

"And you think Sandy's the only woman who can give

that to you?" Scrunchy asks. I take a big drink of wine. I'm a little confused. Today had been amazing. Scrunchy is the best traveling companion I've ever had. I can honestly say I haven't thought of Sandy or Dillon or work or anything other than being here, with her, all day. I have no idea where this is coming from.

"Ah," I stammer. "I guess not, logically."

"I'm sorry, Joe," Scrunchy says. "Today was just, well, it was wonderful. I know things are more complicated than that."

"It's ok," I reassure her. I can't help but drift closer and wrap my arm around her waist again. I let my hand slide down to her hip and pull her in for a side hug. She lets me, and I leave my hand on her hip. It fits perfectly in my palm. I'm not super great at reading emotions, but even with my handicap, I can tell something's wrong. My mind drifts back to the night at the Greek place where she accused me of not really knowing her.

"Tell me what is on your mind," I ask.

"Joe," Scrunchy starts.

She pauses and seems to wrestle with herself. She turns her head and body away from the sunset to settle on me. Her eyes almost glow blue in the ever-darkening evening. Her cheeks are slightly pink from the hot water, her lips full and round. I feel her hands under the water slip over my shoulders, and for a moment, I swear she's going to kiss me and I freeze. The world stops as we look into each other's eyes, but just as fast, she's pushing away from me.

"I fucking hate you sometimes, Joe," Scrunchy growls. "Let's go see about the live music."

"Ah, ok," I hear myself say.

"I'm going to shower. I'll meet you in the lounge in thirty?"

"I'll be there," I respond, even more confused.

As promised, Scrunchy shows up at dinner freshly showered. Her hair, still wet, is pulled over one shoulder. Her face is plain and make-up free. If she's wearing any jewelry, I can't see it. A light blue halter top accentuates her cleavage and leaves her slightly muscled arms bare. Loose white-washed material I can't identify hangs from her hips and then billows around her legs, disguising her pants as a skirt. I find myself watching her figure as she walks to our table to join me. Has she always looked so sexy?

We spend the evening dancing to music neither of us had ever heard in a language we don't understand. We have dinner under the stars, where I get to hear for the millionth time about poor Rombald from her game. I would be annoyed, but I love her passion for role-playing. I can't wait to have her in one of my games. I walk her to her hotel room door, much later, both of us tipsy from the wine and exertion.

"Were you going to kiss me in the pool?" I find myself asking with a chuckle.

"Oh. My. God. Joe," Scrunchy says dramatically. "Get over yourself and your newly forming beer belly."

"You like it. It matches yours," I say as I move to poke her tummy.

Scrunchy makes an outraged noise and attempts to play-punch me first. I easily catch it and whip out her room key with my other hand.

"Hey, where did you get that?"

"You left it on the dinner table. Sleep well, Scrunchy."

"What the fuck does that nick-name even mean," Scrunchy asks as she opens her door.

"I've no idea," I admit. "Before I knew your name, it's what I called you in my head at the gym."

"That's funny," Scrunchy giggles.

Her eyes look me up and down, and she bites her bottom lip before quickly opening her door and slipping inside. "See ya tomorrow," she says with a wave. The door clicks shut, and I chuckle and run my hand through my hair.

It isn't until much later that I realized two things. One, that I wanted Scrunchy to kiss me. And two, that I do know what her nickname means. It means I'm falling in love. And the sudden realization of that terrifies me to my core.

I know I look like hell when even Kevin apologies as he comes into my office needing something. Unlike the past, when he seemed to enjoy giving me more shit to do, this time he comes in with a plan that includes spending as little time in the server room as possible. The buddy system is killing us. I can only watch one person at a time. And then I'm watching them do their job, and I can't do mine.

I was already behind before I left, but now, I'm a step beyond overwhelmed. I understand why so many people are refusing to travel at the moment. This is insane.

"And you can't keep working on the project until this gets pushed through?" I confirm.

"That's correct," Kevin says. "Did you have fun in Italy?"

"I did," I respond. I start to put Kevin's request on the bottom of the stack of requests and stop. I have an idea, a bad idea, but still an idea.

"Fuck it," I say. "You got time right now?"

"Um, yes," Kevin mumbles, both confused and hopeful.

"Not a word to anyone," I insist.

I pick up his request and read it over to make sure he filled out his paperwork correctly. He has. Kevin's not one of my problem children on that front.

I pull out two more requests for access to the same server room and collect my ducklings and badge them in one at a time with my ID in parallel. I'm actually surprised it works. This has to be a security violation of some sort. As each one gets done, I badge them out the same way. I can be three people's buddy at once. There's nothing explicitly saying I can't be.

"Are you going to get in trouble for this?" Kevin asks as we both badge out.

"Probably," I respond overly lightly. "Spread the word to my teams only. I don't know what other team leads are doing, so keep it on the down-low. But, as many requests that can come in together to get access to rooms, at least until I'm shut down, will get approved ASAP. Now, I need to go reorganize a pile of requests."

"Yes, sir," Kevin says.

I turn and look at him, expecting sarcasm or a biting remark. "Sir" is a much more respectful title than I believed him capable of using. To my surprise, he looks completely serious and gives me a nod before walking off.

PAULA LUBELL

Luis and I are seated on the same side of one of the square tables at a fancy Italian tapas restaurant. It's not the type of place I usually go. With a Michelin Star, they serve incredibly beautiful and creative food and pair it with wines way overpriced for my taste. I have taken a picture for my family of literally every dish that has come out. Mom, the only other woman in the chat, asked for a picture of my date. Luis, the gentleman he is, posed nicely for me. I'm having a lovely night. Luis planned the date, like he plans everything, and the food matches the pictures we're going through on my phone.

"Who's this?" Luis asks, flipping around my phone.

"I told you not to swipe," I say light-heartedly. "I haven't gone through them yet to take out the bad ones."

"Would this one be a bad one?" Luis asks, shaking my phone a little to draw attention to it. There's an unfriendly note to his voice, and I take the phone from him.

It's the picture the waiter took of me and Joe in the mineral water with the sunset behind us. The backlighting leaves our faces a little shadowed, but it's quite romantic, really. There's even a little wavy reflection of Joe and me on the water.

I can feel myself blush. Both because I don't want Luis to draw conclusions and because of my actions after it. Of course, Joe hadn't kissed me when I set him up for it. I'd been half-naked in a pool of hot water with his hand on my waist, and it hadn't even occurred to him that kissing me was an option. He'd been trying to comfort a friend. Despite my embarrassment, I'm glad it happened. It helped drive home the message that Joe isn't interested, not even a little, and I need to invest my feelings elsewhere. Easier said than done, but Luis will help with that.

"It wouldn't be a bad one," I say honestly. "That's Joe, my travel buddy."

"You look like more than buddies in this picture," Luis accuses.

I turn my head to look at Luis as an unladylike snort fills my ears. Luis is jealous, and that idea makes me laugh. "Right. First, you can't be jealous, the man doesn't realize I'm a woman. This picture exists because the waiter didn't speak good English, and it was easier to just let him take it than try to explain why I didn't want it. And second, I asked you if you wanted to join me, and you said no."

"I hadn't realized how romantic your trip was going to be."

"Well, Joe didn't find it romantic, even in the slightest," I say bitterly.

"Did you want him to? It sounds like you did."

"Not really," I lie. "I shouldn't be talking to you about this stuff. You're my boyfriend, what I really wished was that you were there with me."

"You can talk to me about anything," Luis responds tightly.

He wraps his arm around my shoulders, and I lean into his warmth. Luis has a right to be jealous. That picture is with another man, and him being jealous means that he really likes me, right? That should make me feel good inside, but all I feel is guilt. Luis had been far from my mind. I need to make it up to him. I need to really try harder.

Maybe it's not that I'm crushing on Joe still. Maybe this is all just me projecting my new-found insecurities onto a situation. Fucking running and Luis's and Joe's comments about my weight. I was happy with myself. I haven't felt this insecure since high school. What is going on?

"I'm sorry I haven't let you in more," Luis apologizes, interrupting my thoughts. "And I'm sorry for putting work above spending time with you. But work is important to me."

"I understand that."

"No, it's more than just important. I've not opened up, and I should have. I've had a lot of loss in my life. My mother killed herself when I was fourteen. It destroyed my family, everyone blamed everyone else. She was our only income, and what was left, my dad gambled away. We lost the house, everything. My senior year of high school, I floated around on my friends' couches instead of living with my mess of a father."

"I'm so sorry." I wrap my arms around Luis and let him continue.

"My college fund was gone. I worked two jobs to pay for my education while eating ramen noodles. I even started running because it was free. I will never go through that again, nor will my family." I can feel the tension thrumming through his body with his words. "Paula, when I look at you, I see all the strength of my mom and none of her weakness. You're just incredible."

"Incredible insecurities," I joke.

"Tell me about them," Luis demands. "My past is in the past. I just wanted you to understand why I work so hard for my future."

"I understand," I say honestly. "But we don't need to talk about my insecurities."

"We do. I want us to be a team, talk to me."

"I'm a big, broad woman," I say slowly, my worries seem so petty compared to the death of his mother. But Luis smiles at me, nodding encouragingly. "Joe's ex is an adorable Asian. Kevin just got a girlfriend, and she's an adorable little Brit. And with our diet stuff, I lost six pounds. I don't usually even weigh myself. I'm just feeling like I'm making something matter that doesn't."

"Don't worry about your weight," Luis says quickly. He brings a hand up to my face and turns my head for a quick kiss. "We will get back into training meals together, and you can lose more than that."

"That's not exactly what I mean," I say carefully, hurt by his implication that I need to lose more weight. "I don't think losing weight is going to make me feel more secure."

"No, but losing weight is always a good thing," Luis insists. "And it's something we can do together. I know you're looking for more stuff like that. I'm sorry I didn't go with you to Italy, I didn't know it was important to you to have a friend there. Paula, I really like you. You're smart, funny, adaptable, and independent. I've never had someone in my life that just fit into my social group so well. I've dreamed about having a woman on my arm that can run with me, keep up with me. Be the perfect mom to my kids, and you would be! I see it every time you double check that my shoes are tied before we run. When you ask the waiter if there are nuts in the desert because you know I'm allergic to them. Your need to make sure the people around you are safe and happy is unconscious. You even took that picture with Joe to make a waiter you didn't even know happy. You make me happy, Paula."

I'm saved from responding as Luis brings me in for another kiss. I let myself lean into it, feeling the emotions and the love behind Luis's words. Luis is really into me, I just need to be really into him too. We haven't had the opportunity. Between my distraction with Joe, and Luis's very active social life, it has been a relationship mostly about Luis. Of course, his little speech was one-sided. I've not put as much into us as he has, but we already have plans to change that.

"Are you looking forward to *D&D* this weekend?" I ask excited.

"I'm excited because you're excited," Luis says.

He kisses me on the forehead, and I brighten. *D&D* concepts and stories start falling out of my mouth like sparkling raindrops. He's going to love it.

JOE SMARTIN

"I said it would be your job if I caught you doing something behind my back again," Harrison says lowly. I can't help but feel his anger is unjustified concerning the situation.

"I didn't realize I was doing something behind your back," I respond evenly. "It was just an idea I had, and when I tried it, it worked, so I assumed it had been cleared with security."

"Smartin, logically, you had to have known you can't badge into the same room five times in under a minute," Harrison growls.

"You're right, sir," I admit. "Logically, it didn't make any sense, but when it worked, well. I thought that you'd spoken to security about our problems and taken action. It never occurred to me that it was a security breach."

Harrison looks me over. I'm good. I didn't get to where I am by not being good. Kissing ass and networking are two skills that I mastered young. The contractors might be rubbing off on me, but when I need it, I can still roll a 20 in charisma. Well, this is more manipulation and flattery, so maybe deception. But that makes it sound bad, though bad is subjective. Let's call it performance, a 20 in performance.

"And how far behind are your teams since you started doing this?" Harrison asks, clearly trying to hold back his anger.

I can see the gears turning in his head. My gamble wasn't completely wrong. If the system was letting us do this and my numbers could show it was working, Harrison could take credit for the idea. I just gave him credit for the idea, but if the higher-ups come down on him, he can re-point their fingers at me easily.

"Still four months, sir," I say. "And honestly, it's mostly working because we're behind. Looking at my books, it's not that often that two people need to go into the same room at the same time. But we will get caught up." I hand him a paper with the numbers proving my words. Harrison snatches it from me.

"A little too prepared for this, aren't you, Smartin," he says.

"I don't know what you're talking about, sir," I respond, my shoulders straight.

"How was your holiday? You're looking tan. Where did you go?" Harrison's interrogation catches me off-guard.

"It was good. I was in Italy," I answer, confused.

"Not many people taking trips right now," Harrison states, still scanning the paper and not looking at me.

"I just learned why," I say, attempting to be more at ease.

"Don't do it again," Harrison orders. "I'll announce it formally soon, but Command is putting a freeze on vacation."

"Understandable," I agree. Until I get the formal announcement, I won't believe it. "And my work-around for the buddy system?"

"Until you hear otherwise, we didn't have this chat," Harrison seethes.

I repress my smile as I see myself out.

SEVENTEEN

Campaign: Where is your god?
Scenario Four: Conspiracy theories? Or the foundation of wives' tales?
Scene: It's all about those trolls.

POOH - KEVIN'S WIZARD

I'm deep in my wizard trance. Neither Ixar's squeaky voice nor Byke's unending questions for Pebbles register as I use my magic to explore the troll's home. I feel my breath hitch as I sense something odd. The uneven breaths blur my senses, and I have to re-center myself. Once centered, I look for it again. There, more of the odd "revenant" energy.

I let my trance fade, my mind and body reconnecting on Pebbles trash-covered floor. Yes, trash. Despite living in the twenty-first century, trolls still decorate their lairs with trash. I will admit it's fairly artfully strewn about...but still trash.

Pebbles' wife comes in and refills our mugs with more steaming liquid. Similar to her husband, her skin has a grey hue to it, her large flat face has random bumps and patches of hair. Both of them are huge, approaching seven feet, their bodies lumpy with muscles and scattered pouches of what I'm hoping is fat.

Pebbles stands and lifts up his club as if to smash Byke's brains out. I obviously missed something.

"We didn't know you could be a troll and work magic, is all," Byke exclaims.

Pebbles grips his club again and then sets it back down, sitting.

"You know little," Pebbles says bitterly.

"We didn't know Rombald was a friend," Ixar squeaks.

"More than friend. Legend."

"Why did you ambush us?" Ixar eventually asks. "And for that matter, why did almost all of the supernatural community show up for our 'secret' exchange."

"Meant to kill and make Rombald complete," Pebbles admits to the first part. "Didn't know others knew about plan. Rombald's essence powerful, but not battle worthy. Teresa would know why...but Teresa gone. And now owe you life debt. Not fair!"

"You have a mole," Byke says knowingly.

"I HAVE MOLE!?" Pebbles roars, looking around his house for a rodent.

"No, I meant..." Byke tries to placate the troll.

PAULA LUBELL

I crack myself up. Unfortunately, I seem to just be making my players frustrated as they have to shorten their words and talk carefully to Pebbles. Eventually, they get the hang of it, and information starts flowing out of my troll's mouth like a waterfall.

They abandoned the mole concept quickly, although they were exactly on the money. I keep waiting for Kevin to bring up the energy he felt in his wizard trance, but they've gotten a little stuck on the details of the tunnels that run under all of Yorkshire. To be fair, they've realized the troll faction is much bigger then they thought, entire communities existing underground.

An hour of real time later, they are still talking to Pebbles. On one hand, it's good. They've confirmed what Farmer Brooks said. Teresa might have had a faerie mother, but she'd be a part of the troll faction. And that leads them to the unrest in the diverse troll faction.

Hedge witches live next to shapeshifters, who babysit fae babies. As the group's grown, they're starting to have internal issues. Pebbles isn't willing to elaborate too much, but their leader has a plan to unify the group. There are individuals that want to see the group broken up into smaller pieces again, specifically, Audry Lakeland, the witch that owns the kitchen supply store that was in the trash war.

"Rhymed," I stop to point out.

Kevin groans. I remember distinctly back to when he was rhyming on purpose to try and get my attention, but I don't point it out. I guess I know the truth on that one now. I let the rhythm roll off my tongue a second time.

"Does this unification plan have anything to do with a relic you might have recently come across?" Kevin asks Pebbles in the game. Oh, thank god, I thought he'd forgotten.

"All right, roll me Empathy, um, everyone," I ask.

At least one of them has enough plus signs showing, and I breathe a sigh of relief.

"I not know what you ask," I say in my best broken troll.

"You all know he's lying," I add in my own voice. "You can

see fear fill his eyes at the mention of the relic, his body language changes as he stands." I switch back to my troll voice. "Brain hurts. No friends troll underground. Life for life. You need, I come."

They try to ask him another question, and I have Pebbles and his wife chase them out with their seemingly endless supply of clubs. I smile to myself when Ixar jumps onto Pooh's back. Their characters are getting along really well.

"All right, it's daylight when you manage to make it back to the surface," I tell them. "I'm assuming you head back to the office?"

"No," Joe says quickly, "I'm booking it to Valley Gardens and screaming madly while waving a toe around until I'm unshrunk, enough is enough."

"Fair," I laugh.

"I will come with you," Byron states.

Joe looks at Kevin who doesn't meet his eyes. "Sorry, if she really is the queen of faerie, then it's not going to be a fight and I think our time would be better spent investigating the spa. I'm taking Clint, but, if it makes it any better, I think we should explore the tunnels as a group."

"Right," Joe says, disappointed.

I turn to Kevin and Ed, "Let's get this show on the road then, shall we?"

POOH - KEVIN'S WIZARD

"Is that what ah thiynk it is?" Clint asks me.

We're lying on massage beds. Although I have stripped down completely, wearing only a towel around my waist, Clint isn't as comfortable with this spa concept. His boxers stick out from under the towel on his waist, and his socks and cowboy boots still cover his feet.

"Maybe, what do you think it is?" I respond, studying the ceiling.

Covered in a fanciful mural full of magical curiosities, the ceiling radiates power, and I would bet runes and magic circles are hidden its details. "Ixar would know for sure. But they sure look like magic circles to me."

"Too bad I'm not there," Joe interrupts.

"Only two beds per room, so you couldn't be even if you came," I shoot back.

"Children," Paul barks. "Have the two of you developed a crush on each other or something? Joe, take your phone and go play in the corner."

I flush as Joe takes his phone from Paul and gives me a wink.

"I don't have a crush on Joe," I quickly stammer.

Joe barks out a laugh as Paul once again tries to get us to focus on her game.

I reach for my phone to take a picture of the ceiling, but remember that we had been required to put everything in lockers before we came in.

"Why didn't you put your phone in those boots?" I ask Clint, starting to get up.

"It's an ole Nokia, it can't take pit'ures anyway," Clint responds.

The door to the room opens, and two lovely ladies come out, dressed in very skimpy matching outfits, complete with little hats reminiscent of old hospital caps. This could be the opening to a porno, easily. One of them guides me onto my back, and the other one asks Clint to roll onto his front.

"I can't rub your feet with those on," I hear a lovely voice say.

"Ya wouldn't wanna touch those theyer everhoo, ma'yam," Clint responds.

She giggles but doesn't press him. Soon I feel my body completely relax as scented oils are pressed into my skin by warm hands.

"Roll Notice, both of you," Paul advises.

"I knew it!" I exclaim.

"Ugh, I zeroed out," Ed relates after rolling.

"Um, negative one?" I say timidly, even worse than Ed's roll.

"All right," Paul says. "Shitty rolls, my favorite. Ed, your notice skill is ranked higher than Kevin's. I'll let you notice that everything might not be right with this massage – if you let her take off your boots."

"But my boots will still be in the room," Ed double checks.

"Assuming you're still in the room," Paul responds sweetly, holding out her hand for Ed's FATE chip.

I start shuffling through my spells. I can smell combat in the air!

"Stay down," I roar as I send a bolt of ice magic into the face of the trow.

Leathery brown skin covers her body that is, funnily enough, still covered in the skimpy white outfit. Dark stumpy bat wings protrude out of her backside and are outlined with spikes that follow her spine. She's potbellied and hunched over, standing on a stool. The brown and silver tones of Clint's magic dance around her fingers before being sucked into the ceiling. A hideous cross between faeries and trolls, trow are easily enthralled and used as minions. Like Clint's, my magic also gets sucked into the ceiling before it can do any damage.

I flip to a standing position on the table. Claws sink into my leg as my masseuse also sheds her human skin, laughing.

I shoot another blast of power at her face, but it's once again sucked into the ceiling.

"Yes, keep feeding our relic," the trow hisses.

I release my magic and fly at her, fists and arms ready to strike. Her leathery skin feels like wood as I beat into her with everything I've got. A decorative vase flies across the room in my peripheral vision. I drop to the ground to sweep her legs, but as she tips, her wings pump and she kicks me hard in the side. I fly toward the wall.

"Ah need ta git ta maah Justins!" Clint hollers.

A chair go flying off to my side and Clint vaults over the massage table, claws ripping into his shoulder as his trow quickly recovers from the projectile, sending him off course. I dive toward him and catch him before he can fall.

"Ah need a fuckin' focus," Clint growls. "Something to attach my magic to."

My eyes search around again, but there's just nothing. The trow have us backed into a corner. Their sagging breasts jiggle as they laugh at their assumed victory.

"I have an idea..." I start to tell Ed.

"Nope, you're in the middle of battle," Paula cuts me off. "Do, or do not, there is no discussion."

"This is going to be cold," I warn Clint.

I grab his hands and focus, creating the shape of a gun over each one. I can see his eyes widen as my ice sculptures encase them. "Will this work?"

"Got any ice bullets ta go with these?" Clint drawls.

"It's never enough for you, is it?" I joke.

Focusing again, two balls of ice appear floating in front of my face. Clint gestures for me to pop them into the gun.

"We're gonna teach what pahrts ahr ina gun whe-yn this is all over," Clint tells me.

Time slows down, and I let myself sink into a wizard trance. My ice bullets start spinning with Clint's magic as he anchors it to them. His power seeps into the back chamber to give the projectiles as much speed as possible. I just hope they cut through the mural's spell.

I can't help but look up at the mural when I think of it. The runes now glow in my magic sight, a few of them remind me of the lines on the relics. More than that, I can feel the stolen energy moving, I know where it's going.

"It's now or never," I exclaim as the trows start advancing, drawing my attention back to the room.

Clint aims and releases the two super-fast spinning balls, one aimed at each trow. The ice bullets cut through the mural's spell and hit their targets, sending both flying backwards.

I surround my fists with my ice magic and launch myself at them, with a "keyup," I jump into the air, my fists connecting with a head and my feet on the other's chest. I feel a breeze around my hips as my towel flutters to the ground.

"We gotta gitty-up!" Clint tells me.

As he says it, I can hear voices in the hall coming toward our room. I flip to my feet, and the two of us tear out of the room, surprising and pushing aside spa employees in our hurry. Clint has reclaimed his boots, and we manage to grab our stuff out of the lockers before dashing to Clint's truck.

IXAR - JOE'S WIZARD

"On the brightest night, during the darkest hour, choices will be made by the four. Surrounded by foe, friend, and feline, the future will know nevermore," I repeat Byke's most recent prophecy.

I can't help but feel myself up once again, overjoyed to be the correct size and in clean clothing. It seems the trash faerie is, in fact, the faerie queen, Betty, who wants as little to do with us as possible. My trip to Valley Gardens had been fast and uneventful, though I'm now very suspicious. Faeries are not known for their forgiveness. Other than scaring the piss out of us with the sheer amount of power she now controlled, her new pet rock back on her staff, she'd done nothing.

"The last one had the word nevermore in it as well," Byke points out.

"Though dead, still connected. Though feared, still loved. The power that connects the spirit will rise nevermore," Pooh recites.

"I think we need to be on the lookout for ravens," Byke declares.

"Ravens?" I ask.

I can't help but look over at Scrunchy. Her poker face is too good, and she gives me a big grin, knowing I'm looking for a hint in her facial features. She shakes her pointer finger at me before pointing around the table.

"Nevermore was used most famously in an Edgar Allan Poe poem specifically about a raven," Byke explains.

"Do we think the prophecies are connected?" Pooh asks.

"I've no idea," I summarize. "It never hurts to look out for menacing birds. They could always be a sign of the supernatural, even if Byke isn't right. But it sounds like we're finally on to something. We know the relics are collecting energy, but we don't know why or how many of them there are. We know Farmer Brooks and the trolls have a relic. The energy from the spa led us to Betty's Tea House and the faeries; we're pretty sure there's another relic in there. Though I'm just as sure I don't want to mess with Betty. There's a relic under that big lake under Harrogate." I turn my gaze on Pooh. "I think we need to go back to the underground lake. Together, all of us."

"Agreed," Pooh says.

I look hard at the kung fu wizard.

"All four of us, together," I say again.

"I think we have spent too much time running and not enough time relying on our allies," Pooh admits.

"Aww, I can feel a Disney moment in the air," Scrunchy says cheekily. "I'll give you each a FATE chip if you make it awkwardly sexual."

I bark out a laugh and Kevin glairs at Scrunchy.

Pooh and I come up with a very manly and straight-laced secret handshake and soon find ourselves back on the Ilkley Moor. The four of us search the area we picked Pooh and Clint up in after they emerged from the tunnel connecting to the underground lake.

We end up finding two doors. The door Pooh and Clint emerged out of is shut tight, even my hell fire won't melt it. On our way back a second an ancient, decrepit door in the hillside is spotted by Byke. It crumbles and breaks as we try to open it, but enough room is left for us to squeeze through. The place hasn't been touched for years. Oversized dishes, tables, and chairs fill one side and a bed the size of a giant fills the other.

"Rombald's home?" Byke asks the stale air.

We don't know for sure, but it's a good guess. A few minutes later, we find a portrait of the giant himself, holding…a mermaid in his arms?

"Where did you find this?" I ask Byke.

"It was in that drawer," Byke relates. He points to a massive bedside table, a single drawer pulled askew. "He kept it near him. She must be close to his heart."

"Where on earth would a mermaid be this far inland?" I ask.

"You did not," Kevin exclaims, turning to Scrunchy.

"What did she not do?" Ed asks politely.

"There's a conspiracy theory that Helmwith is actually a submarine base," Kevin explains. *"Long story short. It actually got published in the papers years ago, but the idea just gets more elaborate with time."*

"Are we anywhere near a coast?" I ask.

"Nope," Scrunchy says happily. *"About sixty-some miles off."*

"Does this rumor exist in the game world?" Ed asks.

"If it exists today, it exists in my world," Scrunchy confirms.

"You work on the base. You should know better than to keep spreading conspiracy theories," Kevin chastises.

"If it works for Juan," Scrunchy says with a smile. *"Now, get over it. You were going to explore it again anyway, this just gives you double incentive."*

EIGHTEEN

Campaign: Reality
Scenario Nine: Emotions are complicated.
Scene: The games we play.

JOE SMARTIN

"Those guns I made on Ed's hands were epic," Kevin exclaims happily.

"I was more impressed that Paula set something up to force the two of you to work together," I respond. "That doesn't really seem like her GMing style."

"Huh, you don't think it just happened?" Kevin asks.

"Very little just happens," Ethan comments. "Especially if she gave Edward a *FATE* chip to make sure he didn't have any weapons for the fight. She wanted something to happen, maybe not that specifically, but something."

"Clever girl," I say, mimicking Jurassic Park.

"I wish I had Friday nights free," Harriet gushes. "I've never played under another woman GM. They are so rare."

"Yeah, Paul might not be the best first one," Kevin chuckles.

"Is it that bad?" Ethan asks.

"She can just get a little wordy sometimes," Kevin relates.

"I think she's great," I quickly add. "Her style is not what I would choose to run with, but she's a storyteller. *FATE* suits her, not that I've played *D&D* with her. I can't believe how much research she's doing to keep the game relevant to us here in Yorkshire."

"Yeah, you're new to town, so everything is still exciting," Ethan adds. "But she does a lot of fun research for her characters too, so I can see it."

"I can't wait to have her in one of my games," I say absently.

"Are you planning on running one?" Harriet questions.

I fix my gaze on the little welsh woman. She blushes slightly. Her pixie cut is adorable. I can tell she likes what she sees when she looks at me, and to my surprise, I find myself flirting back. I have a weakness for petite doe-eyed women.

"When I do, you'll be the first one to know," I purr.

She blushes scarlet, and Kevin rolls his eyes. I suddenly realize that I feel like old Joe for the first time since moving to England. Even thinking of running my own game doesn't immediately make my thoughts go to Sandy. The smile that has been plastered on my face since coming back from Italy widens. I hadn't realized just how grumpy and unhappy I'd been my first few months here.

"Jesus, Joe, it's like they just fall down at your feet," Kevin whines. I turn to him and am surprised to find humor instead of anger in his eyes.

"It's a gift," I chuckle, giving Harriet what I hope is a reassuring smile.

Harriet looks like she both wants to murder Kevin and hide under the table at the same time. I start to apologize but remind myself that Kevin and Harriet have been friends for a while. We're saved from my awkwardness, as the *Star Wars* theme sings out of Ethan's doorbell. He moves to get it. My face falls a little as I remember why we're here and my only regret from Italy. I should have kissed Scrunchy, and now, instead of exploring my own romantic interests, we're here to meet her mystery boyfriend.

Ethan's dining room reminds me a lot of mine. Mostly matching woods, his table is square instead of round, but still a big eight-seater. A poster of a psychedelic Scottish bull sits on the wall with no windows or shelves.

Ethan will sit at the head with the window behind him. Kevin, Harriet, and I have taken the side facing the door and left the other side of the table for Scrunchy and her date. I clearly hear voices in the hall, and I tense as I think I recognize one. There's no way.

"Bathroom is just down the hall," Ethan is finishing his little mini-tour. "And we're playing here, it's a little early for alcohol, for me anyway, but let me know if you want a beer or soda."

I feel my jaw lock as Scrunchy pulls Luis Harrison by the hand into the room. Luis Harrison, my boss, my useless asshole boss that I don't like and disagree with on everything. But also my superior that I maintain a polite professional relationship with for the sake of my job. Shit. For a moment, I see red, and then I feel Kevin's hand squeeze my arm. I immediately relax and school my face into something neutral.

"Hey," Scrunchy says.

She has on a simple tan skirt and one of those long-sleeve flannel button-downs she loves. Her hair is up in a bun on her head. A few pieces left out around her face are curled. Gold jewelry accents her neck, ears, and wrist. She looks lovely. She looks lovely for him. I force myself not to focus on it.

Luis is not dressed in the formal suit he usually wears to the office, but a pair of dark jeans and a cashmere sweater. His hair is just as greasily slicked back as ever.

"Luis, this is my travel buddy, Joe," Scrunchy starts to introduce us around. I stand. Kevin and Harriet follow my lead.

"We've met," I say evenly, taking Luis's hand in an overly firm handshake. He returns it.

"So have we," Kevin says next to me, not offering Luis his hand.

"Oh, wow, sorry," Scrunchy says. "I forget how small the base is. You haven't met Harriet yet, though."

"Nope, I'm new. How do you do," Harriet chatters. The first person to remember pleasantries.

"How do you all know each other?" Harriet asks.

"It's a magical thing. All Americans are born knowing each other," Ethan says, trying to diffuse the tension. Scrunchy barks out a laugh and pulls out a seat for Luis.

"As this is a learning game," Ethan explains as we all settle in, "I've prepared some characters that we just need to put the finishing touches on, and then I've got a short one-shot setup. Harriet, you might have played it before. I couldn't remember, so if you have, just don't give away my ending."

"I won't," Harriet promises.

I focus on Ethan's words as he continues. My eyes fixed on the paper in front of me and not Scrunchy. Her hands glide over Harrison's arm and shoulder as she points things out on his sheet and answers his questions. I hear my phone ding, and I find a message from Kevin.

Kevin: This can't be real, he's 1000x worse than you.

I look up, unsure how to respond, and Kevin nods at me. Luis is my boss, my superior officer. We shouldn't even be in the same room together socially. I shouldn't be having those thoughts about him at all. He outranks me. There's an order for all of this.

"And you do this twice a week?" Luis asks Scrunchy skeptically.

"Just give it a chance. This is just character creation," Scrunchy adds. "Do you not like your character? We can change it."

Kevin gives me another look as Harrison makes a few noncommittal comments. Clearly not very excited to be trying out Scrunchy's hobby. It hurts me to type out my response to Kevin. Everyone is too connected for heated words.

Joe: He's our boss, just play it cool. There could be a side of him we don't know.

Kevin: No way, but I'll follow your lead, for now.

———————

"Paula, this is such a waste of time," I hear Luis's voice from the hall. I'm not sure if they've realized that, even with the door closed, the walls are paper-thin. I look around the table, and no one moves to tell them. The last three hours have not been so much fun. Luis's half-hearted attempts to get into the spirit of role-playing had been terribly see-through. I think the only thing that has really happened is that a general dislike for Luis has formed, even from Harriet, who doesn't have any preconceived notions.

"It's not a waste of time," Scrunchy stands her ground. "I'm sorry you're not having fun, and I appreciate that you're willing to give it a try. We're almost at the end. Just see it through."

"You're running that 10K with me in Amsterdam, right?" Luis demands. "If I see this through, you're going to train for it, for real, and stop complaining about running."

"I'll never stop complaining about running," Scrunchy answers playfully. "And you still agreed to try some board games as part of that deal."

"I haven't forgotten," Luis admits. "They can't be stupider than this."

"Stop, really, Luis," Scrunchy pleads. "I like you a lot, but I grew up playing *D&D*. It's what my family does still when we get together. My dad ran all our campaigns. It's what I want to do with my kids. You don't have to like it, but don't belittle my hobbies. I don't do it to you."

"I'm sorry," Luis says immediately. "I didn't realize. This seems like a great thing for kids. Imagination and learning to count. I hadn't thought about it that way."

"That's not really what I meant," Scrunchy says, frustrated. "Look, I have tried a lot of things in your social life. I even wore a dress and pretended to smell quince at your hoity-toity wine class. I don't even know what the fuck a quince is."

"Please don't swear."

"Sorry, I forgot," Scrunchy retorts. "Please show my hobbies a little respect, that's all I'm asking. We're almost done."

"You know I can't say no when you say please," Luis's voice softens, and the soft sound of kissing drifts through the door. "But you're still training with me, three times a week."

"Fine, as long as it's not in the mornings," Scrunchy counters. "Can we go over the details again later? Everyone's waiting on us. Just try to have fun?"

We hear shuffling as the pair rejoin us, a fake smile plastered on Luis's face and, surprisingly, just as fake a smile plastered on Scrunchy's. It hurts to see it. Scrunchy's a woman of many emotions, but fake is not one of them. Any concern that I had over wanting another man's girlfriend vanishes as I study Scrunchy's face.

"I summon Leviathan," I growl.

"I don't think you can do that in this game," Scrunchy says lightly, a real smile tugs at the corner of her mouth.

"You guys go through the final door," Ethan begins, rushing us to the end. "The wizard you met at the pub in the first place cackles maniacally. 'It was me all along,' he announces dramatically. Roll for initiative."

Edward (Ed)

"She's dating Luis Harrison," Kevin says for the third time, clearly in shock.

"There's no way," Juan adds. "She's smarter than that."

"Other than the obvious, why is this such a big deal?" I ask, a little out of the loop.

Harriet messaged me saying tonight was not the night to skip out on the beer crawl, and I find myself seated at Major Tom's. The super trendy bar is one of Paul's favorites. Long benches and tables line the middle of the room. The corners are filled with leather couches and low tables. Iconic pictures of the eighties cover the walls, along with faerie lights.

"Because he belittled role-playing," Harriet says too quietly. "He didn't even try to understand how much it meant to her...to us! The friendships you make role-playing, they're special. You open yourself for criticism and judgment, your expose parts of your personality that you normally keep hidden, and they are accepted, loved. Luis just spit all of that back out at her, at us."

The sounds of the busy pub fill my ears after Harriet's words.

"Well, I was just going to say he's our boss," Kevin

eventually adds. "Well, Joe's boss and Joe's my boss. He's also a control freak with a temper."

I look over at Joe. He has been super quiet. Apparently, he was upset enough after the game that he went straight to the gym to take his temper out on a punching bag.

"He treats her well," I add, trying to relieve the rooms worry.

"You knew?" The hurt in Joe's voice quiets all of us as he looks at me.

I duck my head. "I hadn't put together that he was your boss. But, well, you know I'm into history, and Luis has taken Paula to several events that I also attend. He seems friendly enough and spends a lot of money on her. I mean, I knew you guys did well on the base. But 150 quid for a bottle of wine at the cinema? I'm sorry, I shouldn't press, but it's one of those lingering questions."

"I don't do that well," Kevin mumbles. "And I'm a contractor, we get paid more than the government employees, usually."

"She's not a gold digger," Joe snaps in her defense.

"I by no means meant to imply anything of the sort," I quickly interject. "She doesn't know her wines, I doubt she even realized it."

"Look," Juan takes control of the conversation. "We need to put our shit aside."

We all look at Joe and Kevin, the two men in turn look at each other.

"We have a common enemy," Juan points out.

"What's she doing? Luis is such a piece of shit," Kevin blurts out, instead of acknowledging Juan. "She missed beer night to drink wine she doesn't even like."

Joe's phone rings. The picture of a blond guy with nice hair shows up with the name Dillon Dempsy.

"Hey, Dillon, is everything ok?" Joe says into his phone. "Is it Sandy, the baby?" Joe stands and walks away from us.

I raise an eyebrow and look at Juan, who just shakes his head.

"Everything all right?" I ask as Joe when he reappears.

"Yes, my best friends from the states found airline tickets and wanted to make sure it was ok to buy them," Joe explains.

"Cool, when are they coming?" Kevin asks.

"Two weeks." He hesitates and then says. "Sandy's pregnant, I guess it's been harder than they expected or have been telling me. They want to come out before her morning sickness gets worse."

"You don't sound excited," I observe, a little confused. These are the friends on his phone he's often distracted by, right?

"I don't know if I am or not," Joe answers, sounding just as confused.

"You said they were your best friends? Why wouldn't you be excited?" Kevin presses.

"It's complicated."

"We don't need details," I quickly say before Kevin can speak again. "But, Joe, we're your friends if you need anything."

"The next round's on me," Kevin announces. "I know we're kinda frenemies Joe, but, well, you're not so bad."

Joe looks up at Kevin and gives him a nod before finishing his drink. I silently approve of the exchange. It's past time these two get over their differences. Especially if Paul is in as much trouble as the table seems to think.

NINETEEN

Campaign: Where is your god?
Scenario Five: Love, long ago.
Scene: Fact or fiction.

Joe Smartin

"Nice place, Joe," Scrunchy says.

"It is," I confirm.

I eye our group as they poke around my flat. Byron's out of town with the kids this week so I volunteered.

Scrunchy rolls her eyes at my confidence. The interior is a little out of date and filled with all my too-big-for-England furniture, but the view's nice anyway, up on the 17th floor looking over all of Harrogate.

"Damn, I didn't grab our miniatures," Paul grumbles.

"No one did, don't be hard on yourself," I defend her immediately.

"I can't believe you're using a debunked conspiracy theory," Kevin complains.

"Debunked?" Scrunchy responds with dramatic surprise.

"I'd no idea it was debunked. I'm pretty sure I work on a submarine base."

"You do not," Kevin insists.

"It's my favorite of the conspiracy theories as well," Byron agrees.

"And it's got thirty years of history behind it," Scrunchy continues. "At what point is it no longer a conspiracy theory but a legend? Do you think in 100 years there will be some landmark and people will have folklore about giant underground boats that made the sixty-mile journey?"

"It's too far-fetched. I mean, we're so far away from the ocean. Harrogate doesn't even have a major river going through it," I add logically.

I'd no idea there were conspiracy theories about what the base did. A super-secret military base in the middle of Yorkshire. It does make sense, though.

"But Yorkshire has such a history with its cave network," Scrunchy insists. "If the passages were already here, and just needed a little help, it would be the perfect place to hide your submarines. No one would guess in the middle of England."

"It's a fun idea," Ed humors her. "I'm unsure of your understanding of the direction water runs."

"Not uphill," Kevin adds for clarification.

"Doesn't change the dream," Scrunchy says happily. "Legends are not about what is, but what might have been."

"All right, you guys exploring the hatch you found? Or doing something else?" Scrunchy asks as we all settle around my table that takes up half my dining room. My collection of old-fashioned battle mats wait for us, we're so spoiled by THE CAVE.

"We explore thuh submarine," Ed confirms, slipping into character.

POOH - KEVIN'S WIZARD

I don't like how we got here, but with the door sealed, what other options did we have? We gave Pebbles the bag of holding with Rombald's body parts in it so they could properly mourn. It was only after we'd left that evil Ixar admitted that he still has Rombald's family jewels as insurance. Pebbles had already warned us that the trolls are not our allies and despite all of this, we'd used magic and bribery to slip back into The Den. Back down to the underwater lake and the hatch, untouched for years.

It takes three of us to peel it opened. The sound of metal grating against metal hurts my ears and the smell of rust fills my nose as we get it open. We leave Byke guarding the opening as we climb down, our wizard lights hovering in front of us.

Intuition tells me that we're exploring a submarine. Long abandon, we learn the hard way that we need to check the oval doors that are sealed shut for flooding before spinning the pressurized hatch wheels on their front.

"Is it flooded?" Ixar asks me.

"It's not," I say, feeling for the elements behind it.

Ixar nods at me, and I heave on the rusted wheel. With a painful squeal, the hinges rotate, and I blink, surprised to see something completely out of this world. The other side is a large clear room, somehow already dimly lit. Inky black water is held back by an invisible force. The floor crunches under our feet with sand as we move into its center. Our reflections look back at us, rippling unnaturally.

"It's all magic," Ixar whispers in awe. "This bubble, it's not glass. It's pure active magic."

"Shit, we ain't alone," Clint says what I just realized.

Before any of us can react, there's a hollow boom as the door shuts behind us. Motion draws my eyes as two figures step through the magical barrier holding the water at bay. Their passing doesn't even leave a trace, though water drips off them onto the sand floor.

"It's been almost 25 years since our last visitor," a male voice says sweetly in perfect British English. A soft singing slowly fills my ears, not much more than a lovely white noise, and I forget it immediately.

I move my wizard light so it illuminates their faces. Covered in green, blue, and silver scales, the creatures are barely humanoid. Long sharp teeth stick out between their lips. A cross between kelp and dreadlocks hangs like wigs on their heads, all a dark, unnatural green. Both wear no clothing, though there's nothing between the man's legs, and the woman's small hints at breasts have no nipples. Her eyelids blink vertically across her large black eyes. Despite her alien appearance, her hips move with purpose as she walks. I can't pull my eyes away from her.

"Pooh, down," Ixar's voice cries, and a weight slams into me, shocking me out of my stupor.

"Sirens!" Clint shouts.

His guns blaze as I roll and jump away from the woman. Her mouth opens and sounds too beautiful to describe fill my world. Once again, I lose myself to her. I want her touch, despite the sharp teeth and webbed hands. I would die happy if she'd only bring me into her fold.

"Pooh," I hear my name yelled again, and for a second time, I'm thrown to the floor.

This time, I strike out at my attacker, and I hear Ixar grunt painfully. The sound of Clint's guns blazing brings me back to reality, but I still can't move against the siren that has trapped me with her song.

An inhuman cry of pain draws my attention. I see the male fall to the ground, green blood oozing out of a massive hole in his chest. A blur of motion pulls my attention as the female turns from me, releasing my body to my control. She rushes Clint; siren and cowboy disappear through the magical barrier.

"Shit," I spit, finally in control of my own mind.

I start running, but Ixar's hand on my shoulder stops me.

"We have to be smart about this," Ixar warns me.

"Clint will drown," I growl, wrenching my shoulder out of his grip.

"I know," Ixar says calmly, and he begins chanting.

Paula Lubell

"You're being drown by a siren and you want to ride it?" I repeat slowly.

"I've not gotten to use that aspect yet," Ed answers logically. "I grew up on a huge ranch, it's in my back story, and my aspect from that is 'I can ride anything.' I would like to tag it. She's swimming, correct? You just said we're going inhumanly fast through the water, so she can't still be in human form, at least not completely."

"It could be magical," I mumble, searching through the papers scattered in front of me. Byron's gaming table has spoiled me horribly. I find the *FATE* manual and thumb through a section.

"I like this character. I'm not going to let you kill Clint yet," Ed emphasizes.

I don't look up from my searching. Kevin and Joe both look excited to see this happen. I can't find the rule I'm looking for. Fuck it, I'll make it up.

"Um, roll me Athletics and Physique," I request.

Ed rolls. Not so well on Athletics but three plus signs on Physique. It's a sign. This will be entertaining.

"Physique is how strong I am, right?" Ed double checks.

"It is." I give it a dramatic moment before announcing, "You have a grip on her."

Ed gives an uncharacteristic cheer, Joe and Kevin joining.

"You can't see a bloody thing, the water's going too fast, and you've no idea exactly what you're holding, but it's between your legs. Something rigid and painful is wedged literally into your butt crack, but at the moment, it's part of the reason you have purchase. Take a mild consequence."

"Ouch," Ed responds.

"I can ride anything," Kevin reads Ed's aspect, stressing the word ride.

We all giggle like fifth-grade girls. The slightest of flush appears on Ed's cheeks.

"I'd not realized the sexual implications of that until just now," he says carefully.

We laugh again, Ed joining us this time with his polite chuckle.

"All right," I eventually control myself. "Your hands are wrapped around, your best guess is, two big handfuls of hair. I'll let you roll with two extra dice on your ride skill. But I need a *FATE* chip from you."

Ed quite happily hands it over and rubs his dice between his palms. I watch as they bounce around Joe's fancy dice tray before coming to a stop.

Although Clint manages to control the siren, he's still trapped underwater. No one's surprised when I describe a mermaid coming to his rescue, her skin so pale it's almost translucent. Blue veins make a spider network over her skin and up her neck where it meets with milky, unfocused pink eyes. She is beyond old and wise.

Joe has summoned Leviathan. His scaly part-dragon part-octopus demon easily eats the siren before pushing the wizard and mermaid back into the bubble. Happily, but still evilly, Leviathan frolics around in the water. Pleased to be free for this brief time and guarding the bubble from anything else that might attack.

Back inside the bubble, my mermaid's fin turns to legs, and she stumbles trying to stand, her arms dropping her precious cargo.

"The relic tumbles end over end," I describe. "It's surface a pearl white, the lines at the top loop and peak, their edges inlaid with onyx."

"I dive for it," Kevin announces, rolling.

"You keep it from hitting the ground, and it's now in your possession," I confirm, looking at his dice. "The ancient mermaid moves some of her stringy moss and kelp-filled hair to one side. 'Please, don't hurt my God,' she whispers. And we will end here for tonight."

"The relics are gods!?" Kevin exclaims.

"And we will end there for tonight," I say again.

I love leaving them on cliff hangers. I start to clean up my mess of papers.

"Do you want to get dinner on Monday?" Kevin asks me, changing gears. "I've got Lyla questions."

"I can't," I say, disappointed.

I feel l like I say that a lot right now, Harrison's been planning so much for us. He seems to think that if I do enough of his things that I'll like them, but it's just not working. I so badly want to be in love this time. Luis had made me so happy in the beginning.

"It's Harrison, isn't it," Kevin immediately snaps. "He's an ass, you need to ditch him."

"I'm not having this conversation with you!" I exclaim. "You're my friend, you should be supporting my choices."

"Not when they are bad choices, Paul," Kevin yells angrily. "Harrison isn't one of us!"

"You said that about Joe, too," I point out.

"And I was wrong, but I'm not wrong this time," Kevin admits, standing. "You said you wouldn't go on any more dates with me because you wanted 'real love.' Well, the look on your face at the end of Ethan's game was pure misery. Hypocrite."

Joe's flat is awkwardly silent as Kevin storms out the front door. I can feel myself shaking. I can't tell if I want to cry or deck Kevin. His words ring a little too true.

"He needs time to cool off," Ed breaks the silence.

"The world's not black and white." I wipe the side of my eye, grateful I don't feel moisture, and take a calming breath.

Ed nods sympathetically, and I refuse to meet anyone's eyes as I continue gathering my papers.

"Joe, is everything alright?" Byron asks.

I glance over to Joe. He looks so conflicted, his eyes boring holes into me.

"I've just got a lot on my mind," Joe answers, finally looking away.

I take a deep frustrated breath and finish gathering my stuff. Why is love so complicated?

TWENTY

Campaign: Reality
Scenario Ten: Sometimes you just have to get it sorted.
Scene: The comfort of friends...

PAULA LUBELL

M y eyes bore holes into Joe as I will him not to ask the question I know is about to slip out of his full, perfect lips. He's drinking more than normal for a weeknight, not near as much as Ireland, but enough. His Adam's apples bobs sensually to my inebriated brain as he takes another nervous mouthful of beer and swallows it down. Can an Adam's apple be sensual? I force myself to focus on the painfully transparent words that have been leading us to this moment all night.

"Ah, yeah, so, I need to chat with Dillon alone, and I was hoping you could entertain Sandy for me. I don't want her to be alone in a foreign country in her condition," Joe asks.

I pray that my unease with his request doesn't show on

my face. I quickly cover my expression with a big gulp of beer as Joe watches me, waiting for a response.

"You think Sandy and I would get along?" I ask, searching for a way out.

"She's a little abrupt," Joe admits. "Her heart's in the right place, and you guys love a lot of the same things."

I have never told Joe that I dislike Sandy. Nor does he realize that the fact that he is still in love with her makes me hate her even more. We're not going to get along.

"Does she like cats?" I ask, instead of being honest.

"I don't think she doesn't like cats."

"How can you not know if your possible baby mama likes cats or not?"

"Well, I've actually been thinking about that a lot."

"Shit, Joe," I joke. "I didn't think cats were that deep."

"No, not that specific question," Joe amends flatly, not even giving me a chuckle. "But more about the things I know and don't know. I'm really bad at expressing this stuff. I just think that maybe I can do better than Sandy, but I never would have known it if I hadn't moved."

"Jesus, Joe," I say, honestly shocked. I put my hand on his forehead to see if he's running a fever and then check his pulse, both normal. Joe laughs. We're seated in a red leather booth at the most masculine pub in town by the train station. Rather fitting of our bromance, if I do say so myself.

"Joe, we have to lift in like, six hours," I finally say.

"Just say you will spend some time with Sandy," Joe begs. "Or if you have a pack of girlfriends, set up a girls' night maybe. I just, I need to talk to Dillon, and I don't want her left alone."

"You know she's pregnant, right?" I say sarcastically. "Not terminally ill."

Joe gives me a pitifully dramatic look that I'm sure is fifty-percent acting and fifty-percent actual lack of understanding of pregnancy. I cave. "Fine. But when I'm pregnant, you better not treat me like glass."

"Are you pregnant?" Joe asks me seriously.

"No," I say quickly. "It was supposed to be funny, Joe. I just drank six pints of beer. If I was, it would probably be pickled by now."

"I don't want you to have Harrison's baby," Joe mumbles, not picking up on my humor. Obviously, a little drunker than I thought, I forget what a lightweight he is for being such a big guy.

"All right," I grumble. "Let's get you home. We will skip the gym tomorrow."

"If we skip tomorrow, then we go Saturday," Joe says.

"Deal, and then we will go check out Valley Gardens," I add.

Joe agrees but adds on lunch, and I agree but add on a walk through the Stray and so on and so forth until we have an entire sixteen-hour day planned together. I have no idea if we will go through with it or not, but I love it either way.

Blue fills the sky as Joe and I walk through Valley Gardens. After months of winter, spring has finally come to Harrogate, *and* it happened on a Saturday! At the gazebo, I pull out a plastic toe. Joe's laughter pulls the attention of the entire garden to us as I make him take pictures of me pretending to be the faerie queen Betty, removing the curse from Ixar.

"Now, leave my presence!" I command dramatically.

"But, your highness," Joe plays along, "I would like to ask you some questions...lights have been seen at your most luxurious and famous tea shop and there seem to be some relics..."

"I said be gone, summoner," I command again. I raise my toe in the air and imagine magic spilling out of it, but it remains a plastic prop. Joe and I both laugh as we carry on with our day. Comfortably, just like we drunkenly planned on Thursday, we wander all the little parts of town from my game.

"What are you doing?" Joe asks as I bend down to frame dog shit for a picture.

"I'm taking a pic for Mason."

"Of dog shit?"

"Yep. Oh, Joe! Get in the background for some bokeh."

Joe does as I ask, his confused face perfect.

"It's something my brother Mason and I do together," I explain as we start walking again.

I feel like Joe is walking closer to me than usual. I want to reach out and take his hand, but I don't.

Luis would never do this with me. He wouldn't make a fool of himself in a park playing make-believe with my stupid plastic prop. Our relationship is mostly about him. Fuck Kevin, I'm not a hypocrite, am I? Shit.

The Stray's filled with white and purple crocus flowers. I saw them last year, but it's Joe's first time. We take the long way before meeting up with our normal crew at the Blues Bar.

"Who's messaging you?" Joe asks me after I ignore my phone for the third time after we're seated.

"It's Luis," I admit. "He's been, well, overbearing since we got back from Italy," I explain. Joe frowns. My phone goes off again, it's Luis telling me he's at the Little Ale House. Is he looking for me?

"Hey, Joe," I ask. "Do you want to come over and watch a movie?"

"I'd love to," Joe answers. I feel butterflies fill my stomach and remind myself that Joe doesn't like me that way as we take the long route back to my flat.

———

I blink, trying to figure out if I'm asleep or awake. I have my ankles resting on Joe's thighs and my phone turned off. Lord, my cat, has taken up residence draped across Joe's lap and part of my feet. I'm pretty sure I fell asleep for part of the movie because I can't quite figure out what's going on.

"Good morning," Joe teases.

I frown at him for noticing my sleepy state and give him a half-hearted middle finger.

"It's not my fault, you wore me out," I say sleepily to Joe.

I turn my attention back to the movie before my mind can wander. Joe had been trying to get Lord to sit on his lap. I knew my cat would probably do it as long as part of me was on his lap; hence I was bold and inserted my feet. Lo and behold, magic, my cat is now on Joe's lap.

I glance over as Joe shifts my cat enough that his hands can wrap around one of my feet. I hold back a groan as he starts rubbing.

"Good looking and gives magical foot massages," I say. "Maybe you're the wizard, not Ixar."

"Why not both?" Joe asks.

I giggle. Of course he would say that.

"And dripping in self-confidence this evening," I add. "You seem to be doing a lot better."

"I am," Joe answers.

His hands move to my other foot, and I enjoy the massage until the credits roll. Yeah, I probably slept through more than half of the movie, Joe better not want to talk about it.

"Tell me about your family," Joe asks.

To my cat's horror, I pull my feet out of Joe's lap and cross them to face him, one eyebrow raised.

"You don't want to talk about Sandy?" I ask, her visit right around the corner.

"No, I don't," Joe snaps.

I narrow my eyes at him, and he relaxes. "I don't. I've talked too much about Sandy. The baby's either mine or it isn't. Either way, my life shouldn't revolve around her, and I have let it, for too long."

"It should never revolve around anyone but yourself," I clarify.

Joe gives me that half-nod that means he isn't sure if he agrees with me but doesn't want to talk about it.

"Regardless," Joe insists. "I want to hear about you."

I give Joe another skeptical look before I start talking, skimming over the details. "You already know about my brothers, we're all super close. I had the usual trauma growing up. I was chubby, uncoordinated, and not the shining star of intelligence, but I did ok. I had a run-in with an incredibly incompetent teacher that almost got me held back a year, but my family got me through it."

"Everything can't have been easy," Joe insists.

"Well, no," I admit. "Then it wouldn't be life. But not every person needs a defining moment that makes them who they are. Life is as much a collection of the little experiences as much as big moments."

I feel my hands start moving to get my point across. "Think of it like lifting. I remember when I met my goals the first time, that feeling when 135 pounds finally went down and back up on my bench press. But it was years, literally years, of crawling up a few pounds at a time to get there. And my new goal is 150. And, eventually, I want to bench my own body weight, which will remain a mystery for obvious reasons. Do you feel you have a defining moment? An origin story, if we were superheroes?"

"Well," Joe collects his thoughts, his hands wandering forward to trap mine. "In the past, it would have been my first day at basic training. When I realized I would never have to deal with my alcoholic dad again. When this skinny nerdy little shit managed to impress our drill Sergeant before I did. My world both got bigger and smaller at the same time."

"Pretty picture, Joe," I say.

"But I'm not so sure anymore," Joe continues. "Because I think maybe my true origin story happened when I moved to England, and I met you."

I blink a few times, unsure if I should laugh or not. The comment is uncharacteristically romantic and sweet. We're mostly sober. I know, rare, but Joe's looking at me like I'm his world. Not even a bit of humor in his voice.

"And you met me," I repeat with a bit of humor in my voice. "Joe, I know you're not trying to get into my pants. You don't have to say cheesy shit for us to stay friends. It's cool, I'm happy with things as they are."

"That's not..." Joe stops what he was going to say and releases my hands.

"I think I get it," I try again. "The rug was pulled out from under you back home and moving here, it changed everything and is helping you look at your life a different way. Maybe not a defining moment, but it's a decent origin story. Though you need to be bitten by a radioactive spider, or fall in radioactive goop...there seems to be a theme here."

Joe barks out a laugh and stands. He runs his hand through his hair. "I should let you get to bed," he says. "You're running with Harrison in the morning, right?"

"Ugh," I answer, my mood already darkening. "Don't remind me."

177

"If you hate it, stop doing it," Joe demands.

"I'll remember your advice, Dad," I say sarcastically.

I show Joe to the door. To my surprise, before he leaves it, he pulls me in for a hug. Strong arms surround me, and I let myself breathe in his smell, his comfort. When he lets me go, his hand comes up and cups my cheek.

"I'm leaving for Scotland next week," Joe whispers. "I need to get my life straightened out, but when I come back. We are retconning this evening, and I'll be rolling with advantage."

"Um," I say, confused.

Joe leaves the lightest of kisses on my cheek before letting himself out. My bromance with Joe just got weirder.

No, it can't be. I slow as Luis and I approach the cenotaph toward the end of our run. I have some random running playlist with upbeat techno remixes of pop pumping into my ears. My desperate attempt to convince myself I'm dancing rather than, once again, doing this hated activity. Luis doesn't notice as I stop.

It's a dog poop that has been pooped on by a bird. It's a double shit. What are the chances of that? I take out my phone. It's not going to be very artful. It's even on the pavement, but this moment must be shared. I open the camera on my phone and kneel down to frame the shot. As I go to take the picture, a hand grabs my arm and hauls me up. I jump, startled. Luis's angry face is talking, and I take out my earbud.

"...your best time yet, we were in the yellow zone," I hear him finish. God, I hate his color-coded zones for heart rate.

"Sorry," I say quickly. "I saw this shit. It's a shit on a shit," I say. Luis looks at me like I'm insane. I quickly explain to him that A, I'm not swearing, it's the technical term, and B, my poop picture battle with my brother. I can feel a little bounce of excitement in my steps, despite the fatigue in my legs from our six miles so far this morning.

"Why would anyone want to look at feces," Luis asks, bringing down my mood. "That's the stupidest thing I've heard."

"It can't be the stupidest," I say defensively, hurt. "You told me your wine smelled like cat pee the other night."

"It's ammonia," Luis corrects. "And it's part of the aromatic textures in quality wine, especially Sauvignon Blanc."

"All right," I say slowly, fighting not to roll my eyes. "Sorry, I'm not as cultured as you, but this is something I do."

"Paula, we're fixing that," Luis explains, his voice reasonable. "You need to want to learn some of this stuff and make our goals important to you. You could have made a personal best today if you hadn't been distracted by something so gross. Let's sprint it out, get our heart rates up high for the final half-mile, try to salvage this."

I feel myself agreeing, my natural ability to go with the flow kicking in before my emotions catch up. Half-a-mile later, I'm breathing hard, a stitch in my side, Luis's approving smile blessing me for doing what he wants. I suddenly realize I hate that smile, I hate running, I hate most of the things I do with Luis. Fucking Kevin, I am a hypocrite.

"I don't think this is a good idea," I find myself saying. I'm breathing hard, taking short steps to control my airflow. Luis seems fine, more than fine, though he's also walking. The sky is partly cloudy, unlike the brilliant blue of my day with Joe yesterday.

"You never think running's a good idea," Luis laughs at me.

"No," I wheeze. I take a few deep breaths, thinking about how to phrase this. "I think we need to take a break."

Luis is at my side almost instantly, his hands on my elbows. "Are you breaking up with me?"

"Sorta," I placate.

The stitch fully releases from my side, and I move the two of us to a bench. Sunday mornings are deserted in Harrogate. We're seated at the bottom of the Stray where the big tour buses usually drop people off, looking up at the steep hill, surrounded by budding trees. It could be the apocalypse for how dead town is.

"Look, Luis," I start. "I like you, but...I just. Well. To be frank, I'm not falling in love with you. We don't enjoy the same things. And well, I was reminded recently that that's what I want, to feel head over heels for someone."

"Paula," Luis says quickly. "I love you. I'm head over heels for you. I'm sorry if I haven't seemed supportive recently. I'm just pushing you to be your best. I will back off. We still need to play a board game together, right?"

"No. I don't think we need to," I force myself to say. "My friends don't want to play with you again, and all my favorite games are four players."

"You know you even sound like a kid talking about games," Luis remarks.

"Maybe we should all feel like kids more often," I say quickly, twisting his hurtful words into something positive.

"Now, I didn't mean it like that," Luis's tone darkens. "Look, let's grab a quick shower and get some hot food. You're always more agreeable after you eat."

"I don't want to do that," I stand my ground. Luis and I are still on one of his "diets," and if we go eat together, I can't cheat. Why am I even on a diet? I hate dieting, I love food. I love a lot of things that Luis doesn't approve of, and there is nothing wrong with that. I'm just going along with him because I want to be in love. I don't want to fail in another relationship, but this isn't healthy, and I'm drowning in my fantasy.

"I'm sorry. I want a giant waffle covered in ice cream," I apologize, simplifying all my thoughts into an edible object.

"You know that kind of food will just slow down your run time," Luis chastises.

"I don't care about my run time!" I yell standing. "And you would know that if you were actually interested in me, and not designing your own girlfriend."

"Where did that come from?" Luis asks.

It's a fair question, I hadn't really planned on saying that. It just popped out, and it feels right now that I said it.

"Did one of your friends say something? Did Joe say something about me?" Luis asks angrily also standing.

"No, of course not. Joe's a fucking saint who never says anything bad about anyone. No, I feel like that. I feel like you're trying to change me, and I'm letting you. And I can't anymore."

A tear slips from my eye. I scrub it away. I'm not crying about this. Luis slips an arm around my shoulders, and I let him bring me into his embrace as another tear slips out.

"I'm still breaking up with you."

Luis doesn't answer me as I pull myself together. It's the running that's making me cry. There's no way it's years of unresolved body image issues combined with the realization that I'm not in love. Again.

"Paula," Luis says calmer. "I don't want us to break up. I know in your heart, you don't want us to either. You're amazing. We want so many of the same things in life. I'm sorry that I wasn't more open to your hobbies. It's hard for me to socialize with your friends because most of them are my employees. I'm not trying to change you. One of the things I love about you is your ability to fit in with my social group. Everyone loves you at wine class. Just give us another chance. We will take a break from training for a bit. But I know you like feeling stronger, and once you settle in, running will make you feel just as strong as lifting."

"Luis," I start, trying once again to assert myself.

"You don't have to decide right now," Luis reiterates. He backs away from me with his hands up. "We're on a break, just like you asked. Go get your waffles and ice cream. Dinner, Tuesday? Just friends?"

"Just friends," I confirm. Why does everything Luis says sound so agreeable?

"Jesus, Joe, I just saw you three days ago. What happened?" I exclaim from my seat on the floor. Even larger than usual bags dip under his eyes, and he hasn't shaved, the scruff looks unkempt and out of place on his usually clean chin.

On the other hand, I feel great! I'd even taken Kevin up on his dinner invite, and we'd gotten our friend ship squared away and did some brain storming for him and Lyla. Given it was easy when I told him Luis and I broke up, even easier when he got to be right about his assessment of my hypocritical actions. Though I made him apologize for, once again, losing his temper.

"I'm swamped," Joe tells me. "Harrison called me in on Sunday. I ended up working fourteen hours and sixteen yesterday, but he keeps piling work on my desk. He's revoking my time off to go to Scotland. I'm still trying to find a way around it."

I freeze. There's no way Luis would be so petty as to take out our breakup on Joe, is there?

"I can't believe you're at the gym," I manage to say. My body starts moving again. "Should you be here?"

"Probably not," Joe laments. "But this is my only headspace to get away from it all, and I need that more than sleep right now. Sandy will be here in a little over a week. Do you think the baby's kicking already?"

"How far along is she?"

"Five months, give or take."

"Probably not. I know Mom felt my little brothers super early…given, it was pregnancy four and five." Joe holds out his hand and I take it, moving to a standing position. He doesn't let go of my hand, and I shiver with the memory of his lips on my cheek.

"We're getting the paternity test done while she's out here," Joe says quietly. "If it's mine, I really don't want to miss those moments…"

"Joe," I interrupt. "Think about what you told me Saturday night. If it's yours, they are your best friends. They will find a way for you to be there for your baby. Running yourself ragged thinking about it's only going to make you sick. Both mentally and physically. Now, I'm declaring it leg day. Suit up."

Joe groans but does as I say. I love how we take turns bossing each other around. I just like Joe. If Luis is running him ragged and it's my fault, I will fix it. Joe deserves time with his best friends more than anyone.

Edward (Ed)

"Are you by yourself?" I turn at the sound of Paul's voice. I'm seated, my food already ordered at my favorite eatery in town. White table cloths and polite conversation surround us.

"I am," I confirm, surprised to see Paul here.

"Mind if I join you…um…Luis will be coming along shortly…"

"Not at all," I respond. "Luis seems a nice enough chap."

"Nice enough is a good description," Paul's lips flatten into a line.

I take a deep breath remembering our groups conversation about Paul and Luis at the pub the other night. Maybe I didn't want them to join me, but it's too late now.

Paul moves off to find a waiter, as only an American would do, and soon two more places are set at our little table.

"I don't usually see you here," I point out to make small talk.

"Luis picked the place," Paul confirms. I nod, unsurprised, slightly upscale French seems more *his* style.

"So, just a warning, but you're my backup," Paul suddenly says. "I didn't know you were here, but as you are…You don't need to do anything, but Luis and I broke up, and now that I'm here, I really don't want to be alone with him."

I cringe. "Paul, I really don't want to be put in this…"

"Paula, you're not alone," Luis's voice interrupts me.

"Ed was already here, and I realized I wanted a neutral ear during our conversation," Paul says quickly.

As if emphasizing the point, my food arrives. Bugger.

"Well, it's not what I was planning," Luis hesitates. "But I'll take what I can get."

"Perfect, sit."

Luis does, and we all look at each other.

"I'll order us a bottle of wine," Luis states.

"I want a beer," Paul counters. "Ed, what do you want."

"To leave," I stress, very uncomfortable.

"Sorry," Paul says immediately, her eyes begging me to stay. "A bottle of wine is fine, keep it simple."

Luis narrows his eyes at me before taking a breath. "Paula, I'm not trying to change you."

"I'm letting you change me, whether you're intending it or not, and your actions sure feel like you're trying to change me, even physically."

"You know my history," Luis stresses, glancing at me again. Not knowing what else to do, I just sit and look at my plate. "I just want everything to be perfect."

"But that's not life," Paul points out. "I'm not perfect, nothing is perfect, I've never even seen you rate a bottle of wine as perfect. It's not attainable."

"You're right, I lost track of that," Luis agrees.

The waiter shows up, and once again an expensive bottle of wine is ordered. At least I'll get a glass out of the arrangement this time.

"Why's Joe swamped at work?" Paul asks once our glasses are full.

I raise my eyebrow, not where I thought this conversation was going.

"New projects come in all the time," Luis says lightly.

"Three days before he leaves for Scotland?" Paul presses. "So much work that you had to revoke his time off?"

"Joe's a very capable manager," Luis states, a cunning smile on his lips. If this was in our game, I'd be asking to roll Insight. "He's managed to get more productivity out of his teams than any of my others."

"So, you're punishing him for being a good employee?" Paul asks.

"Look, Paula," Luis explains. "Projects come and go. They go faster when upper management can focus on their jobs and not their personal lives."

"I see," Paul mumbles.

I narrow my eyes as her shoulders fall. I don't understand what's happening here.

"So, if you were to have a date, Joe could still go to Scotland?" Paul asks.

"Well, the two are not directly related," Luis admits with a smile. "And it would need to be with someone who I care for, and deserve a second chance with, but, essentially, yes."

The table goes quiet, and I reach for my wine. I've missed something.

PAULA LUBELL

It's not that I've been dreading meeting Sandy, exactly, but I have. My door buzzes and Lord's unceremoniously dumped off my lap as I answer it.

"Hi, Scrunchy," Joe says to me brightly from behind his friends.

The chilly evening air wafts through my door, the night blessedly dry.

Sandy looks even more adorable than her picture. She's short and petite. Her long black hair is caught under what I recognize as one of Joe's scarves. Her light blue, slightly slanted eyes are wide with lovely eyelashes. I hate it that it makes me hate her more. This is going to be a long night.

Dillon's one of the most well-groomed men I've seen. His hair is short on the sides, but long and styled on top. A good six inches shorter than Joe, his frame is narrow and lanky. He moves his arm from around Sandy's shoulders as she steps into my house.

"Do you want to come in?" I ask Joe and Dillon.

"No. We're just dropping Sandy. We'll be back in an hour or two. Fish and chips still, Sandy?" Joe says.

"Yes," Sandy agrees happily.

Joe gives me a weird wave as I move out of the way and get Sandy out of the cold. Some awkward small talk later, we're sitting on my couch with mugs of herbal tea I bought just for this occasion. I'm not much of a tea drinker.

"So, Joe says you're headed to Scotland this weekend," I prompt.

"I was so worried when Joe's time off was revoked," Sandy answers. "But it all worked out! We're going to see castles, coves, and visit distilleries. I'm driving. We've, well I, planned a circle from Glasgow up to Inverness, and then across and down to the Kingdom of Fife, ending in Edinburgh."

"That's a lot of driving," I point out.

"I'm happy to do it. I mean, I wish I could drink. Scotch *is* my favorite, but pregnant and all. The least I can do is facilitate Joe and Dill."

"Are you comfortable driving on the other side of the road?"

"Why wouldn't I be?"

"Have you done it before?"

"No. You just keep yourself in the middle and don't turn the wrong direction."

"All right," I say. "Fair."

I didn't find it that simple. Most people don't. Joe has admitted to me that even months in, he still has moments of self-doubt. Hell, when I dream about driving, it's back on the right, and I struggle for the day. I really don't want to get into anything with Sandy, so I don't voice any of my thoughts.

"I don't need to stay if you're uncomfortable," Sandy says after a moment of quiet that's just a heartbeat too long. "Joe and Dill are just really protective. He didn't need to dump me on you."

"No, sweetie," I respond too quickly. "You've not been dumped on me. Joe talks about you a lot, I'm happy to put a face to your name."

Sandy gives me a skeptical look but doesn't offer to leave again.

"And you win again," I huff.

God, all I want is a drink. If this is the kind of woman Joe likes, no wonder I don't exist. My suggestion to watch something on the TV had been countered with the request for a boardgame of some sort. Which meant talking.

"Are you even trying?" Sandy asks politely.

"I am." I pick up my phone and text Joe to see if they know when they are headed back yet. He doesn't respond.

"What do you think Joe and Dill are talking about?" Sandy suddenly asks.

I watch her putting away her cards and chips. The bright colors of *Splendor* reflect against my living room window.

"I don't know. Joe's a mess. He's been really slow to make friends out here," I answer.

"Joe's a mess?" Sandy asks, perplexed.

I narrow my eyes, trying to decide if she's messing with me. Even from just this interaction, I can tell that Sandy is not the most emotionally in-tune person. It's possible she hasn't noticed.

"You don't like me at all, do you?" Sandy asks. "Dillon says I'm really bad at reading people. You haven't smiled since I walked in your door, and I made the effort to smile at you. Most people smile back when you smile at them. And Joe says you're always smiling."

"Joe's talked about me to you?"

"He has. He makes it sound like you're the only reason England isn't terrible. Though I can't see how that is true. It's England, the home of legends and knights in shining armor and castles. Even the streetlamps look English!"

"They're streetlamps, in England," I say dryly.

Sandy gives me a small smile.

"Why's Joe a mess?" she asks again.

Lord jumps up on my lap, eyeing my guest. Sandy's smile falls, and I see tears bead in the corners of her eye. "Fucking hormones," Sandy cries, wiping them away. "I dislike this part of being pregnant. And the morning sickness. My mood swings are terrible." She takes a deep breath and looks me in the eyes. "I don't like the idea that Joe is a mess. He's never a mess. Joe is the most together person I know, well, maybe other than Dill."

"Sandy," I start, but I don't know what to say here.

"I didn't find out I was pregnant until after Joe's orders came," Sandy continues. "Joe says you know everything already. I like Joe. I love Joe, but I fell in love with Dillon. It wasn't the hot rush of lust I'm used to. It was something slow, something trusting. Dillon's really special. He makes me want to be a better me. Joe, well, Joe never did that for me. He's supportive and a great guy, but it just never clicked."

"You kept sleeping with him," I can't stop myself from pointing out.

"I did. We did," Sandy corrects. "I'm not defending it because it isn't something that needs to be defended. Joe could have left us any time."

"Joe thought he was a part of the 'us,'" I snap.

I can't stop it from coming out, and Sandy looks up at me, surprised.

"He was a part of us," Sandy affirms.

"That's not what you just said."

Sandy lowers her eyes. "It's what I meant. Why's Joe a mess?"

"I'm not getting into the middle of this. What's going on between you and Joe is between you and Joe."

"Please, Paula," Sandy pleads. "Joe and I have never been great at talking. I'm scared. I will love the baby either way, but I want it to be Dillon's. It would break Joe's heart to have another man, even Dillon, raising his kid. I won't leave

Colorado and Joe would be miserable without the military. Dillon's in Colorado, and my mom. I need my mom. I don't know how to be a mom."

A tear slips out of one of Sandy's eyes and then the other, and she puts her fingers in her mouth as if to push her words back in.

"I don't know why I'm telling you all of this," Sandy cries.

I stand and find a box of tissues and put them in front of her. Sandy blows her nose, and thank god, it honks. If her nose blowing had been as cute as everything else, my sympathy might have left me.

"It's ok," I say. "Believe it or not, my first trip with Joe ended similarly. Crying is good."

Her puffy face nods. I leave her to collect herself for a moment and go to my kitchen for a few things. Sandy's not been super successful at stopping her tears by the time I get back. I refill her tea and sip the rum and coke I just poured into my coffee mug.

Sandy's a weird combination of exactly what I was expecting and someone softer, younger. It changes everything that she didn't know about the baby until after Joe's orders. It means a lot that she acknowledges how worried she is about hurting him. I had this picture of a cold hard bitch in my mind. Not a crying, confused teenager. Not that Sandy's a teenager, but, well, I'm only five years older than her, but those five years feel a lot further apart right now.

"Have you talked to Joe or Dillon about any of this?"

"Not yet," Sandy admits with a sniff. "I was going to wait until we had the paternity test results back. I don't want to hurt Joe."

"Joe wants it to be his," I say. Sandy nods miserably. "You've already hurt him by picking Dillon."

"He promised the three of us would be friends no matter what," Sandy whispers.

"He's trying to keep that promise," I try to keep my words soft. "But it's hard when emotions run high."

My phone buzzes.

Joe: On our way back, is everything ok?

"They really-are treating you like you're made of glass, aren't they?" I ask, messaging Joe back to set his mind at ease.

"I've had to go to the hospital twice for dehydration. We didn't tell Joe. But Dillon knows. The doctors call it hyperemesis gravidarum. In layman's terms, really extreme morning sickness, but 'morning sickness' just makes me sound like such a wimp."

"It doesn't," I assure her. "Should you be traveling?"

"Honestly, it's been nice," Sandy non-answers my question. "My body and the baby have no idea what time of day it is. As much as I can, I'm only eating things I don't usually get to, to keep us all guessing. So far, so good. Just some minor vomit a few times a day and heartburn."

"That doesn't sound so nice."

"It isn't, believe me. Don't say anything to Joe?"

"I won't," I promise her. "But the two of you need to talk."

"Now you sound like Dillon," Sandy accuses. I'm unsure if that's good or bad, so I leave it there.

TWENTY-ONE

Campaign: Reality/Where is your god?
Scenario Eleven: Preconceived notions/Love, long ago.
Scene: The big reveal...?

PAULA LUBELL

I only need to strip off two sweaters this evening. Spring's finally seeping into the bitter cold of winter on my windy base. My phone dings, and I smile as another message from Joe comes in. The first one had pleasantly surprised me. I'd been sure that he would be so lost with his friends, he wouldn't even think of life in Harrogate. But I seem to have slipped into his reality, it's not like he's messaging me every minute. Just a pic every now and then.

Despite my self-imposed rule to not use my phone while GMing, I pick it up and peek.

"Wow, it must be important," Byron comments. "I've never seen you get out your phone unless it was to google something game-related."

"Joe's making a big fire and set up his kindling to look like a barbell," I explain.

"Right," Byron responds, slightly confused. I don't elaborate.

"Joe's in Scotland?" Ed confirms.

"In Fife," I relate "I guess they rented a cabin that has a fire pit in front of it. Anyway, sorry, game time."

"Don't be sorry," Kevin smiles. "Things going well with Joe?" he asks cryptically.

I give Kevin a flat look. How he went from, "Stay away from Joe," to now rooting for the two of us to get together is beyond me.

"Joe's my gay BFF," I laugh. "Stop looking for things that don't exist."

"You'd be a pretty good match. Better than Harrison anyway," Kevin reminds me.

"Well, I'm not going to argue with that," I agree.

"Didn't you and Luis go on another date?" Ed asks, very confused.

"You went on another date with Harrison!" Kevin exclaims. "You told me you dumped his ass."

"I gave him another chance," I explain, leaving out his not so subtle blackmail. "And thank you for asking, Ed. It was fine, he tried to recreate our first date."

It wasn't fine, it left a bad taste in my mouth, though Luis had acted the perfect gentleman.

"POOH!" I stress the name to get the focus off my personal life. "You're holding a relic the mermaid just called her God. Clint, the mermaid's naked in your arms," I recap, starting the game. "Her body trembles as gravity pushes down on it for the first time in five hundred years."

"Where am I?" Byron asks.

"Guarding the entrance to the submarine," I tell him.

Byron nods and starts playing a game on his tablet.

"I dry her off using magic," Ed tells me.

"I give her my shirt," Kevin adds enthusiastically.

"I'm surprised it's still on for you to give it to her," I laugh.

My players quickly realize that the mermaid doesn't speak any English. Ixar has one "speak all languages" potion on him and even though Joe isn't hear, I let them pull it off his character for the game. As it works, the ancient mermaid's jumbled mind begins speaking.

"I was in love," I say in my best wizened old lady voice. "I was in love with two men. One of them the god of all, and one of them the god of my heart. It's what trapped me, left me in this dark hole. I'm still beautiful, yes?"

"Of course, a beauty beyond belief," Byron says smoothly.

"I'm not sure Byke would say that," I laugh. "Carmen may have trained Byron well. But Byke's a goblin with Rapport not even listed on his character sheet, and she's hideous. The only thing on her face that's not white is her teeth that have some sort of green moss in between their sharpened points. And Byke isn't even here! Keep your comments to yourself."

"I kissed that?" Ed asks.

"She was giving you air, saving your life," I placate. "I think you can let it pass this time."

Clint and Pooh start talking to my mermaid, her mind in and out of reality, her conversation often coming back to her two lovers. My phone dings again, but I ignore it this time. When I'd read Joe's backstory, so much of it reflected on things he was dealing with. I've never thought about how many of my issues subconsciously come out in my game. But here we are.

"What's the significance of having two lovers at once? What does this have to do with the relic?" Pooh flat out asks the mermaid.

"There's no significance," I find myself saying. "It doesn't matter if I had one or seven, all that matters is happiness and the love born from it."

"Paul, I hate this NPC," Kevin whines.

In his defense, I have been letting her talk them in circles for like twenty minutes.

"Happiness," Ed muses. "And the love born from it."

"Did she have a child with one of them?" Byron asks.

I shoot him a look, Byke isn't supposed to be in the room, but I answer anyway.

"My daughter was so beautiful," I say dreamily in the mermaid's voice.

"Is she in the relic?" Kevin asks me.

I roll my eyes; do they not remember anything from last week?

"The mermaid's daughter is not in the relic," I deadpan.

This is going to be one of those nights.

TWENTY-TWO

Campaign: Reality
Scenario Eleven: Preconceived notions.
Scene: Turning over a new leaf.

JOE SMARTIN

The air is crisp and clear in the highlands of Scotland. I take a picture of the setting sun over the beach before the three of us walk back to our room at the Glenmorangie House. I hadn't thought of beaches when I thought of Scotland, but this far north, the sea has once again met with the rugged Scottish traditions. The highlands are incredible. Green sweeping valleys are dotted with ruined castles and jutting rocks. The new buds of spring sprout in every corner.

"I wish I could drink," I hear Sandy say for the five hundredth time.

"I would take a turn being preggers if it worked like that," Dillon laughs. His voice isn't slurred at all, but the warmth of whiskey fills his cheeks, as it does mine.

"Would you take your turn too, Joe?" Sandy asks me sweetly.

"You know I would." I see her near me and reach my arm out, pulling her into my side. She laughs and snuggles in. This feels so right. Sandy has us stop and take a selfie with the last of the sunset as we pass one of the many small ruins scattered around our trail.

With the sun down, the air suddenly feels colder, and the three of us hurry our steps back to our room. I automatically take Sandy's coat as Dillon heads for the gas fireplace in the corner. This is one of the nicest rooms I've ever been in. Rustic for sure, but the finishing of the 17th-century house makes it seem especially grand.

I can't take my eyes off Sandy as she wanders over to the massive king-size bed in the middle of the room. She turns and flashes me a smile before peeling off her sweater.

"I need some help with my pants, or trousers, as we're in England," Sandy tells me causally. She moves so that her knees are balanced on the bed so I won't have to stoop to kiss her. "Getting too round to see my toes," she jokes.

If anything, she has lost weight. It worries me, but not in this moment. In this moment, I remember Sandy's soft skin under my fingers. Her passion igniting my own.

I automatically move. I haven't gotten laid since moving to England, and my dick reminds me of that fact as I run my hands along Sandy's hips. I can't stop my hands from wandering to her stomach, her baby bump clear despite her inability to put on weight.

Her hands remind themselves of my build before hanging off of my neck. Our mouths meet, and I close my eyes. For a moment, I lose myself in the past. I just enjoy Sandy, and then, with an unhappy groan, I pull back. Dillon's already behind her. He stops kissing her neck at my sound and looks at me.

"You two talked about this already," I say, my voice husky with lust.

"We did," Dillon confirms.

I listen to the sounds of the house, the creaking of old boards and the low hum of the fireplace.

"I didn't," I finally admit.

It hurts to say it. An image of Scrunchy fills my mind. I never enjoyed sharing as much as Sandy and Dillon. Yes, some parts of it had been incredibly hot, but like I told Sandy all those years ago, I'm more of a one-woman man. I don't want to be Sandy's second choice. I deserve more.

I move and pick up Sandy's sweater. She takes it with a surprised look on her face. I ignore her glances at the obvious tent in my pants. A man is more than the hormones that drive him. Sometimes, especially with Sandy, I don't remember that.

"We're not having sex tonight," I say. I look at Dillon, who nods encouragingly before slipping to the door.

"I'm going to go check on our dinner reservation," Dillon comments. "Don't kill each other, please."

The door clicks shut behind him, and the silence grows thick between us.

"Sandy, I'll always love you," I start. I pull her into a brief hug before sitting on the edge of the bed, leaving distance between us.

"You're breaking up with me, with us," Sandy sniffs.

"You don't sound surprised."

"Dillon's all but said it," Sandy admits. "He can't keep a secret to save his life."

"That he can't," I chuckle.

"I'm going to miss the sex, a lot."

"Not me?" I ask.

"You too," Sandy laughs. "But mostly the sex. I think that is part of why I'm not more upset. Is that wrong?"

"Dillon would tell us that what we're feeling is never wrong."

"He would also tell me that it's not an appropriate time to share," Sandy counters.

"It's always an appropriate time to share with me," I tell Sandy. I can't help but push some of her silky black hair behind her ears, just like I did on our first date.

"One last roll in the sheets for old times' sake?" Sandy asks, catching my hand.

"Sandy," I warn, taking my hand back. She pouts, her adorable lower lip sticks out. My hormones fight with my self-control as Scrunchy's face appears in my mind. "Go find Dillon, I'll meet you two at dinner."

"No fun," Sandy teases. Her eyes light up when I say Dillon's name. I watch her exit out the same door Dillon had earlier, a smile filling my face. For the first time, I'm honestly happy for my two best friends.

"Hi, Scrunchy," I purr into my video chat.

"Jesus, Joe. It's like one in the morning. Are you ok?"

"I'm amazing." I'm sitting in a big chair in my room after an emotional, but clearing, evening with my friends.

"And drunk?" Scrunchy accuses.

"Not really." I'm not. Actually, very little liquor had been involved tonight.

Her screen tilts and then goes black. I assume it's fallen forward, and I hear the sounds of shuffling. Scrunchy reappears, backlit, her face resting on her arms. Attached to very bare shoulders.

"Are you in bed?" I ask stupidly.

"Joe, you woke me up. I'm not fucking getting out of bed to have a video conference with you."

"Are you naked?" I ask stupidly again.

"I'm wearing tighty-whities on the bottom. Don't be intimidated by my delts. If we keep training together, yours can look this good too."

"Really, it's your TRAPS I'm looking at," I manage to joke, mispronouncing traps.

"Aww," Scrunchy says sarcastically. "It almost sounds like tits, so you think it's funny."

"I know you're envious of my traps," I come back with. I subconsciously flex.

"I am. They line your neck perfectly. What I would love more is the knowledge of why I'm being called at one in the morning when I would have thought you would be all snuggled up to your besties."

"Maybe I just wanted to hear your voice," I say honestly.

"Aww, Joe, did you guys smoke something good?"

"Really, Scrunchy. All joking aside. I had a good talk with Sandy. This place is amazing. Did you get my picture of the sunset? It was over a sand beach."

"I would call that a weedy beach."

"It was still a beach."

"I can see you're in too good a mood to be swayed by my half-awake arguments," Scrunchy relents. "I'm glad you're having a good time."

"There's one thing that would make it better," I say, my voice lowering.

"Alright, I'll bite," Scrunchy laughs. "And what would that be?"

"If you were here." And I honestly can't think of anything better. In the moment, kissing Sandy had been all I wanted. Once that moment was over, my first thought was of Scrunchy.

"Oh, Romeo," Scrunchy says dramatically. "If only thou'st understood my afront to orgies. Thine eyes would quicken.

And thy heart respect." It takes me a minute to process her half-Shakespearian half-made up word sentence.

"Scrunchy, I didn't sleep with Sandy or Dillon," I say, the humor leaving my voice.

"Joe, I'm not judging you," Scrunchy says quickly.

"It's not about judgment, Scrunchy. It's important to me that you know I didn't. If it's my baby, I want to be a part of its life, but that's it. I think Dillon and I will always be close, and I'm sure Sandy and I will stay in touch. But I'm done with that part of my life. I want something different now."

"Wow, Joe." I see one of her big smiles fill her face, and I almost sigh in relief. "I'm impressed. You must feel like a weight has lifted."

"I hadn't thought about it that way, but I do. I wish you were here to share the moment with me."

"Joe, you're too sweet sometimes."

"Only to you."

PAULA LUBELL

"Joe called you in the middle of the night?" Harriet confirms. "He likes you…like, like-likes you."

"But he didn't kiss me in Italy! I was half-naked in his arms," I hiss quietly.

"Weren't you dating Luis at the time?" Kevin points out.

"Kevin! This is girl talk, butt out," Harriet screeches, scandalized.

"You two are in the middle of a pub crawl with mostly guys," Kevin points out. "And I can be one of the girls, don't be sexist."

"I was dating Luis," I admit.

"Joe seems very formal to me," Ed sticks in.

Harriet and I both give him a glare, and Harriet mouths, "girl talk."

"You still owe me from that horribly awkward dinner with Luis," Ed points out before continuing. "Maybe he just doesn't want his personal life to get messy. I don't."

"This is no longer fun speculation," I point out. "I'm going to get another beer."

"It seems my timing is perfect," Luis's voice comes from behind me.

I squeezed my eyes shut momentarily before speaking. "Hi, Luis, what are you doing here?"

"Getting you a beer," Luis answers smoothly. "What are you having?"

I rack my brain. I do not want Luis to buy me a beer, I refuse to be in debt to him. We left our date as "good friends." Though I really didn't even want that, Luis can just be so persuasive and agreeable.

"I'm out too," Harriet pipes up. "I'm drinking barley wine and Paul, the chocolate stout? It's my turn to pay, put it all on tab fifteen please."

As Luis wanders off, I find Harriet's hand and give it a grateful squeeze.

"It's what girlfriends are for," Harriet offers.

"Who invited Luis?" Juan's voice finds us moments later.

"No one," I clarify. "We're on a break, and he's probably just trying to make a point."

"Do you want us to chase him off?" Juan offers.

"No," I say quickly, thinking of Joe's job, almost everyone at this pub crawl is under Luis's management, fucking tiny base. "No, just play nice. This isn't really his scene; he will get bored and leave."

"If you say so," Juan says skeptically.

Fortunately, the conversation has moved on by the time Luis returns with two barley wines and my beer. Despite there being no room on the couch, Luis perches on the arm, resting one of his hands possessively on my shoulder. I leave it, not wanting to give Juan any reason to provoke his boss's boss.

"It doesn't taste anything like wine," Luis says after taking a sip.

"It's wine made of barley, though still 14% alcohol," Harriet giggles.

"What something's made of is very important," Luis comments. "Vines only produce grapes if they are one of the lucky few to not get trimmed back during the winter." Luis's fingers put pressure on my shoulder. "Only the best-viewed vines make the culling."

"And who decides which vines are best?" I ask, already knowing the answer. Luis smiles and squeezes my shoulder again.

"What the fuck are you talking about, man?" Juan laughs awkwardly.

"Making wine is a very delicate process," I agree, reaching up and squeezing Luis's hand back.

Ed gives me a strange look, but I bite my tongue and plaster on a fake smile. I just need to make it through the evening. Just like our last date, I can do this.

"See, that wasn't so bad," Luis purrs.

My trainers are quiet on the cobblestones leading to the taxi stand. It's a walk we've taken many times, but tonight it feels wrong. Luis attempts to put his arm around my shoulders, and I dodge out of the way.

"Luis, we're not getting back together," I spit. "You're threatening to fire my friends. What is wrong with you."

"I never said that," Luis states.

He stops walking and grabs my arm, pushing me against a nearby building. His mouth hungrily devours mine, and I push him away. His arms still pin me to the wall on either side of my head. I can taste multiple barley wines on his breath.

"Paula. You're amazing. You could be even more amazing. Tonight, all we talked about was beer and movies and stupid games. There's so much more to the world. You're smart, adaptive. You're waisted amongst these people."

"I don't think you should be judging what people choose to talk about in their free time."

"No, Paula," Luis explains as if I'm a child. "Don't take this personally. You didn't start those conversations. That's what I'm saying. You just go along with the people around you. I want you to be around me always, moving in my flow. Move in with me."

"What the fuck, Luis!" I exclaim. I quickly duck out between his arms and cross my arms defensively over my chest. "Did you just insult all my friends at once, my intelligence, and then ask me to move in with you?"

"I asked you to move in with me," Luis reiterates, ignoring the first part of my question. "We're perfect together."

"You've had too much to drink," I say. "Luis, you're trying to blackmail me into having feelings for you. Love doesn't work that way."

"You can learn to love someone," Luis counters.

"I'm going home now, unmolested," I deadpan. It's the only thing I can think of to say.

"I would never force you to do anything you don't want to," Luis reassures me. "I love you, I'm obsessed with you. Your strength, your care. You don't even realize that people gravitate to your joy, the ease they feel in your presence. I'm going to love you like no one else can, treat you like the princess you are."

He moves towards me, and I flinch back. Despite being a strong woman, I'm very aware that I'm alone in the middle of the night with someone I don't trust. Someone who could hurt me or my friends if he doesn't get his way.

"I know you wouldn't, sweetie," I say, opposing my instinctual reaction.

"Let me walk you home," Luis insists.

"You've never needed to before," I point out, sweetly.

"Times change, as do peoples jobs," Luis growls.

I take a deep angry breath, but what else can I do?

A few blocks later, we are at my door and he gives me a sloppy kiss on the cheek, exactly where Joe's had been. I shudder.

"You will see things my way." Luis turns, walking back the way we came.

I suddenly wish my door had more locks as I secure it behind me. I met Luis and Joe on the same day, given Joe was from a distance. The same day the dice gods had rolled a twenty and a one out of my pocket. The D6 was even broken. How have I so badly mixed this up.

TWENTY-THREE

Campaign: Where is your god?
Scenario Six: Knowledge is power.
Scene: You can't always get what you want.

Joe Smartin

"Let me get this straight," I explain, after the recap of the week I missed. "While I was gone, we kidnapped a mermaid, who has a relic that has a god inside of it?"

"She wanted to come with us," Byron interjects.

"We were then captured by trolls, who took said mermaid and relic, and then locked us in the same cellar under The Den. And then, in exchange for your freedom you gave me to the trolls. Who immediately sent an unregistered wizard who needs to keep a low profile into a magical library for a book they can't even read?"

"Don't forget you kept Rombalds family jewels, and Pebbles has figured out we still have them," Byron adds, looking at his sheet. "We have leverage."

"It sounds really bad when you say it like that," Kevin nods at my summery. "But, scout's honor, it was the best thing we could have done."

"We got a ton of information too," Ed sticks in. He takes out his notes and paraphrases. "Although we still don't understand if the relics call gods or are just storing consciousness, we do know that they need to be charged with magic. The type of magic seems to be important. Farmer Brooks is using blood magic. Betty's using trow minions, those were the masseuses at the spa, to gather, well, sex, the magic of lust.

"Pebbles' implied that there is a split in the trolls. Audry Lakeland's at the head of it while somehow being involved with the faeries. And last, and most importantly, Teresa, our missing faerie, is actually associated with the trolls, though all trails on her have gone cold. It's part of why the trolls hate us so much. We don't have the foggiest on what type of magic the trolls are powering their relic with."

"Have I been discovered at the library?" I ask Scrunchy, reminding the group that I'm not with them.

"You have not," Scrunchy says very slowly, making me doubt her words. "When the mermaid discovered that she'd been trapped for three hundred years, she became irrational, desperate to find out what happened to her child. In exchange for that information, she has agreed to tell you all about the relic. Though at this point, it's no longer in her possession, so that's all she can do. That's part of the reason you agreed to go to the library. So, Joe, join me in the hall so I can tell you what you found there in private?"

I grin cheesily at Scrunchy once we're in the hall. I just got back late last night, and we haven't seen each other in a week. It feels so much longer than that. I only video-called her that one time, but I sent her many texts. Sandy'd given me some ideas of how to tell Scrunchy how I really feel about her. Honestly, talking about Scrunchy's easier for Sandy and me than talking about our own emotions. Scrunchy smiles back, but it doesn't stay on her face.

"Is everything ok?" I ask.

I want to give her a hug, but she's keeping her distance, her arms crossed.

"Not really, but let's just focus on the game," she says, barely taking the time to breathe. "We can chat later. I'm just stressed. I'll be better after we play for a bit. You're currently in the magical library located deep in druid territory across from the Stonefall Cemetery. You got here by bus. Your iconic trench coat and all your magical tools are with the trolls who are holding your friends, however Pebbles did give you your bag of holding back. I've moved Rombalds' family jewels into it. You've already taken the book the trolls needed, but while in the bowels of the library you discover the MPD's not quite as incompetent as you would have hoped.

BYKE - BYRON'S WIZARD

"Sshhiiittt," I hear Clint yell. "Puh-lease tell me ya ahr joking? MPD pokey house, rey'lly Ixar?"

I put down the ball of wires and metal I was fiddling with. I still can't decide if it's going to be a bomb or a mechanical toy. The trolls kept our phone above the cellar in case Ixar needed to communicate, and he did. One of the trolls is currently gripping Clint's legs from the bottom of the steep stairs leading up to cell phone service. Another is sitting, and the third is picking its nose near the keg that covers the hole to the submarine.

"Byke got the pic," Clint announces, much calmer after another minute of listening.

I absently open my phone, recently returned to me, and look at the family tree Ixar sent me. I don't know if he truly understands what he has found. I need to talk to Cleodora, the mermaid, and Betty. We're focusing on the wrong thing. I start to open my mouth, but my brain starts to get the fuzzy, a feeling I've come to associate with prophecies. I desperately try to bring up the video mode on my phone. When the fuzz leaves me, who knows how much later, I discover I didn't quite make it. A few pictures of the floor, and one of my blurry crotch as I dropped the phone, are all I see.

Pebbles has appeared in the cellar with us. His ugly troll face looks at me like he's seen a ghost. An evil ghost that needs to be destroyed. He raises his club above his head. Pooh's madly typing my prophecy into his phone behind him, Pebble's threat unnoticed.

"Oh, god, don't hit me, please," I beg of Pebbles. "It's not my fault."

"Giant moths!" Pebbles roars as he charges me.

I stand and squeak as I run behind Pooh.

"Tarnation?" Clint bellows.

No longer on the phone, he puts his hands out and explains my curse, and Pebbles slowly relaxes.

"Not curse, gift," Pebbles says after he understands. "Maybe use gift more often, and you spend less time in troll cellar. Trolls no like Rombald slayers."

"Too late for that now," Clint quips.

"Pebbles, can you get us our stuff and get us out of here?" I ask.

Pebbles gives us an indiscernible look.

"Ixar bring back book, you return rest of Rombald, you go free," the troll states.

It wasn't Pebbles who captured us, though he did warn us

he was our only ally on troll lands. Now that I'm thinking about it, Pebbles is known to be the second-in-command to whomever the first-in-command is. I start to open my mouth to ask exactly who ordered us down here when Pooh starts reading off his phone.

"In power it combines, in time it rhymes, in places it chases, and in our hearts, it's forgotten. Nevermore will the threads be separate, for combined rhymes chase their truths."

"My prophecy?" I confirm, memorizing the words.

"Indeed," Clint twangs. "We 'ave a problem. Ixar's gawt yo-wr book, but Ixar's gotten himself caught eend thrown in thuh MPD jail. So, this hair is what we cahwl a stalemate. If wer stuck down hair, we kay-yun't gitty-up rescue 'im an git yo-wr book now kay-yun we?"

"Huh?" Pebbles says, scratching his head.

"We need to rescue Ixar," I summarize Clint's drawl.

I listen closely as Clint outlines our exact situation.

For better or for worse, Ixar's ex, Cercia, is still at the MPD and, apparently, in the same cell as Ixar now. He's been roughed up, search and separated from his belongings. Pebbles seems fairly uninterested until Clint reminds him that Ixar's belongings now include both the book he was sent to retrieve and Rombald's family jewels. At that reminder, Pebbles perks up immediately.

"Tunnels under clink," Pebbles states.

"There's no way the MPD was stupid enough to build their magical jail above troll tunnels," Pooh scoffs.

"Not troll, forgotten," Pebbles corrects.

"Where is the MPD jail?" Ed asks out of character.

Paula brings up Google Maps on the big TV and types in Harewood House & Bird Garden. The map zooms in and out to a large expanse of grey with dots of green and blue representing the expansive grounds with the Victorian manor house right in the middle.

"Not Lord Harewood," Ed gasps.

"Turns out he was a very powerful faerie," Paul says knowingly. "You would need to be to keep penguins alive and happy in the middle of the Dales. Anyway, he was too organized and too smart. He loved his magic and his birds more than the new world order, and the MPD took him out and confiscated his lands."

"His beautiful manor house," I moan dramatically in Byke's voice.

Kevin starts quizzing Paula on details as my mind wanders to my last visit to the brightly colored and perfectly restored Victorian estate. It had been filled with art and antiques. Even the vaulted ceilings were painted and patterned.

"Sounds like a daisy ole fuh-ashioned jailbreak t' me," Clint says, bringing me back into the game.

"We need a plan," I say quickly, my worries forgotten. "Pebbles, can I have my pack back? How big are these tunnels?"

IXAR - JOE'S WIZARD

Cercia's skin is smooth under my fingers, her body warm against mine. I press my lips into her back, muffling my summoning, hiding my use of magic in her necromantic aura. Leviathan dances unhappily as I once again make a minor contract with a lower demon instead of calling on her. In my mind's eye, I see the twin demons I have summoned as they metaphorically sign themselves into my service. As I mumble the final words of my casting, Cercia wiggles her hips, putting unwanted pleasurable pressure on my crotch.

"This is really not the time," I growl.

I don't move away. I can't; the MPD have cameras and patrols everywhere. They think I have no magic. I'm the only one in here with no magic damping band. They only brought me here because I broke into a magical library.

I pretend not to see my two wispy demons as they find radiators sticking out of one of the walls and melt into them, hopefully following them down and down. I hope Clint's info on the tunnels is correct.

The room we're in was once beautiful, but now it's divided up by ugly black bars and cold metal floors. The restored paint peeling, the amazing plaster works destroyed. The jail cells are more like livestock pens, stacked two high, most filled with two or more supernaturals.

Cercia's relishing her new position as my magical scapegoat. I slowly back up, away from her touches until my back hits the cell bars, where she lifts up my shirt and begins kissing the skin right above my belt line. A few whistles and catcalls ring out, and I feel heat rise to my cheeks.

"Enough, Cercia," I demand.

She stops, but meets my eyes with a lustful grin. I wipe my thumb across her lips and give her a hard look. She pouts, but agrees, and the two of us sit. Cercia pillows her head on my lap. My traitorous fingers brush through her hair. I quickly close my eyes, feeling for my magic and my two demons. They have found tunnels, but much deeper than Clint made it sound. I take a deep calming breath and let myself sink into a wizard trance to wait.

JOE SMARTIN

I accept a few pieces of paper clipped together from Scrunchy as she turns to the rest of the party. Clint, Pooh, and Byke begin to follow Pebbles, my duster and magical supplies with them, through the tunnels that snake under all of the Dales. I know my character isn't there, but I listen to the descriptions of the various tunnels anyway. It really sounds like they are from different eras. Some man-made, some clearly troll, and others still natural, full of obstacles and beautiful mineral formations.

As my party gets distracted by a dusty locked door, probably from the 90s, I look down at the packet again. It's a list of names, each one accompanied by a little story. Although some of them are written by Scrunchy, most of them look to be copied and pasted from the internet. I read through the first few.

"Are these all the people in jail with me?" I ask.

"They are," Scrunchy says after Byke epically fails a roll to try and shrink a golf cart they found behind the door in an attempt to take it with them. I'm glad to see her relaxing, all her work clothing is gone, the tension that filled her shoulders at the beginning of the game has been channeled into her characters and world descriptions.

"As you're the only player there," she continues. "I'm not taking the time to play out a bunch of interactions, but the magical jail is pretty chatty and very overcrowded. The country club, as the MPD jail's sometimes called, is super underfunded. Anyone caught doing minor offenses is placed in the pens you're in. No uniforms, just three basic meals a day, until they can be processed by the magical offenses panel."

I go back to reading as my party finally gives up on the golf cart and goes back to looking for the underside of Harewood House. I can't stop my chuckle when I see the name Goku. His offense, eating an inhuman amount of food, making him a suspected unregistered magic user. Obviously based on a popular character from *Dragon Ball Z*, an anime.

"What kind of magical dampening keeps Goku in jail?" I ask.

"Oh, good question," Scrunchy intones. "Roll."

As I roll, Byron's doorbell rings and he excuses himself. Carmen and the kids are all out tonight. I don't think much of it as my dice land on lots of plus signs.

"It's like you're channeling your inner Byke," Scrunchy tells me enthusiastically. "The bronze bracelets that you see on almost everyone suspected of magic, so not you, are a simple but genius device that tap into the magic of the person they are wearing and uses their own energy to neutralize itself. They need a key to unlock, a key that's kept in the administration wing along with all your confiscated belongings."

"Would these people help me escape?" I ask.

"All right, I need an Empathy roll for that," Scrunchy answers. I roll again, and movement catches my eye. I look up as Byron walks into the room, Harrison right behind him. I feel my mood go sour. What's he doing here?

"And what are we drinking tonight?" Harrison asks, overly friendly.

I take a calming breath. Kevin did mention that they left together after our most recent pub crawl. I need to stay calm. What they are doing has no bearing on my plans. I'm going to be honest with my feelings and let Scrunchy do with it what she will.

"What are you doing here?" Scrunchy asks Harrison, her voice unfriendly. Her relaxed posture's gone, replaced with that tension again. Her legs, usually crossed under the table, flatten out, and she physically pulls back.

"Sweetie, you play games every Friday," Harrison purrs. "I was excited to see this gaming cave you raved about and figured I would walk you home once you were done playing."

Scrunchy picks up her phone and glance at the time.

"That's very thoughtful of you," she bites out. "But really

not necessary. It will be probably another hour, maybe more. Are we still running tomorrow morning?"

"We are," Harrison answers. "I just didn't want to wait that long to see you again. Byron, that drink? Mind if I sit?"

Harrison takes the empty chair at the opposite end of the table before Byron can answer.

Our host seems conflicted. Hell, I'm conflicted. What's coming out of Scrunchy's mouth is one thing, and her body language is something completely different.

"If it makes you happy," Scrunchy says after the two eye each other for a minute. "I think it was cosmos tonight. I'll have another one too if you don't mind, Byron."

"Of course," Byron, who still hadn't sat, moves to his bar.

The sound of clinking bottles and shakers fills the tension.

"Joe," Scrunchy turns back to me as if nothing interrupted us. "You don't think anyone in this jail gives a whit about you or each other, but all of them want out. You can see a mix of supernatural races, including some with known mind control and elemental powers. A random druid looks pretty strung out in a far corner. A mass jailbreak, if successful, would erase all records of who came in or out in the last few days."

"I have an idea," I tell Scrunchy. "I need to communicate with my party."

"Well, then you need to have two ideas," Scrunchy corrects brightly. Her body language perks up, but then back down as her eyes dart to Harrison. I feel the need to punch his smug smile off his face, but force myself to calm.

———

PAULA LUBELL

215

This should have been amazing. Joe's now summoned three different types of demons successively. His messenger demon sends broken notes between him and Byke, and eventually, his party finally finds the tunnel under Harewood.

Just after sundown, they roll. Simultaneously Byke, Pebbles, and Pooh start drilling a magical hole directly under the administrative offices. Joe unleashes a small army of minor demons into the destroyed ballroom of Harewood House.

"I still casting through Cercia?" Joe checks with me.

"You are," I confirm.

My comfort at describing anything involving Joe and Cercia, even though they are just our made-up characters, has vanished with Luis's appearance. He's so comfortable walking into my social life, like he belongs…it leaves me sick to my stomach. I never told him where Byron lived or invited him here. I swallow thickly. His threat against Joe and all my friend's forefront in my mind. I try to take a sip of my Cosmo, but it's already gone.

"Another?" Byron asks me.

I shake my head and find my water bottle, licking my lips nervously. I really do want another. Anything to calm my nerves, but Luis is walking me home, apparently, and I need a clear head.

"Where was I?" I mumble.

I gather my nerves, gaining strength. "Right, Joe, would you like to describe the chaos you've caused with your little army, or shall I?"

While Ixar creates a confused jailbreak above, Byke's devised a massive magical auger and has been drilling toward the energy of Rombald's family jewels. With a flair of drama, Clint comes out of the new hole in the floor in the middle of the MPD prison, only to find the room filled with black plastic unmarked evidence boxes and locked with a complicated password-protected control panel. Between Byke, Clint, and Pooh, with only a few clues from Pebbles, who shouldn't have known anything, they crack the code. Ixar and Cercia tumble into the room, but they still don't have Ixar's bag. Only the auger's hole being on the left side of the room gives them any clues as to where to even start.

"The cry of an MPD bull horn emerges along with the sounds of whizzes and bangs of magic flying. The cavalry has arrived. You can see Kevlar-covered bodies running down the hall toward you. You have seconds," I say, my voice lacking its usual dramatic flair.

Joe scramble for his character sheet as I have Cercia dive into the auger's hole, followed by Pebbles and Pooh, to keep his eye on Cercia.

"Can I just call my bag to me?" Joe asks.

"I need a skill or a *FATE* chip," I say.

Joe frowns, it's his last one. But he hands it over, and I gift him with a bag of holding. The three wizards still in the room dive down.

Reunited, my party, Pebbles, and Cercia included, dash back through the tunnels, the MPD hot on their heels. They manage to find their way back to the door that had the golf cart behind it. Clint hotwires the thing, although, if they had just searched the two skeletons on either side of the door, they would have found the keys. With a whoop from Clint, they drive the golf cart recklessly fast into the unknown.

"And we will end there for tonight. Sorry we ran a bit late," I say.

I'm not sorry. I'm avoiding having Luis walk me home.

"It's not a problem," Luis says evenly.

I tense, I hadn't meant it for him.

"It's whenever," Kevin confirms helpfully.

Pooh had been instrumental in the final chase scene,

coating the walls and floors in slippery ice, even filling the base of the auger's hole, slowing down the MPD. Despite Luis's unwanted presence, I'm actually quite pleased with myself. Everyone had been pretty equally involved in this encounter.

"Interesting. Very creative sweetheart," Luis praises.

His voice has a judgmental, derogatory edge that makes his words the exact opposite. I don't understand his logic. Does he really think that demeaning my hobbies is going to change them?

"Great session. Really well-balanced between your players." Joe's simple, honest praise briefly lifts my spirits.

Everyone's packing up their areas. I slowly follow suit, dreading my walk home. It's late, there's tension in the air from Luis, tension I'm not about to get anyone else involved in.

"Ah, I'll talk to you tomorrow?" Joe asks. "At beers?"

"At beers," I confirm.

Joe holds out his hand, and I look at him, confused for a minute before I remember I still have his phone. I don't think he needs me to take it anymore, but habits die hard. I hand it back to him, and his hand presses into mine, pulling me slightly forward.

"I don't know what's going on, but just let me know if you need anything," Joe whispers. His words are fast and low and gone even before they register. He gives Luis a polite nod and leaves with Kevin and Ed.

I take a deep breath, my stuff gathered and stand, Luis copying my movement.

"Shall we?" Luis asks, holding out his arm. I swallow thickly and plaster on a smile.

"Thank you for hosting, Byron," I say.

Byron gives me a concerned nod. "Call me when you get

home. There was a stabbing last week, and if I don't get a call soon, I will call the police."

"I will," I say as if Byron asks that every week.

I hope the two words express the amount of gratitude I'm feeling as I wrap my hand into Luis's arm.

TWENTY-FOUR

Campaign: Reality
Scenario Twelve: Crossroads.
Scene: The drawback and benefits of family.

PAULA LUBELL

"Rob, is Mom there?" I ask my youngest brother. "What are you doing at the house?"

"What are you doing not at the house?" Rob asks me back.

I hate my brothers. Not really. I love to hate how much they frustrate me. At the moment, the familiar emotion feels like a painful loss. All of us still have our childhood bedrooms at my parents' place in Texas. Honestly, until I moved here, I was just as guilty as my brothers of random pop-ins for no real reason.

"Just get me Mom," I cry, frustrated and now homesick.

I can feel the tears already forming in my eyes, and I try to scrub them away before Rob notices. No such luck.

"Are you crying?" Rob asks.

Ugh, I am. Luis had been a perfect gentleman. Walking

me to my door. Telling me what an amazing mom I was going to be to our kids with all my creativity, and I had just silently nodded. Every one of his words filled me with silent dread. I hate the future he paints for us, the future he's attempting to blackmail me into.

"Do I need to fly out there and beat in someone's head?" Rob asks.

I realize I've stopped answering him, and I quickly make eye contact through our video chat. Rob, like everyone in our family, is from the same cookie cutter. Tall, broad, muscled. None of us are twins but we look eerily similar.

"No," I manage to croak out.

What I really want is to say yes. Siccing my overly protective pack of muscled brothers on Luis sounds amazing, but I need to fix my own problems. That's half of why Dad sent me out here in the first place. Forced me to manage. I don't deal well with conflict. In part, because my brothers often came to my rescue. I took a lot of shit, a lot of it from them, but if they caught word of someone outside them picking on me, it stopped.

"Hey, Paul," Rob's voice is soothing as he sits in front of the computer. "What's up? I've not seen you this upset in a long time."

"It's girl stuff, Rob. GO GET MOM!" I half cry, half yell.

Rob's face pales a little, and he nods, standing and heading out the door. My eyes search the familiarity of my parents' office. The room is lit, I know, by a window behind the computer screen my face is on. It's lined with bookcases and filing cabinets. I can't see it, but a matching desk will be next to this one, with my dad's laptop, probably covered in disorganized papers. I feel another bitter stab of homesickness rush through me.

It takes Rob a suspiciously long time, but my mother's form fills my screen. Her eyes are light blue, where mine are dark. She keeps her hair short, the white natural from age, not the layers of dye jobs I put mine through. We look so much alike. I'm blown away by the image of me in thirty years that looks back at me with concern and love-crinkled eyes.

I don't even say hi before the tears come again and I pour my heart out to my mom. I've been so good about only telling them the good stuff, trying to live in only the good stuff, but I just can't anymore. I hate England. I hate the weather. I hate the terrifying roads. I hate being a manager. I hate this tiny base that's like a fucked-up replacement for my family. I hate Luis, and I hate Joe. And hate Lord, my stupid cat who has abandoned me and my crying mess.

"Yesss, let the hate flow through you," I find the *Star Wars* quote coming out of my mouth, and I manage a sobbing snort. I hear the bark of a laugh. I scrub my eyes and look at my mother accusingly.

"Is everyone watching this?" I ask. Mom stands and shoos someone out of the room. "I'll tell you about it later. Just give us some girl time."

"You don't hate your cat," Rob's voice comes from a distance just as Mom shuts the door. I laugh a little. Lord's sitting in his cat tree looking at me like I have betrayed him by making my lap so uninviting. Rob's right. I don't hate my cat. Mom sits back down.

"I would give anything in the world to be able to hug you right now," Mom says. "But I can't. Tell me more about what's going on with Luis."

I don't hold back, it feels so good to admit to someone how lonely I feel. Despite filling my days with work and my nights with social stuff, I still come home to a dark apartment. I take back some of my hate. I don't hate England. I do hate the weather, but it's not England. Living here has made me realize how important my family is to me. How badly I want a family of my own. How that need, that loneliness, led me to Luis. Despite obvious signs that he's bad news, I kept seeing him, hoping for something that just wasn't there.

"I can't call the police," I finish my story. "I can't contact security on base. It's just the word of a little radome contractor who isn't even good at her job against a high-ranking government official. He hasn't hurt me. He hasn't technically done anything wrong. He isn't really threatening me even."

"No, he's threatening Joe through you, right?" my mom confirms. "And Joe's the man you went to Italy with?"

"Not like that, Mom," I explain. "Joe's just a really good friend. He doesn't like me like that."

"I'm not there," my mom starts. I can tell she wants to say more but changes topics. "You're not bad at your job."

"I am, Mom," I insist. "I don't hate my job. I hate managing. I'm not a ladder climber. I don't need to make more money. I like using my hands, not listening to people's bullshit and filling out ten forms to change a light bulb."

"Do you want to come home?" Mom asks.

I squeeze my eyes shut. Another tear spills out of the corner of my eye. I do, I want to go home. I want to leave all of this behind. Love, drama, my insecurities at work, my loneliness. I want to feel my mom's arms. I want to go back to the world where I just did the work required and then went home without worrying about contracts, if people are getting paid, and if my work is good enough. I have no doubt, especially after hearing about Luis, that Mom would have me on the next flight. If Rob is home, he could even fly out and take my place; it wouldn't even affect the company. I could be safe, in my room, by this time tomorrow.

As I think those things in my head, Joe's face fills my mind. What would happen to him if I just disappeared?

Would Luis take it out on him? What about the escort office? I agreed to be a part of their expansion, assuming Joe and I get the details worked out. God, even Joe, Kevin, Byron, and Ed have started to work as a real team in my game. I won't find out if they can put all the pieces of my story together if I leave now.

"No," I finally say, my voice gaining strength. My mom nods, the pride on her face is something I don't think I have ever seen before.

"Good for you," I hear my dad's voice in the background.

"Dad," I say, scandalized. "How much did you hear?"

"Just your mom's offer to get you home," Dad assures me.

I don't believe him, but I don't want to fight. As if to confirm his lie, he continues. "Take care of yourself. I don't care who Luis thinks he is. If this escalates, you get help. I know a few people myself. You're not some faceless girl. If you don't feel safe, talk to security, and go stay with Joe."

"How do you even know who Joe is?" I demand.

"Just because I don't talk much in the family chat doesn't mean I don't read it," Dad responds. "That picture of the two of you in Italy. He might not know it yet, but he cares about you much more than he's letting on."

"Dad," I say, embarrassed now.

"We love you, sweetie," my mom continues. "We'll chat again soon."

"I love you too," I say.

My laptop screen goes dark as we hang up. Lord jumps off his tree and sits on the floor in front of me, his little nose twitching as if smelling to see if it's safe for cuddles. I scoop him up and bury my face in his fur as he meows like I'm killing him and I drop him back on the floor.

"You're right, Lord. I need to get some sleep and make a plan. I'm not some faceless girl. I am Paula-fucking-Lubell, and Luis needs to know that."

JOE SMARTIN

I get the text from Scrunchy while I'm at the gym. My notification sound momentarily fades my music before it blares back to full volume.

Scrunchy: Still feeling sick, won't be at the gym this week.

Joe: Feel better, can I bring you anything?

I shake my head as I send her the response, but I'm doubtful that she's going to message me back. My mind immediately goes back to Saturday night, she wasn't at beers either. Kevin told me that was how she got when she wanted to break up with him. Scrunchy and I are not dating. I don't understand what's going on. I was extra surprised when Luis showed up at the second pub, also looking for her.

Something doesn't feel right. I force myself not to rush through my lifting set, our set. She should be here, spotting my bench. I hadn't even been in town this last week. I doubt she's upset with me, but I could be wrong.

No messages have come in from her still when I have to turn my phone in at security. When I get to my desk, I can't help myself. I pick up my desk phone.

"Security Escort Office, Deb speaking," Deb answers.

"Hey, it's me, Joe. Did Paula come into work today?" I ask.

"She did, early even," Deb says. "I already have more paperwork turned in from her today than the entire year she has been working here."

"Ok, thanks for telling me," I respond. Is she avoiding me then?

"Hey, since I've got you, how are things going with you know what?" Deb asks, referring to our plan to get the escorts underground.

It takes me a minute to switch gears. "Ah, right, yes. Well, really well. I think my reports have gotten the desperation of the situation across, and your work with Paula to get the foundations all laid out has been instrumental. The director has OKed it. I can't name names, but we're just waiting on the final contract."

"Paula has really shown me a side of her I didn't know she had," Deb praises. "I'm excited, as is the rest of the office. Is that why you're looking for her?"

"It is," I easily lie.

"I can get ahold of her for you," Deb offers. "It might take a while, especially if she has wandered to a random as she's known to do..."

"No," I say, quickly interrupting her. "It's not important. Thanks, Deb." I hang up and absently pull up our presentation notes. It's a risk, a huge risk to be planning without Harrison's approval.

I'm in disbelief that he hasn't gotten wind of it yet, but I'm not looking a gift horse in the mouth. When that last contract agrees, Scrunchy and I will run the final implementation meeting together. I take a deep breath as I feel a decision settle in my chest. I don't know why Scrunchy is avoiding me, but it ends tonight.

PAULA LUBELL

I jump when I hear my door buzz. Curled up on my couch, it shouldn't look like anyone's home. The blackout curtains are pinned shut, and I'm even using my laptop and headphones to watch a movie instead of the TV. If I ignore it; whoever it is will hopefully leave. Especially if it's Luis, I told him I was sick and wanted to be left alone.

The buzz sounds again, followed shortly by a text message, both making me jump. I'm getting paranoid.

Joe: Are you home? Is your buzzer working?

I close my eyes as my heart tears itself in half. It's Joe at the door. As much as I long to invite him in and tell him everything, I don't want to make things worse. It's not his fault Luis turned out to be a dirtbag. I need to make sure it looks like I'm not home. Luis is too knowledgeable of my comings and goings...I'm probably being paranoid, but what if he's watching me? My text message notification goes off again, and my eyes scan it without my permission.

Joe: What did I do wrong?

My heart squeezes, Joe's hurting enough, I shouldn't just leave him hanging. Overly cautious, I trot over to my front door unlatching my two new locks.

Joe gives me a quizzical look. "Um, do you want to turn on a light?"

"No," I whisper as I pull him into my dark flat.

"You seem to have acquired more locks," Joe points out, trying to be funny.

I grab his arm and drag him onto my couch. Joe looks extremely confused, his large frame slightly hunched. His usual jeans and hoodie that he throws on after work cover his build.

"Um. I can explain. Make yourself comfortable." I sit as well, scooting toward the opposite side, legs curled under me while I try to think of what I'm going to tell him. The truth, or make something up? What would I want to hear?

"I actually came here to tell you something," Joe says quietly. "Why are we speaking quietly?"

"Did you work things out with Sandy?" I whisper back.

"Stop doing that," Joe snaps.

I bristle, my frayed nerves flinching as the sudden noise. "Sorry, I didn't mean to snap," Joe quickly back peddles. He seems to wrestle with himself before speaking more normally. "I did work things out with Sandy but not in the way you mean. We had a really good talk. We're always going to be friends, but that chapter of our lives is over. That's not what I came here to tell you."

My phone beeps, and I glance down at it. It's Luis. Hesitantly I pick it up.

Luis: Is Smartin at your house?

"Where did you park?" I ask Joe.

"There was a spot right in front."

"Shit."

Luis: I'm going to come check on you, sweety. I'm so sorry you're not feeling well.

"Shit," I say again. "Joe, I promise I will explain. Luis is on his way over right now, and we're both in big shit if he finds you here." I'm interrupted by a knock on my door. I freeze, and I can feel the color drain out of my face. Luis knocks again, louder. Was he watching my house? It's the only way he could have gotten here so fast.

"I know you're sick. Just let me in so I can make you some tea and check on you," Luis's voice sounds like acid to my ears through the door. I don't look like a sick person, I'm still wearing my work pants and even one of the sweaters. I quickly point to my bedroom.

"Get under the bed," I hiss.

Joe doesn't move, and I grip his beefy arm and pull him up, shoving us both in that direction. I motion for Joe to wiggle under my bed and quickly discard my work pants and throw on my little green-and-blue checkered PJ shorts and a wrinkled tee. I close the bedroom door behind me and attempt to comb my hair with my fingers as I wander over to my front door.

I make a pitiful sniffle as I crack it open. "Luis, you can't just show up at my house like this. You woke me up."

"I'm sorry, sweety. I saw Joe's car right in front of your house, and I just got worried you needed something and couldn't get a hold of me. May I come in?"

"No, Luis, you may not. I'm sick, I just want to go back to sleep."

"Think about your friends, especially Joe. He's been struggling so much…"

"If I let you come in and look for Joe, will that make you go away?"

"You must be sick," Luis chides. "That doesn't sound like someone in love at all. And you will fall back in love with me, I promise, we are perfect together. Look. I won't look for Joe. I trust you. Let me just make you some tea and tuck you in with a movie."

Luis pushes his way in before I get the door fully opened. He not so subtly looks around my flat as he slowly makes tea. I hold my breath when he peeks in my dark bedroom and flips on the lights, but he doesn't do much more. Fifteen minutes later, I'm swathed in blankets with tea in my hand and Master and Commander up on the big screen. Luis gives me a kiss on the forehead, and I pretend to be too sick to acknowledge it before he lets himself out.

I wait for a solid three minutes before I unwrap myself and bolt the new locks. Warm water scrubs across my forehead to rid me of the feel of his lips before I dump out his emotionally tainted tea.

Joe's already out from under my bed sitting too still on its edge, his eyes trained on the floor when I enter. I turn on a small lamp in the corner. Luis knows I'm home now; no reason to stay in the dark.

"There are a lot of cat toys under there," Joe points out calmly, too calmly.

I lean against my door frame and cross my arms.

"How long has Harrison been using my job to get you to do what he wants?"

"It's my fault, Joe. He took away your time off to go to Scotland with Sandy and Dillon after I dumped him. He told me he would give it back to you if I would give him a second chance. One thing led to another. It's only been this bad for a few days, really. I'm going to find a way to save your job."

"Scrunchy, stop." He stands and turns. One of his fists makes contact with my wall.

Plaster goes flying as his second fist makes a second hole. Great, there goes my security deposit. I give Joe a minute as he pits his frustration against 300-year-old Victorian masonry. I can see blood on his knuckles already. I slip out of the room and into my bathroom for a wet towel and my first aid kit. Joe's still breathing hard, both his knuckles bruised and bloody when I come back. Some of the anger has left his shoulders.

Gently, I wrap my hand over his beaten knuckles. First, to get his attention, and second, if he's still seeing red, at least I'm holding what's going to fly at my face. I learned that dealing with my brothers. Joe's hand stays still, and I gently press him back to a seated position on my bed and join him.

"I don't have any bonuses in first aid," I joke, trying to bring some *D&D* humor into the situation. I let the warm towel seep into his new bruises and soak up the minimal bleeding.

"Scrunchy."

"Joe, it's not your fault," I interrupt him.

Before I can say more, Joe's hand caresses my cheek, his other hand buries itself in my hair, and then he's kissing me. His wide mouth, hot on mine, his tongue demanding entrance. I feel a burning desire tingle through my entire body, and I move myself so I'm straddling his lap. His hands trace my sides and hips before gripping my butt and pulling me forward. I feel up his muscled arms as I open my mouth and encourage our tongues to dance. I savor this moment, my entire body thrumming with joy and heat. Joe is kissing me! I have wanted this since I first laid eyes on the man. Too soon, the moment passes, and the reality of what's happening breaks through my haze of lust and joy.

"Joe, I'm ok," I say breathlessly.

I push away from his mouth, my hands resting on his chest. "It kills me to ask you to stop because, God knows, I've wanted to jump you for months, but you don't need to do this."

"What?" Joe asks.

I can see confusion in his eyes as his brain tries to switch modes. I try to move off his lap. Joe's strong arms pin my hips in place.

"Joe, I know you don't really want this," I explain slower. "I'm never going to be smart petite little Sandy. You're still my best friend in the world. Boys and girls can be friends without this. I will still protect you and your job, as much as I can anyway."

"No," Joe growls. I can see his brain catching up. "No, Scrunchy, that's not at all what I want. All I have thought about since Italy is why I didn't kiss you in the pool. This is my fault. If I hadn't been so blind, we would have gotten together in Italy, and I could have been holding you in my arms every night." Joe's hands tighten on my hips. "You were so patient with me, so amazing." Joe moves me off his lap so our eyes are level on my bed.

"Don't ever compare yourself to Sandy," Joe says, his voice raw with emotion. "There's no part of you I would change." His lips are on mine again before I can respond. His hands explore my hips and move under my wrinkled tee. He stops only to gently push me flat against my bed, where his hands brush against my stomach as his lips feather kiss from my

231

jaw to my throat. I can't stop the moan that escapes me, as if drawn to it, his mouth returns to my own.

"Joe," I breathe his name when we break for air. "Are you sure you want this?"

"Yes," Joe says. "I've never been more sure of something in my life."

"Were you going to tell me about Harrison?" Joe asks me.

I've lost track of time. Actually, I've lost track of everything in Joe's arms. Joe's just as wonderful as I imagined. We just fit. It doesn't hurt that his past adventures in the bedroom taught him some toe-curling tricks. I try to pinch myself, except I've lost track of where I start and Joe ends, and I end up pinching Joe.

Joe yelps. "What was that for?"

"Sorry, I was pinching myself to make sure this is real," I giggle.

Joe chuckle rumbles in his chest as he pulls me tighter.

"Were you going to tell me about Harrison?" Joe asks again. I groan. I want to stay here in happy land, but I can't, can I? There's real life to deal with. I sit up, bemoaning the state of my sheets that will definitely need to be changed before I sleep. Oh, shit. I'm not on birth control. Oh, god, I didn't even ask Joe about STDs. Fuck, why is sex so complicated?

"What time is it?" I ask.

"Time for you to answer my question," Joe reiterates. I sit up and find my phone, unwilling to deal with reality, my mind focuses on everything else.

"Scrunchy," Joe says louder.

"Sorry," I say to Joe, calming my racing thoughts enough to answer his question. "I hadn't decided if I was going to tell you, honestly. I was going to see if I could fix it first. I know how much you love your work."

"You can't fix it." Before I can stand, he reaches his arms around me and pulls me back to him, bringing us eye to eye. "I've broken security protocol," Joe tells me calmly. "I had verbal permission from Harrison, but he can easily twist it if he wants to."

"Joe, no, how can you say that so calmly?" I ask quickly.

"Because it's a fact. When bad things happen in life, you stand up to them and you deal with them, one at a time."

JOE SMARTIN

I love the feeling of Scrunchy in my arms. She fell asleep much faster than either of us expected. Her body completely relaxed, with the world's smallest snores filling the room. I wish I hadn't been so oblivious during her game when Luis showed up.

As much as she says it's not, this is my fault. I feel the need to punch her walls again, but to do that, I would need to move her sleeping body and I just can't. Eventually, my thoughts, equal parts happiness and dread, slow. Sleep claims me.

I wake up to knocking. For a moment, I don't remember where I am, and when I do, I worry I'm dreaming. My legs are still tangled with Scrunchy's. Her long hair tickles my face. The knock happens louder. I give Scrunchy a kiss as she stirs and tell her not to move. Quickly, my jeans pulled over my lower half, I make my way to her front door. The clock on her microwave reads 5:32 AM. It takes me a minute to figure out her locks, but as I do, I open the door wide, knowing exactly who this is.

"Harrison," I say calmly.

My boss looks at me, confused for a minute, and then smiles sadly, as if disappointed. He pulls himself up to his full height. I have maybe an inch or two on him, even with his attempt to intimidate me.

"I guess not a lot needs to be said," Harrison states.

"I guess not."

"If you change your mind about the dishonorable discharge in the next, oh, let's say five hours, you come and see me."

"Yes, sir," I answer.

He narrows his eyes as if seeing if I'm being sarcastic before turning. I quietly shut the door behind him, redoing all the locks only to turn and see Scrunchy's amazing naked body leaning against the door frame. Her breasts are pushed up from her crossed arms, they look amazing.

"Joe, your job. We could have found a way."

My arms are around her in seconds as I silence her fears with my lips.

TWENTY-FIVE

Campaign: Where is your god?
Scenario Six: Mortals tremble and supernaturals obey.
Scene: Back to the druid board.

IXAR - JOE'S WIZARD

"What about the mermaid?" Scrunchy points out.

"What about her?" I answer. "She had Rombald's baby, the trolls are going to take better care of her then we are."

"She had a relic," Scrunchy points out again.

"We're not collecting relics," Kevin answers this time. "This book tells us more about them than her bat shit crazy brain probably could."

"Fair," Scrunchy sighs, shuffling something around with a frown.

I know exactly what's happening. Scrunchy planned on us going back to the trolls, only she didn't give us enough motivation, and now she has to come up with something else. I move my foot into her space and tangle it with one of hers. As a player, I love *messing with the GM's plans, but as her boyfriend, I want to be supportive. She smiles when our feet connect.*

A shiver of foreboding tries to climb up my spine as my imagination seats Luis at the table with us once more. He's vanished from Scrunchy's life as if they'd never dated. Our interactions at work are overly cordial, but there's a gleam in his eyes that makes me uncomfortable. He's up to something.

"You're at your office," Scrunchy sets the scene as she changes THE CAVE's table. *I push Luis out of my thoughts as she carefully moves her little cat miniature onto Byke's desk next to the two books we found.*

"They're trying to raise a god," Byke declares.

I'm leaning against Byke's desk. The books, open to a family tree and a page on relics, respectively.

"You shaw 'bout that?" Clint asks.

"Yup, pretty shaw," I mimic Clint's accent. "It's the only thing that adds up. Plus, it fits with Byke's prophecies."

"Look," Byke explains, putting the pieces together. "We don't know all of the who's, but it says right here, the relics contain the building blocks of gods. It's a combination of the energy going into them and the relic itself that decides which god comes out of them. This book's like an encyclopedia of the different creatures you can bring back to life using this method. It's like a weird happy necromancy book for immortals."

"Could I have a look at that?" Cercia pipes up.

"No," I quickly say.

Cercia pouts, but keeps to her spot in the corner, playing with her phone. We don't really know what to do with her. She seems happy to just follow me around for the moment, and the last thing we need is another problem, so here she is.

"Here's the fun part. Teresa, the kidnapped friend of our original client," Byke continues holding up the family tree. "She's so much more than just a faerie. She has four different supernatural magics running through her blood. Troll, mermaid, faerie, and druid. She's the great-great-granddaughter of the union between Cleodora and Rombald. She's like a melting platform of powers. Not super powerful herself, but you could channel anything through her. She would make a perfect vessel for a god."

"Do we want a god in England?" Pooh asks.

"Well, they have done little good in the rest of the world," I answer. "The ancient gods were petty, bored, and super powerful. It's why they were put to rest by our ancestors."

"So that would be a 'no' the-yn," Clint confirms.

PAULA LUBELL

"Could you two stop making googly eyes at each other?" Kevin complains. "Good for you, finally figuring out you like each other, but you don't need to display it to the world. Paul, you're supposed to be GMing."

My face flushes, and I attempt to return my foot to my personal space. Opposite my reaction, Joe gives Kevin a wink and pulls my foot further into his. I sigh as Kevin and Joe have a little stare down. I guess some things will never change.

Although my players toy with some options, at this point, they've figured out my game. They either need to pick a side or try to stop the ritual to raise a god from completing. The clues to find Teresa are long gone. The spa cleaned out, Betty one step too many ahead of them. The trolls, extra not their friends after they refused to return Rombalds' balls and escaped Pebbles grasps.

"We still don't really know where the ritual's taking place," Kevin points out, looking right at me.

I grin and put my hands behind my head. "I could use another drink, Byron," I request nonchalantly.

Byron laughs and moves to his bar as people flip through notes and play on their phones, hopefully thinking about what to do next.

"Well, there's one powerful NPC we haven't 'pissed off' as you American's say it," Ed eventually adds. "Farmer Brooks."

Kevin groans audibly.

Soon enough, Farmer Brook's farm is displayed on the table. I don't make them fight any crazy sheep this time.

"As you follow him into his dimly lit barn, his relic throbs with "reverent" energy, ready to burst if rubbed just the right way," I describe with a giggle. "Cercia, a young necromancer, is immediately enamored with everything here. Ixar, her attention leaves you as she focuses on the evil druid."

"Well, introduce them," Byron encourages Joe.

"Um, Farmer Brooks, this is Cercia," Joe says in Ixar's voice.

"Farmer Brooks comes forward," I describe. "His hand traces Cercia's cheek as he looks into her eyes."

"You brought me an apprentice," I say in my best powerful old man voice. "A beautiful young necromancer would do well under my teaching."

"Can I roll to see if this is a trap?" Kevin asks.

"Sure, everyone can roll." Dice bounce around in their trays.

"Oh, wow!" Ed exclaims.

I look over at his tray, all plus signs.

"In addition to knowing this is not a trap," I relate. "You know that Farmer Brooks is truly enchanted with Cercia. That he really loves his sheep, despite his propensity for slaughter, and you get the feeling that, though he's still probably evil, there is some good druid left under all that darkness."

"Shades of grey, in even those using the darkest magic," Byron adds sagely.

"Like contractors," Joe adds with a snort.

"Or military meathead," Kevin shoots back.

"Now children," I say calmly, but unlike our first game, our words are playful.

"How about just Americans in general?" Ed adds.

"We'll all give you that one," Byron laughs.

"All right," I laugh with them. "Now that we're all officially shades of grey...what do you ask Farmer Brooks?"

"All right, the goal is to keep the gods out of England," I say after the party has confirmed their information and gotten the location of the god-raising ceremony from Farmer Brooks. "We're ending here for tonight. Please email me with what you do to prepare; you have about sixteen hours, some of that must be spent sleeping. Unless it's super extravagant or you want to go on some adventure for more information, you can assume I'll probably be ok with it."

"I'm making armor for our cat," Byron says immediately.

"We're not taking the cat," Kevin argues.

"It says in the prophecy that a cat is there," Byron says for the millionth time. "It might as well be our cat."

"It is possible everyone's working together to raise a god?" Joe asks skeptically.

I roll my eyes at Joe, no one's working together, that at least should be loud and clear.

"Paul's scene-setting at the beginning was pretty clear," Ed adds, echoing my thoughts. "I think it's too much of a stretch to think they are working together. We also had that big fight at the cenotaph, clearly no one's friends. We must be prepared for shenanigans. I doubt we will be dealing with just the druids."

"How many different historic English gods are there?" Byron asks.

I give him a huge smile. I've been waiting for this question all night. "There are around twenty-five well known Celtic gods and goddesses. You don't know much about them, but you do know each one is tied to a different type of magic and worshiped by different groups of people. They probably each have their own type of preferred magical energy."

"Right," Byron says. "Would I have time to do some research and make our cat armor?"

"You would," I confirm.

"What about Rombald's rocks?" Joe asks the table.

"I'm not sure if Rombald would have died if we hadn't gotten involved," Ed points out logically. "The fight at the cenotaph was certainly about more than just Rombald. His power could be helpful according to the book, but it's only earth magic and only amplification of magic. It isn't necessary. No one, other than the trolls, has come looking for his bits either. I think he might have just been an innocent bystander."

Ed looks over at me, and I mouth, "Murder."

"Again, email me with what you plan to do," I emphasize. "And don't forget that you might have collected items along the way that could help you. I look forward to the birth of a god next week."

"Some faith," Ed asks.

I give him a grin.

TWENTY-SIX

Campaign: Reality
Scenario Thirteen: The final act.
Scene: All that hard work.

PAULA LUBELL

"Joe, you look very official in uniform," I tell Joe.

We're in the largest meeting room in the underground compound. Set up with stadium seating, much like a small college lecture room. A few early birds have drifted in, but it's only the two of us at the front at the moment. Joe gives me a heated once over and returns the compliment before going back to his notes.

I'm dressed in black dress pants and a white blouse with blue flower details around the collar and cuffs. I've left my long hair down and am wearing the simple pearls my mom gave me when I turned eighteen. I'd read through my good luck messages from my family before turning in my phone to security. I hold them close to my heart as I feel my nerves pick up. People begin to filter into the meeting room, time going both too fast and too slow.

"Joe," a voice hails.

I turn as the two men greet each other.

"Paul, I'd no idea you were in England," Joe greets his friend. He beckons to me and I join them.

"It's just temporary," Paul responds. "I'm actually here to facilitate this transition assuming everyone agrees. You must be Paula Lubell."

"Everyone calls me Paul," I say.

"It's a great name," Paul tells me.

I give him a nervous smile as he continues. "Joe seems especially good at finding talented women."

I raise an eyebrow and force myself to roll with the slightly sexist comment. "I met Sandy a few weeks ago. Joe got her a job as a contractor, right?"

"Let's not joke around. I got her that job," Paul laughs.

"Now, now, Paul," Joe chides. "It was a joint effort."

I give the two men some space to reminisce and go over my talking points one last time. We start about five minutes late, giving everyone time to filter in. Joe introduces us, and my eyes narrow as I dim the lights for our presentation. Luis Harrison gives me a winning simile, standing in the back of the room. He's not supposed to be here, but I can't stop to question as Joe has already started speaking.

The presentation goes well. We practiced it enough. I've never in my life wanted something to go well so badly, and I find my need fusing with my nerves. My voice rings even, if a little fast, as I smoothly pick up my lines from Joe. Suddenly I'm saying my final bit, and a smile of pure exhilaration cracks my face. It's quickly wiped away as Luis reappears in the back as the lights come up. I can clearly see now that he's not alone, two armed officers stand at his side dressed in black Kevlar, their standard-issue MP5's slung over their backs.

"I want to open the floor for questions and suggestions," Joe announces.

Unlike me, Joe looks cool as a cucumber, like he does this all the time. His calm, deep voice puts me at ease.

"I have a question," Luis's voice rings through the little meeting. "What do they do with officers who create and purposefully maintain major security breaches?"

I suddenly can't breathe. That ease, the adrenalin, it all drops. This is why he'd been so quiet. I feel my stomach sink as I steady myself on the podium next to me. I don't want to, but I look at Luis. Most of the eyes in the room are turning to do the same. He isn't looking at Joe. He's looking at me, and I flatten my lips into a tight line.

"Joe Smartin, you're being relieved of duty. Please come with us," one of the officers barks. I didn't see Joe move, but his voice is right behind me.

"Don't come after me, don't cause a scene. Stay here and finish the meeting. He wants us to make this worse by putting on a show. Don't let him," Joe whispers in my ear as he slowly walks toward the armed officers like he expected this.

I reach for him, but he's long past. His head held high and his shoulders back, Joe does exactly as instructed, calmly and quietly. I manage to take a small breath and then another. I've never seen someone get escorted off base before, and it's fast. Joe hands the two armed officers his badge. They flank him as he disappears out the door, everything he's worked for ripped from him.

Luis stands at the back, grinning like he's won. His smile pushes our past forward in my memories. A string of off-color comments, his subtle attempts to change me, his belittling of my hobbies run through my mind, and I force them out. Wrapping myself in the ease Joe's voice brought me, I take two deep breaths before turning back to the room. At least thirty curious eyes watch me. I glance at the PowerPoint. Joe hadn't turned it to the last page. My trainers are quiet on the carpet as I press the mouse pad on his laptop.

"The floor is open for questions," I announce. I'm pleased with how steady my voice sounds.

"Um, what just happened?" a voice asks.

"A misunderstanding, I'm sure," I explain. "A misunderstanding caused by the ineffective way this base is handling implementation of the new security protocol."

I turn my gaze back to Luis, but he's already gone. Stronger now, and with the focus back on what it should be, the questions start coming.

"You handled yourself well," a woman says to me. I turn, my hands slightly shaking from the adrenalin still pumping through my veins. I'm terrified, not of the adrenalin, but of it wearing off. Luis has won. Although I kept detailed notes as questions and solutions formed, putting the final pieces together for the escort office's new below-ground branch, nothing can be signed off without Joe. This might've been my idea, but it's Joe's project. I don't even work in the building. Even if we can get him the document, I don't even know if his signature is valid anymore. Is he going to be dishonorably discharged? I force my thoughts to stop spiraling and focus on the woman in front of me.

She's short and quite plump from years of desk work, it adds character to her expressive face. Her hair is dyed a lovely shade of almost rose gold. I feel my brain returning to normal as it tries to place her body type in the world of supernatural creatures. A hobbit, definitely a hobbit. I tower over this woman, and I have the sudden urge to bend down or at least sit so we're eye level, but I have no idea how that would go over, so I don't.

"Thank you," I manage to say. "I'm Paula."

"I knew that," the woman laughs. "But that was rude on my part not to introduce myself. My name is Emma Talik, I'm the base Director."

"Like the person that oversees everything on base," I say stupidly. The woman nods sharply. "Ah, that was a stupid question."

"It's fine," Director Talik says. "I'm excited to sign off on your idea. I hope it works because nothing else seems to be."

"I do, too," I stammer. "I know a lot of the escorts, and I think having more meaningful, consistent work will boost morale and keep more employees on base."

"Said like a true manager," Director Talik adds.

"Oh no, I'm not..." I start to explain, but Director Talik cuts me off with a motion.

"I've had a few interactions before this with Joe. I'm surprised by what happened today. He struck me as one of our more dedicated and loyal men."

"Yes, well," I can't help the bitterness creeping into my voice. "Even the best of us can be brought down in the right situation."

Director Talik raises an eyebrow. "Joe's ideas were not sitting well with his direct management. I have no doubt that he stepped on some toes. I can't be involved directly, but like Joe, I also believe that we're all working toward the same goals for something greater. I hope he finds his way back to his office soon."

"Thank you, Director," I say earnestly.

The short woman's quick steps click as she exits the room. I gather the last few pieces of our presentation and sit.

Joe was my escort into the building. Great, now I can break security protocol by wandering around, or sit here and wait for someone to come save my ass. What are we going to do?

EDWARD (ED)

I have to walk past a burly-looking ex-marine, covered in tattoos named Jake to get into the cellar of the Little Ale House. We have our own orc guarding the pub, it's brilliant.

"Ed!" Kevin calls my name, and I weave my way through the packed room. He motions to a seat next to Lyla, though I only know it's her from the pictures Kevin's shown us.

"This must be a weird introduction to Harrogate. I'm Edward, but you can call me Ed," I introduce myself.

"It's marvelous!" Lyla exclaims, looking around the room. "I've never seen so many people come together for one person before."

Neither have I, though I'm not surprised. Joe and Paul have a charisma about them.

"I'm not working for a new guy, again," Kevin states.

"Really, that's what you're focusing on?" Juan berates Kevin.

A "social emergency" has been called in after Joe's dramatic removal from base. I can't believe how many people are here. It's all the usuals from the beer group and a lot of people I don't recognize.

"It's everyone who works under Joe, and honestly, most of Harrison's section as well," Kevin explains to us. "Juan and Paul set all this up. Paul found Jake, and Juan made the list of who's trusted to be here and who's not."

Paul, seated next to Joe, stands and quiets down the room. "I'm not much for public speaking, so thank you all for coming tonight, and here's Joe." Joe stands, Paul reclaiming her seat.

"I know rumors are running wild, and I'm going to put them straight," Joe announces. "Right now. I've been relieved of duty pending inquiry. My system to get our work caught back up was, in fact, a security breach, so I'm guilty of exactly what they say. I believe in our justice system. I hope it treats me fairly and I'm back at work soon."

"That's horse shit," Juan exclaims.

He stands a few feet down from Joe. Joe waves his free hand to cut Juan off, but Juan ignores him. "Joe was given verbal approval by Luis Harrison. I heard it. I will vouch for it. Luis also had a personal grudge against Joe and was actively looking for ways to get him out of the way. I'll not sit here and say cheers as one of the good ones is sunk by the corporate machine. I will fight. For Joe! Who's with me?"

"I am," Kevin yells. He stands, his face animated with excitement. "Joe might be military, but he's one of us. He has gone out of his way for us, it's time we stand up for him."

I know Kevin's not looking at me, but I nod approvingly. I've spent the last four months watching these two slowly learn to like and trust each other. I'm proud of my excitable American friend standing behind his friend.

Paul stands next, then Byron and Ethan. One by one, one by one, everyone gets to their feet, their beers out in salute. Joe looks close to tears. Paul, next to him, whispers something in his ear and gives him a quick peck on the cheek.

"What's the plan?" someone calls out.

"Well, first, it's to take a drink so we can all sit back down," Joe bellows.

The room laughs, but a cheers is called. Soon the room is buzzing with ideas, Paula especially circulates around, listening and commenting.

"Anything useful?" I ask her when she joins us.

"Maybe. The rumor mill is churning."

"Does Luis come from a wealthy background?" I ask.

"Definitely not," Paul answers. "Do you have an idea?"

"It might be worth looking into his finances," I point out, thinking of his expensive tastes in wine.

"I've put all the jewelry he gave me in a box," Paul muses. "He certainly pulled me into a life style I couldn't afford and I do pretty well. A few people have had some weird conversations with him about pleasing contracting companies. Most people are taking the opportunity to chew out his management style, he's not well-liked. I can't believe I ever defended him, I'm sorry Kevin."

"You're paying for it in the end," Kevin says tactfully.

"Following the money is always a good plan," Lyla's sticks in before Paul can respond. "But what exactly is the goal here?"

"To get leverage, or something that clears Joe's name," Paul answers.

She moves back to Joe's side and starts clinking glasses together to get everyone's attention. It takes a bit, but the pub slowly quiets.

"There's no way Luis Harrison's squeaky clean," Paul announces to the room. "Ed and I think he's got something going on with his finances. Now, I'm not suggesting anything illegal, but if you come across anything, pass it onto myself or Juan. If Harrison thinks he can bring down Joe on a technicality, let's teach him the true meaning of background check."

PAULA LUBELL

248

We're in Joe's apartment tonight. I'm seated on Joe's couch with my feet up on his coffee table. Joe's lying across the couch with his head on my lap. I absently run my hands through his hair, humming tunelessly as his amazing view of the lights of Harrogate at night fills my view.

Although I enjoyed that Luis made me feel like a delicate princess, it's moments like these that feel real, that make a real relationship between two people. I can't imagine what Joe is going through right now, but it can't feel good. The fact that he lets me hold him, lets me play the role of the prince while he can be my delicate princess, means the world to me.

Joe's life revolves around his work, the military. It's what he loves. I don't know if he has a clue what to do with himself without it. I pray our army of nerds finds something that can help him. I worry what will happen if they don't. Joe rolls on my lap and presses a delicate kiss to my abdomen.

"I'm sorry I still haven't fixed the hole in your wall," Joe says out of the blue.

It's my turn to attempt to change gears. Not what I thought he would be thinking about, though the hole is still there and he did promise.

Joe takes my silences the wrong way. "I plan on it, I just don't even know…"

"No, Joe," I interrupt. "I'm just shifting gears. I thought you would be thinking about your job, not my flat."

"Are you worried about me not having a job?"

"Not at all," I answer honestly. I run my hands through his hair again. "I'm here for you, whatever happens. I just want you to be happy, and I know that your career's everything to you."

"I won't lie. I'm scared shitless. Maybe this is a chance to see who I am outside of the military. One thing at a time, though. I will only cross that bridge if I need to."

"Who you are outside of the military," I fake exclaim.

"I'm serious, Scrunchy. My work's still important to me, but I want more out of life."

"If the baby is yours…" I start to reassure Joe.

"No. This isn't about the baby. This has nothing to do with Sandy. I don't care if the baby's mine or not. I have spent so much time worrying and being unhappy. Dillon's a good man and wants to be a father. He's that baby's father."

Joe sits up and takes both my hands in his. "I know we have only known each other for a few months, but sometimes you just know. I'm not pushing. I'm not asking. I'm just sharing my dream because I want us to have a family together someday. I don't want a baby, I want a family. It's people, not work, that make me happy. It's our role-playing games, it's lifting together at the gym, exploring the world. You make me happy, Scrunchy, and that's all I need."

"Joe. That's so sweet, and I'm super bad at being sweet. I don't want to ruin this."

"You could never ruin this," Joe reassures before his lips claim mine.

TWENTY-SEVEN

Campaign: Where is your god?
Scenario Six: Mortals tremble and supernaturals obey.
Scene: Summoning a God.

IXAR - JOE'S WIZARD

I feel unbelievably isolated. Mother Shipton's potion is repressing my own magic. In its place, I feel the fake, unusable magic of the druids we ambushed on our way here. I can't even pick out my team as we stand. Well, except for Byke who's stolen green robe drags on the ground sadly. We're hidden in plain sight, in a circle along with eight other druids, our faces, covered in shadow. The only light comes from six massive fires just behind us. We're evenly spread around very short, but ancient, stones that make up the Twelve Apostles at the top of Ilkley Moor. The stars above us seem overly bright as they surround the full moon.

"My brothers!" a deep male voice roars. I want to turn and look, but I keep my eyes pinned to the druid in front of me, intent on doing exactly as he does. "It's time!"

"Huya," I hear the guttural shout from the druids around me as they snap their arms out, their bare hands formed into claws.

I follow suit, as quickly as I can. I notice the locations of at least one of my friends, their motions just as behind as my own. I hear the sounds of a woman struggling, her whimpers and pleas for release cut to my heart. Maybe if we had just focused on Teresa more, we could have saved her this.

"No, please, no. You don't want to do this to me," Teresa's voice cries.

The druids around me begin to chant as the earth rumbles beneath us. I attempt to blend in my voice, but I'm not a druid and have no idea what they are chanting. I move my hands with theirs, slightly shaking them to make it look like power is coming out of my fingertips. Very slowly, a pedestal of stone emerges in the very center of the circle. I see the hood next to me shift awkwardly and lean as if trying to hear my voice. This ruse is not going to last.

The chanting changes as the air around the pedestal beings to move. A single druid breaks rank, carefully placing a porcelain bowl filled with dark liquid at its center. The druid steps back. The volume of the world seems to raise as the magic manipulates the stone, using its speed and power to smooth and carve new shapes into the smooth surface.

As the stone is shaped, the original speaker, dragging a struggling woman enters the circle. Mud stains the hem of her pristine white shift where she has dug her bare feet into the ground of the muddy moors in her struggle. Her oval face is tear-stained, pale blonde hair is up in a beautiful but complicated braid. With just a glance, she looks human, but her face is a little too long, her eyes a little too large. Purple glows around her irises. I can see a dusting of what looks like scales along the sides of her jaw.

The druid pulling her, like all his friends, is covered in

billowing robes. Black in color, his head is lost in the layers of a deep cowl. Unlike all his friends, this druid is huge, almost seven feet tall. With the hand not dragging the young woman, he carries one of the relics. The metals of this one are dark and foreboding, firelight dances off its polished surfaces. He stops when he reaches the pedestal, waiting as the air continues to carve it. And continues to carve it. And continues to carve it.

"I know it's killing the moment, but who's not pulling their weight," a voice speaks up, a little nasally and whiny.

No one answers him.

"Really, guys, we practiced this like a hundred times. Dramatic druid stuff doesn't just happen," the same voice accuses.

"Wer all jus' doin' our bettermost, give us a chay-ance t' git er done," Clint's unmistakable accent cuts through the silence.

Welp, game's up. With a move I learned from Pooh, I jump in the air and attempt to kick the druids on either side of me. I clip the one on my left, but the one on my right dodges, and I land with an ungraceful thump and immediately roll.

I seem to have gotten lost in battle as the circle turns into chaos, Pooh has tangled a druid up in his robes, his shirt is tied around another one's face. I send a bolt of magic into the one with Pooh's shirt and the druid yelps and runs, colliding with another hood-covered Druid. This one curses with a familiar accent. As Clint pulls his hood back, he aims and starts shooting. The sound of his bullets hitting stone adds to the turmoil.

Somewhere nearby, a small explosion rocks the ground. I count three druid bodies not moving. No one has spotted me yet, and I stay still as I drop into my wizard trance, closing my eyes. The relief and joy that fills me as I call Leviathan spreads through my very being. I open my eyes and know they flicker with the same red hellfire that leaks out between her dark-scaled body.

We surround the druid. He pushes his relic into a pouch on his belt, his body shimmering with power as he finishing tying Teresa to the pedestal. Teresa's delicate arms seem to hug the lump of half carved stone. She braces her legs on the ground, struggling to touch as little of its surface as possible.

"My minions are nothing compared to my power," the druid laughs as he pulls back his hood.

"Oh my god, is that a picture of Luis?" Kevin laughs.

"Sure is," Scrunchy says. "Kick his fucking ass."

The Office Cat

Well, I guess they are not completely useless. Byke made me this armor anyway, but I can't lick myself through it. I got bored pretty quick watching Druid Harrison throw the elements of the world at my tenants. After enough circles, I manage to reach my own butt, mostly, but it has mud on it. Mud, I don't like the outside. Where is my carpet? I meow pitifully and then hiss as someone lands on the ground next to me, getting mud on my armor!

I glare at Clint. He groans, one of his arms falls uselessly to his side. Ugh, it smells like blood. And not yummy mouse blood. He doesn't acknowledge me as he slowly gets back up, pulling another gun from somewhere on his muddy, battered, blood-covered body.

Humans are so gross.

I look around for Ixar, but I can't see him from this terrible vantage point on the ground. An explosion shakes the earth, and I hear Byke's giggle.

"Trap his hands," Ixar's voice rings out.

I can't see a bloody thing. I wander over to the whimpering faerie tied to the pedestal. Her eyes glow unnaturally, four balls of color swirling inside of them. I rub myself against her, but she doesn't respond to me. It does get a little of the mud off my armor, so I do it a few more times. Another explosion. Oh right, I wanted to see what's going on. I use the woman as a springboard and vault myself onto the pedestal.

I sit and groom myself for a moment, oblivious to the chaos of battle around me, before I notice something fun. A porcelain bowl with very smelly liquid in it sits very unattended next to me. The liquid ripples as another one of Byke's bombs shakes the world. I feel my butt stick up in the air and wiggle as I give it its first little push.

Pooh - Kevin's wizard

I send another violent knife of ice into Harrison. The large druid blocks part of it with a wall of fire, but his fire's weaker now, and I manage to tear a long bloody gash down his arm. His unnaturally fast and strong body whips around, clipping me hard, and I'm thrown away from him. Clint manages to shoot him in the wound I just inflicted, blasting the majority of his arm off. We're winning, I think? Maybe?

As I prepare to launch myself back at Harrison, movement just out of the circle distracts me. I pause as supernaturals I recognize, and some I don't, step into the firelight. They watch the battle with – well, the only thing I can describe it as is excited anticipation. Each group holds a relic out in front of them.

I don't need my druid trance to see that the relics are

charged and the magics streaking toward Teresa, still chained to the pedestal. Their colors battling for dominance in the air.

"Fulfill the prophecy," Byke's prophetic voice echoes into the night.

I turn back to the battle just as the giant maw of Leviathan snaps around Harrison's head. As the headless druid falls to the ground, the supernaturals all start chanting.

"That fucking cat!" Ixar bellows.

My eyes dart up with movement just as our office cat pushes the porcelain bowl off the side of the pedestal. The bowl smashes to the ground, the sound too loud over the various chanting surrounding us. The air heats and then cools as magic erupts from the shattered bowl. Vivid colors swirl in random patterns, scattering in every direction before forming a thick column right above the pedestal that sways in a wind only it can feel. The energies from the supernaturals behind me rush forward, making the column of magic shimmer and blink as they fight each other for control.

"Leviathan," Ixar's voice is raw and commanding.

I see a look of sheer pain enter the eyes of the demon, echoed in the eyes of its summoner. Leviathan spits out Harrison's head and moves unnaturally fast to encircle Teresa, her body slumped and leaning limply against the pedestal. The demon's skin hardens into a shield just as the column of magic dives for Teresa.

My ears pop as the air pressure changes erratically. The colors in the column begin to swirl angrily, their beauty turning into a mud brown as they beat against Ixar's demon over and over. Suddenly they stop. Everything goes still as the column's colors bubble and ripple in frustration.

"Mer?" our office cat says from her perch still on the pedestal.

Faster than the eye can blink, the column dives forward, engulfing our cat. For a moment, all we can see is a mass of colors, and then power explodes outward. I manage to keep my feet, though I seem to be the only one, and blink stupidly at what's left of the scene. Our cat sits, wide-eyed, her fur sticking out like she has been electrocuted in between the seams in her armor.

A spark of magic runs along her whiskers and sparks. "Mer?"

TWENTY-EIGHT

Campaign: Reality
Scenario Thirteen: The final act.
Scene: Good and evil in all things.

PAULA LUBELL

"Juan wants to know if he can come over," I say to Byron, excitedly.

"Sure, give him my address," Byron answers.

"So, is our cat now inhabited by a god?" Kevin asks. "And if so, um, what god? Can we tell what group successfully modified the original ritual?"

"Your cat has a god in her, for sure. What that means is new territory for all you all," I explain. "You've no idea what god was summoned. Better go get the cat before anyone else asks the same question."

Coming to their senses quickly, my players grab the stunned cat, Teresa, and the now unconscious Ixar, and race through the Moors.

Once driving off, Clint brings Teresa, too, and gets a toe-curling makeout session for his troubles.

"And that's that," I recount, stacking up my notes for the last time. "I mean, you skipped most of the intrigue, you didn't even get into Betty and her war with the trolls, who were being manipulated behind the scenes by the evil druid...but I guess I can use that somewhere else."

I'm honestly disappointed that this isn't going to turn into a campaign. I'm going to miss my crazy wizards and their now cat god. I'm going to miss them a lot, actually.

"Thank you all for learning *FATE* with me," I say, holding back my emotions. "I always enjoy running, but this was something special."

"I think we should all keep our characters, just in case our four wizards need to make a reappearance," Byron declares.

I grin happily at the idea.

"So, what's next?" Kevin asks.

"I want to run a game," Joe interjects. "And believe it or not, I have had a lot of time recently to make some plans."

"Unless you get shipped home," Kevin reminds us bitterly.

Our lighthearted excitement dies with his words.

"I'm here now," Joe reaffirms. "You can only ever deal with one thing at a time."

"Oh, god, no wonder the office runs so slow," Byron jokes.

The room chuckles. Soon Byron's up answering his door and back with Juan, who doesn't even ask, just grabs a beer off Byron's bar, and pulls up a seat.

"Our army found something good," Juan states. "Paula and Ed, you were on the right track." He slaps a pile of papers on the table. "Don't get me wrong. Cool room, but do these lights get any brighter? It's like I'm interrupting an orgy."

Joe Smartin

I don't need to be here for this. Scrunchy took her suspicions and our army's evidence to the Director herself, but I'm glad I am.

I give Juan another side look. I'm starting to wonder if he's the kid of a general or something. He has friends everywhere, it seems. Despite being removed from base and all my security clearances on hold, I find myself with a visitor's badge. Flanked by no less than four security officers. Although I came in with just Juan and Scrunchy, the word is spreading quickly, and people are gathering.

I walk confidently up to Harrison's office. I'm surprised to see the Director and my friend from Colorado, Paul, in there with him. Every instinct I have is screaming at me to let this go. Harrison outranks me, but the wall of support at my back presses me forward. I knock and enter without permission. Two of the four security personnel crowd into the office with me.

"Smartin, I thought I was done with you," Harrison growls. "Welcome back to base. I'm sure you broke security protocols again to make this little show happen."

"The show wasn't my idea, sir," I say honestly.

With little pomp and circumstance, I hand him a few documents. "These were turned in anonymously. They include an account of someone overhearing you giving me permission to badge in groups, as well as your financial records. I'm not a financial analyst, but taking bonuses from contracting companies doesn't look good. I believe it's safe to assume some of these emails promising positions to corresponding companies might look even worse."

"I don't know what you're talking about, Smartin," Harrison says quickly. "I don't even know how you could have gotten any of this."

"Turned in, anonymously," I repeat.

"Sir, you're going to have to come with us," one of the security guards says.

"I will not go with you. Take this man into custody," Harrison demands, pointing at Joe. "He's a liar and a thief. Apparently, a hacker now too!"

"So those are your personal emails?" I ask.

Something inside me shift, the tension in my gut releases. The guilt I feel about doing this vanishes. I will not think in terms of govie, contractor, and military anymore. We're all just people doing our jobs. We need each other to make things work.

"They're not my emails!" Harrison exclaims.

"Sir," the security officer says again. Harrison tries to speak. Before he can get a word out, the officer moves, grabbing his arms and pulling them behind his back as they start dragging him out.

"These lies will not stick," Harrison yells as he's dragged off.

I see a few nods of approval, even a few cheers from the crowd of looky-loos as they part to let security, with Harrison unhappily between them, through. I feel Scrunchy come up on my side, and I put out my arm for her.

"Oh, good. You're both here," Director Talik says as I press Scrunchy into my side. "Let's get this signed before any more drama can happen."

I smile and respectfully incline my head to the Director as she hands me a pen.

EPILOGUE
SIX MONTHS LATER.

PAULA LUBELL

"Really Joe? Why would you ask me to dress nice if you were just going to drag me up all these stairs? I'm starting to sweat!" I exclaim, trailing behind Joe.

Joe looks back at me with a grin, a mysterious twinkle in his eyes. A few steps later, he slows, and we awkwardly switch places in the narrow spiral staircase leading up to the top of Conwy Castle. I slow down as we get to the top. I can feel his excitement for something, and now I want to make him wait for it. Joe grabs my butt and gives it a squeeze. I lean back into the squeeze, encouraging Joe to feel a bit more.

"Keep that butt walking," Joe growls.

I do as he says, slowly, my calves screaming by the time we reach the top. I gasp at the scene in front of me. The warm brown stones of the ruined castle tower are edged in flowers. Orange and purples glisten between green. A few birds of paradise stick out as if lording over the display.

Behind the flowers lay the epic ruins of the castle, its towers and walls mostly intact and almost glowing from the shower that passed over us less than an hour ago. Behind that, the rolling bright green hills of the Welsh countryside crash against the Irish Sea.

I feel Joe's arms go around me as we just gaze at the world around us, my imagination filling the castle with fae and magic. We take in the beauty together, and then Joe lets me go and I turn to him. He's already moving, and my heart stops as he goes down on one knee. A small box comes out of his pocket and opens up to a simple band.

"Scrunchy, Paul, Paula Lubell," Joe says flustered. "You know, I had a whole speech prepared, but now that we're up here, the view, you. You're radiant. I want to wake up next to you every morning, I want you by my side as we keep adventuring through life. Paula Lubell, will you marry me?"

I don't hear myself say yes as my entire body thrums with happiness and joy. I must have because Joe's arms are wrapped around me, his mouth hot on mine. The sounds of cheering drift faintly up from below, and Joe pulls back with a grin. He hands me binoculars so I can see the people on the ground.

I peer through them and my excitement bubbles out of me as my family waves. My mom, dad, and all my brothers are here! Woven between them are our friends. Juan, Kevin, Lyla, Harriet, Ed, and even Byron with his kids. I see Mason smiling and holding his phone out, pointed at the tower. The faces of Sandy, Dillon, and their baby boy, who has Dillon's soft eyes, look up at us from its surface.

"I think there might be an engagement party just waiting to start," Joe says with a smile.

"It never occurred to you that I might say no, did it?" I ask playfully.

Joe's kiss is my only answer.

THE END

Dear reader,

We hope you enjoyed reading Wizards and Wives' Tales. Please take a moment to leave a review, even if it's a short one. Your opinion is important to us.

Discover more books by Kate Messick at https://www.nextchapter.pub/authors/kate-messick

Want to know when one of our books is free or discounted? Join the newsletter at http://eepurl.com/bqqB3H

Best regards,

Kate Messick and the Next Chapter Team

ABOUT THE AUTHOR

Kate Messick is married with three cats and two degrees in classical music. She enjoys lifting weights, reading, playing music, playing games, and traveling.

From a young age, Kate's dad read all sorts of fantasy books aloud to his daughters. Kate found her insatiable hunger for dragons and stories only grow with the years. Kate is living an exciting life. Never afraid to reach for the stars, she founded the Symphonic Anime Orchestra and traveled with her music all over the US. She has worked in many fields: teacher, road construction, spinal technician, data miner, security escort, and more. She has published several music arrangements and a book: *WOOT! Elementary Methods for Clarinet.*

Kate loves life and the people she meets in it. She finds that all games, board games, and most especially role-playing (like *Dungeon & Dragons*), bring out amazing aspects of people's personalities that she loves to explore in her writing.

Kate now lives in North Yorkshire, England, where she word-engineers, travels, and loves.

Lightning Source UK Ltd.
Milton Keynes UK
UKHW020210101020
371334UK00013B/415

9 781715 575182